Praise for the novels of

FIONA GIBSON

Lucky Girl
"Gibson writes like an angel.
She is the voice of modern woman."
—*Marie Claire* (UK)

"A touching tale about embracing family,
imperfections and all."
—*Booklist*

"Lovely, heartwarming, immensely readable."
—Jenny Colgan, author of *Looking for Andrew McCarthy*

"Warm and moreish, like melted marshmallows."
—*Cosmopolitan*

Wonderboy
"Fans of rueful social comedy will chortle over the
escapades of Roo.... [A] witty exposé of the perils
and pitfalls of relocation."
—*Elle* (UK)

"A wonderful story, layered with ironic undertones,
quiet affection and surprises."
—*Romantic Times*

"Addictive."
—*Company*

"Gibson handles the reality of childbearing with incisive
observational humor."
—*Sunday Herald*

Something Good

FIONA GIBSON

RED
DRESS
INK
TM

SOMETHING GOOD

A Red Dress Ink novel

ISBN-13: 978-0-373-89557-1
ISBN-10:   0-373-89557-7

© 2008 by Fiona Gibson.

Excerpt from THE GLASS HEART,
© 2002 by Sally Gardner, used by permission of Orion Books.

www.RedDressInk.com

Printed in U.S.A.

ACKNOWLEDGMENTS

Huge thanks for encouragement and ideas: Margaret King, Jennifer McCarey, Michelle Dickson, Jenny Tucker, Cathy and Liam Gilligan, Alison Munro (for medical info), Kath Brown, Gary Watkins and Marie O'Riordan.
My lovely, inspiring writing group who help to keep the words (and wine) flowing: Tania Cheston, Elizabeth Dobie, Vicki Feaver, Amanda McLean and Margaret Dunn. Andrew McCallum and the Bigger writers. Chris, Sue and Jill at Atkinson-Pryce Books. Anita Naik for Web site advice, and Jenni and Tony at bluex2 (www.bluex2.com) for my Web site (www.fionagibson.com).

Special thanks to Moira and Stephen at Rainbow Stained Glass in Prestwick, Ayrshire, Scotland; my wonderful agents Annette Green and Laura Langlie; and Adam Wilson at Red Dress Ink. Big love as always to Jimmy, Sam, Dexter and Erin.

For my parents, Margery and Keith

"Children," said the queen, "you must take great care of your hearts. They are very fragile and you are very precious."

So the girls did their best to stay out of harm's way.

—Sally Gardner
The Glass Heart

Prologue

A new beginning

They didn't leave in the night, like they do in the movies. They didn't run from the house, heads bent against rain, and bundle themselves into a taxi. The morning was warm and hazy and smelled of the traffic that buzzed along the flyover at the back of the house.

Jane and Hannah Deakin weren't playing in the garden that day. They were sitting together on the warm front step, waiting for Sally to take them away from all this. Hannah pulled her bony knees up to her chin and cradled Biffa, a hygienically challenged rag doll whose ginger-wool hair had been scissored haphazardly into an unforgiving crop. Biffa had been stripped of the lilac felt shift dress she'd been wearing when presented by Max, Hannah's father, a couple of

Christmases ago. The naked doll was now, officially, a boy. On Biffa's polyester chest Hannah had inked a red Biro tattoo, insisting that what looked like a fried egg and two wobbly sausages were, in fact, a skull and crossbones. While her classmates were planning careers as hairdressers and ballerinas, Hannah wanted to be a pirate. She intended to maneuver a galleon through treacherous waters while thrashing a sword in a haphazard manner.

"Where's Sally?" she asked brightly. Her eyes gleamed like fragments of jet.

"She'll be here any minute," her mother said.

"Are we going on holiday? I want my spade. Where's my bucket and—"

"Sweetheart," Jane hushed her, "we're not going on holiday. We're moving to our lovely new house." She tried to quash the tremor in her voice, but didn't make it. Jane had told Hannah this as she'd woken, kicking milky limbs free from rumpled sheets. She'd described each room of their lovely new home: how the sun flooded in, how Hannah wouldn't even have to change schools. "*And* you can help me choose paint colors," Jane had added, trying to make it sound like an adventure.

"Where's Dad?" Hannah asked now.

"Dad's at the shop, love," Jane said, feeling her stomach tighten. She hadn't lied, not technically. Max would be working flat out at Spokes, his newly established cycle shop that devoured virtually every ounce of his energy. Jane had figured that the stark truth was too damned enormous for a five-year-old to take in. Hannah's world revolved around driving a red pedal car at terrific speeds along pavements after school, and trapping earwigs and centipedes in pickle jars in the garden.

Apparently satisfied, Hannah peered down the street in search of Sally's familiar custard-yellow MINI. Her jaw-length black hair was unbrushed, as were her teeth, for that matter. With each exhalation came the rich stench of peanuts. She was sporting her favorite ensemble of bottle-green shorts and a khaki vest with an enormous hairy tarantula on the front. She had yet to acquaint herself with skirts or dresses. Tights were mysterious leg-coverings in which she displayed no interest.

Jane squeezed Hannah's hand. It was greasy from the peanut butter she'd smeared on to her toast. Jane was keeping her gaze firmly fixed upon the patchwork zip-up bag, which lay like an overstuffed dog on the bottom step. This prevented her from turning and looking at the house. If she did that, Jane knew she'd lose it. She'd kept herself mania-cally busy all morning, stuffing clothes into the bag, knowing there were so many things they'd need but being unable to decide what to take and what to leave. She'd darted around, assembling a basic selection of clothes, underwear and toiletries—plus Biffa and Hannah's inhaler—and had tried to write a note to Max, but her eyes and her hands wouldn't behave and she'd flung her unintelligible attempts into the bin. Random words—like *hurt* and *sorry*—had gawped back at her as she'd dropped in a tea bag.

She still loved him. That was the problem, the flaw in her plan. Jane still ached for Max, despite everything.

She swallowed hard and rechecked her watch. Ten fifty-three. Sally was due to pick them up at eleven. Jane had ushered Hannah out of the house too early; she'd needed to get out of there, to shut the door firmly behind them.

Their house, in which Jane had waited and waited for Max to come home from his cycling club. "I called the doctor," she'd said as he'd wheeled his bike into the hall. "It's positive. I'm pregnant, Max." It was the first time Jane had seen real tears roll down his cheeks. At first she'd assumed they were sweat. He'd let go of his bike—his prized possession had clattered against the wall—and hugged her until she could hardly breathe.

Hannah had been born with a fuzz of dark hair and formidable eyes that were so dark they looked almost black. Beautiful, but not quite perfect. Her breathing wasn't right, still wasn't right. Hannah was asthmatic, and regarded her inhaler with the same disdain she reserved for tights. "I want Sally," she announced now, kicking a pebble down the steps.

"She'll be here any minute," Jane murmured.

"I want those flags Dad got for our sandcastles at Brighton and—"

"Hannah, we're not—" Jane began, but her daughter had ceased to listen and was attempting to coax an ant to scuttle on to her finger.

Sally's car lurched into view and bumped up on to the pavement beside them. "Hi, you two," she shouted cheerfully through her open window, as if this were an ordinary day.

"Sally!" Hannah leapt up to greet her.

Sally clambered out of the car, kissed the top of Hannah's head, then pulled Jane toward her. Jane felt the brittleness of her freshly permed hair against her cheek, smelled her baby-powder smell. "All set?" Sally asked, pulling away to inspect Jane's expression.

"Well, as set as I'll ever be."

Sally frowned at the bag. "That's all you're bringing?"

Jane nodded and slung it into the car's minuscule trunk. Hannah sprang on to the backseat, and Jane eased herself in beside her.

As Sally drove, a cluster of keychains—a dangling monkey, a dented plastic lemon and a Feu Orange air freshener— swung jauntily from the rearview mirror. Max wouldn't be back for hours yet. He'd show up at around seven or eight, maybe later; Jane never knew when to expect him. Sometimes she suspected that he wasn't really catching up with cycle repairs or tackling accounts at the shop, but hiding from them—an asthmatic daughter who tattooed her dolls, and a wife who couldn't forgive.

The car radio was playing some lilting song that made Jane feel lighter—as if the dread that had lain in her stomach those past few weeks was starting to rise up out of her, drifting like smoke through the window. Clouds pulled apart, allowing a shaft of sunlight to cut through like a blade. "Which street is it again?" Sally asked.

"Turn right along the edge of London Fields."

"Are we living in a field?" Hannah squealed.

"Not *in* it," Jane said, "but nearly—just over the road. There's a park with swings and a slide and a trampoline thingie. I think you'll like it."

"What's the house number?" Sally called back.

"Sixteen, the one with blue—"

Sally banged her foot hard on the brake, as if stamping on a cockroach. Jane lurched forward and indicated the small terraced house through the window. "This is it."

Apart from a covering of moss and bird droppings on the roof, the house looked pretty well-kept. There was no front garden, but the previous tenants had crammed windowboxes with geraniums and tumbling lobelia, which were still flowering exuberantly at the tail end of summer. A section of loose guttering was dangling down like a doll's broken arm, but that could be fixed. There was a park over the road, a pub you might venture into without fearing for your life, and no overpasses in sight. Jane glanced down at Hannah. Her mouth was set firm.

"So," Sally said, her cheery face looming over the headrest, "what d'you think, Han?"

Hannah tweaked the hairy part of her tarantula T-shirt. "It's—" she began.

"Sweet, isn't it?" Sally enthused. "Wasn't your mum clever finding this place? It's a lovely street. All these trees. Quiet, too, considering it's so close to the main—"

"When's Dad coming?" Hannah interrupted.

Jane's heartbeat quickened. She could do all those Mum things—detangle shoelaces, shoo away nightmares, retrieve a sodden Biffa from beneath a pile of leaves in the garden. She'd been able to make everything all right, until now. Hannah narrowed her eyes.

"Haven't you…?" Sally mouthed over the headrest. She looked shocked, appalled.

"No," Jane managed to say, "I haven't."

"What is it?" Hannah demanded.

Jane was aware of her own blunt-cut nails digging into her palm. She said it then: "Han, Dad's not moving with us. Things aren't good with him and me. I'm sure it'll be fine, and we'll be friends again, but this place—it's just for you and me. Not Dad."

Hannah blinked in slow motion. "Oh."

Jane tried to squeeze her hand but Hannah tugged it away. She'd dipped her head and hunched her shoulders, as if trying to shrink into herself. Then, in one slick movement, she wrenched down the handle and tumbled out of the car. "Han!" Jane cried, scrambling out after her. The words tumbled together: *I should have told you, explained, I was wrong—look at our lovely new house, Han, isn't it…*

Hannah whirled around to face her. "Is Dad still my dad?" she blurted out.

"Of course he is," Jane said gently, crouching down to hug her.

"Good," she muttered. She gripped Biffa tightly to her chest.

Jane felt it then: sunshine, pouring over them like honey. Sally opened the trunk and hauled out the patchwork bag, placing it on the pavement. "Well," she said, "aren't you going to let us in?"

"I like it," Hannah said firmly. "I like our new house."

Jane stood up, dizzy with relief, and fished the key from her pocket. She could tell that Hannah was putting on a brave face but knew instinctively that they would be happy here. Attached to the key was a brown parcel label bearing their new address: 16 Albemarle Street.

A new beginning, that's what it was. It definitely wasn't the end.

1

Ten years later

If Jane hadn't made the cake herself, extracting it from her own oven, she'd have assumed it was some decaying metallic component that had sloughed off a car on its way to the scrap. "Damn," she muttered, glaring down at the pitted slab.

Jane had experienced a wave of good-motherness as she'd glided around the supermarket, loitering in the mysterious baking ingredients aisle to study pots of vermicelli and sugar pearls. At thirty-six years old, surely she should be capable of baking a cake. A bit of creaming and folding, shoving it into the oven at roughly the correct temperature—it was hardly rocket science. Jane had wanted to surprise Hannah, to remind her that she was her *mother*, who loved and cared for her, and not just some irritating adult who happened to inhabit the same house.

The sound of thrashing guitars rattled downstairs. "Go to sleep!" Jane called up. Silence. "Han, can you hear me?" It was twenty past midnight. Of course Hannah couldn't hear; she'd nudged up the volume a notch. Jane sighed and tried to poke a finger into the unyielding cake. Scrabbling among the dented packets in the cupboard, she located a tub of Betty Crocker Chocolate Fudge Icing that she troweled on, instantly doubling the cake's height. Things were looking more hopeful. Jane rummaged again in the cupboard for tiny gummy sweets and studded them all over the cake.

It looked okay. No, better than okay. It might at least raise a smile, if Hannah were still capable of such an expression without cracking her face. Tomorrow she would be fifteen. Her entire childhood had flashed by like a dream that Jane had forgotten to savor.

Hearing the same song starting over again, Jane shut off her ears and jabbed birthday cake candles into the goo.

Happy birthday to you,
Happy birthday to you,
Happy birthday dear Hannaaaah…
Happy birthday to you.

"Gorgeous cake," announced Amy, flicking back hair that had been highlighted with fine golden streaks around her dainty face.

"More like a biscuit," Jane laughed, hacking generous slices for Hannah, Amy, Rachel and herself. A small birthday party—birthday *cluster*, really. All Hannah had wanted this year.

"It looks great," Amy insisted. "You know what my mum's like with her organic-bloody-everything. She still won't have sweets in the house."

"Well, they're—" Jane began, about to say, *they're made from real raspberry and apricot puree and won't, you know, trigger Hannah's asthma*. She stopped herself. Jane sensed that Hannah wouldn't want her asthma mentioned—not even in front of Amy and Rachel, her firm friends of a decade. They'd zoomed toward her in the park the day Jane and Hannah had moved onto Albemarle Street, snatched her hands and run, a chain of three, toward the trampoline.

"Want a piece, Han?" asked Rachel, brandishing a plate bearing a mud-colored mound.

Hannah was sitting cross-legged in the corner of the living room, examining a clear Perspex case of nail polishes in 'difficult' shades—Moss, Lichen and Bark. Amy's present to her. Hannah still detested pink. Clearly, a hastily rescued cake hadn't met with her approval, either. The great twinkling heap was, Jane realized now, entirely inappropriate for a strikingly beautiful daughter with defiant eyes who was virtually an *adult*.

Hannah glanced up and winced, as if she'd been offered some particularly challenging delicacy like sheep's brain, or a trotter. Her hair, which she'd tinted aubergine with a wash-in color, hung messily around her luminous face. "I'm not hungry," she said flatly.

"Go on," Rachel insisted. "It looks a bit sludgy but it tastes okay."

"No thanks."

Rachel shrugged and placed the offending cake on the table. "You okay, birthday girl?" Jane asked, crouching down beside Hannah. Tufts of rust-colored wool were flaking off the rug's edges. They needed a new rug, a new table, chairs and curtains—new everything, really. Their furniture looked way past its use-by date. It had all been acquired, rather than chosen.

"I'm fine," Hannah murmured, removing the silver lid from the "Bark" polish. It was dark brown—not unlike the Betty Crocker icing.

"Are you upset or something?" Jane murmured, wanting to snap: *cheer up, would you? It's your birthday. Your best friends are here. What more do you want?*

"It's just—" Hannah kept her eyelids lowered "—that cake."

"Okay. I messed up." *So shoot me,* Jane added silently. She headed for the kitchen, intending to dispense drinks and leave the girls to play CDs and watch videos. Hannah didn't want her getting in the way. Some mums did that—didn't know when to step back. It happened all the time at Nippers, the day care where Jane worked: women hovering at the windows, steaming the glass, unaware that their looming faces were heightening separation anxiety. She'd see them huddled in their cars, talking fretfully on their cells. Sometimes you had to know when to let go.

The music stopped abruptly. Jane pricked her ears, unable to resist tuning in. "So," Rachel was saying, "what did your dad get you?"

"The usual," Hannah replied. "Thirty quid stuck in a birthday card."

"Lucky thing!" Amy exclaimed. "You know what mine gave me, last time he bloody remembered, which was, like, two years ago?"

"What?" Hannah asked.

"A Winnie-the-Pooh jigsaw."

The girls' high-pitched laughter ricocheted around the house. Jane opened the fridge and took out Hannah's favorite elderflower cordial. They were like wild puppies in there, screeching with laughter as more unsuitable presents— and the general cluelessness and crapness of parents—were howled over. Jane hadn't heard Hannah laugh like that— laugh *properly*—for weeks. At least she could still do it, and her laughing mechanism hadn't entirely seized up. Jane unscrewed the cap from the cordial and picked up the ringing phone.

"Jane? Hi, it's me."

"Hi, Max." She gripped the receiver between shoulder and ear while sploshing the liqueur into glasses.

"Just wondered if the birthday girl's enjoying her day."

Jane smiled. "Think so. Have a listen." She held out the phone in the direction of the kitchen door.

"Has she got some friends round?"

"Just Rachel and Amy. She didn't invite any others—said she didn't want a big fuss."

"God," Max chuckled. "She sounds about sixty."

"I know. She didn't even want to go to the cinema or anything."

The girls' laughter was replaced by sweeping strings and

the film's opening credits. "So…is she okay?" Max asked hesitantly.

"She's…you know. Business as usual." Jane didn't need to use words like *uncommunicative* or *listless* with Max. He just knew. She'd seen it smeared all over his face—that fake jollity—when he'd brought Hannah home from their trip to the London Aquarium. She hadn't shown any interest in the tiny seahorses or the rays with their sandpaper skin and limpid eyes in the touch-tank. "I'm so stupid," Max had hissed, "thinking she'd enjoy somewhere like that at fourteen." Max knew he was losing her. Both of them were.

"She didn't think much of the house yesterday," he added.

"I know. She came back saying you'd lost your mind. Said it's even worse than *our* house. I explained that you're doing it up, that it'll be palatial and she'll love it so much she'll want to move in with you—" She glimpsed Hannah heading upstairs.

"Oh, please," Max cried in mock horror.

"I'm sure she was exaggerating…."

"Come round sometime, see for yourself. It is pretty bad, but it's got…"

"Potential," Jane said, laughing. Her anger had faded a long time ago. That *thing*—Max's drunken night with that woman—was buried so deeply in the past, it could have happened to someone else.

"Actually," Max added, "I was going to ask a favor. Not a favor, exactly—I'd pay you of course. There's this window in the living room… The glass is cracked, and I was thinking some stained glass would—"

"You mean you've bought this place that Hannah reckons was a squat—she said someone's painted 'Fuck Pigs' on the living room wall—"

"I tried to paint over that."

"But the place needs rewiring and God knows what, and you're thinking of blowing your money on stained glass windows?"

"Window," Max corrected her. "Just one. Something simple, bright colors…"

A smile sneaked across Jane's face. "Okay, I'll have a look."

"Tomorrow?"

"I finish work at four. Hannah's got drama workshop after school—she'll probably head over to Amy's afterward. I'll come straight from the day care."

"Great," Max said. Then, almost as an afterthought, he added, "Give her a shout, would you? Tell her her old dad wants to wish her happy birthday."

Jane carried the cordless phone into the hall and peered up the gloomy staircase. "Hannah?" she called.

Silence.

"Hannah! Dad's on the phone."

"I'm on the *loo,*" came the harassed reply.

"Sorry," Jane told him, "Madame's busy with her *toilette.* I'll ask her to ring you later tonight."

"Jane," Max said. "You don't think it's something to do with the house, do you? Has it upset her, d'you think, me leaving the old place?"

"Why would it? She hasn't lived there for ten years…."

"I know, but maybe it was important that she could go

back whenever she wanted. I'm sure that's when it all started. When I told her I was buying this place."

Birthday cake stuck to the roof of Jane's mouth. "We can't do anything about that now."

Max fell silent. Jane could hear his soft breath. For a moment she wished he wasn't alone in an echoey house with its foul graffiti, but right here, jabbing a finger into a tub of icing…which had acquired an unappetizing crust. "I thought she'd like it," he murmured.

"It's probably nothing to do with the house," Jane said firmly. "Isn't this what happens, Max?"

"What d'you mean?"

"The moodiness. Treating me and you like we're… inconvenient. It's just a phase. Our girl's growing up."

"I guess you're right."

What if I am? Jane thought. *When she's really grown up, and there's no growing up left to do—what then? I won't need you anymore, and you won't need me. I'll really lose you then, for good.*

"I'll see you tomorrow, okay?" she said softly, finishing the call and fixing on her best party smile.

2

*H*annah sat on the loo with her jeans bunched around her ankles, wondering when her mother would head out to her "studio," as she insisted on calling that embarrassing shack at the bottom of the garden. She'd had one of its wooden sides replaced with glass, which she never got around to cleaning. The place was crammed with offcuts of lead, sheets of glass jutting from their pigeonholes and a hulking workbench, which was covered in doodles and scarred by Jane's cutting tools.

Hannah hadn't always felt so repelled by the studio. As a child, she'd loved being allowed to play in there. Other mums—like Amy's mum—would have had a hairy fit if they'd seen its potential dangers and mess. The drawers beneath the bench were crammed with paper, pens, glass cutters with oily blades and sample squares of glass in every conceivable color. Hannah had been drawn to the deep blues, greens and turquoises—the colors of oceans and eyes.

Photos of Jane's finished pieces were taped haphazardly on to the inside walls. Scraps of things had been pinned up in clusters: fragments of fabric from Hannah's old dungarees, gleaming wrappers from Quality Street chocolates. By the time Hannah had turned seven or eight, Jane had let her use cutting tools under strict supervision. They'd filled the studio with their chatter, their breath showing as pale puffs on sharp winter's nights…unless the kiln was on, when they'd turn pink and glisten with sweat. Hannah had made a small panel all by herself—a yellow star on a turquoise background—that they'd hung from a rusting hook at the bathroom window.

Hannah shifted position on the seat and peered at it. Weak sunlight eked through the star, forming a golden cast on the cracked washbasin. These days she avoided the studio. It was so chaotic in there that even the warmth of the kiln on a winter's afternoon couldn't draw her in. God knows how her mother managed to produce anything that people would pay good money for. No wonder her little stained glass sideline had never taken off.

Hannah could hear Amy laughing raucously downstairs. She'd left her friends watching the film. It wasn't her thing: too schmaltzy, totally predictable, for people with mashed potato for brains. She could hear Jane chatting with them—with *her* friends. Hannah's friends thought she was the bloody bee's knees. Mind you, they'd like anyone's mum who let them lie about her house for hours and scarf down whatever they liked from the cupboards or fridge. "Jane's all right," Amy reminded Hannah with irritating frequency. "If you were stuck with my mum and her bloody whale music, and her pointing out condoms at the counter in Boots, saying, 'These are *condoms*, Amy,' as if I might've mistaken them for tissues or packets of mints..."

Things could be worse, Hannah reflected grudgingly. She could have parents who hated each other's guts, who tore round to each other's flats to kick over their trash bins, like Amy's mum had before she'd discovered whale music. At least Jane and Max still liked each other. Hannah couldn't understand why they didn't cut all this nicey-nicey stuff and get back together, be done with it. It wasn't as if either of them had met anyone decent in the meanwhile. Jane's love life was beyond tragic. The last man she'd brought home had looked petrified, as if Hannah might actually bite.

Hannah couldn't understand why her parents had split up in the first place. "We were just too young," was all Jane had told her. *Too young for what?* Hannah had wondered, figuring that they must have been around nineteen when they'd met, and wasn't that about as grown up as it was possible to be? Sure, Jane had been young to get pregnant—no way would Hannah end up in a mess like that—but they were hardly kids, for God's sake. By the time Hannah was nineteen she intended to be at art college and living in a gorgeous loft apartment. She'd have an American fridge with an ice maker and none of that depressing, old-fashioned furniture that Jane seemed so keen to hang on to.

She could hear the three of them: Amy, Rachel and her

mum all having a great time wit\
hadn't even noticed she was missing\
cake, most likely. Most mothers—\
have pitched the damn thing. N\
rectify it with ready-made icing an\
made from extract of bloody papaya or solidified mango puree and presented it as if it was perfectly respectable. Hannah hoped she wouldn't be expected to consume so much as a crumb of it. She'd rather ingest poison.

Why couldn't Jane admit she'd messed up? She couldn't face reality, that was the problem. Life was sunny and happy—just the two of them, trapped in a scruffy old house with an ancient telly that took an age to warm up, and a remote that you had to jiggle right in front of the screen, which surely defeated its purpose. "I don't want to be ruled by gadgets," Jane had declared when Hannah had suggested they haul themselves into the 21st century and buy a DVD player.

"It's not a gadget," Hannah had protested. "It's just a thing—"

"I don't want *things*."

Hannah had tried to explain that normal people had DVD players and TVs with functioning remote controls, but Jane had swished off to fire some painted glass segments—naturally, the kiln didn't count as a gadget. It had taken Hannah six months of nagging to persuade her that she couldn't run a business without a computer.

Worse than any of that, her dad had left the old house without giving her any warning whatsoever and bought that horrible crumbly place that smelled like someone had it. New tenants had moved into the old place ready; Max had mentioned that they had a little girl. Hannah wondered if she'd notice that loose floorboard in the back bedroom. Would she lift it up, find those tiny things and wonder who'd hidden them there? They'd be hers then, this strange girl's. Finders, keepers.

"Hannah!" Amy yelled upstairs. "Are you staying up there all night?"

"Coming," Hannah called wearily. She heard the back door creak open. Jane would be in the studio for hours now, out of their hair. Hannah stood up, hiked up her jeans and retied the skinny paisley scarf she wore as a belt. She flushed the loo, even though there was nothing untoward in it, and marched downstairs to join the spectacular throng of her 15th birthday party.

"Hey, Han," Amy said, looking up, "what took you so long?"

"I had a tummy ache."

"Oh, poor you. You've missed half the film."

"Never mind." Hannah squeezed into the space between her friends on the sofa. She thought about the worry dolls—five tiny figures bound in brightly colored wool—trapped under the floor at the old house. They weren't really dolls at all; they didn't even have faces. Yet they'd worked. All through her childhood, once they'd settled into Albemarle Street, she'd realized that she still had her mum and her dad and no real worries at all.

Now everything was different.

3

The little boy extracted his face from his mother's corduroy skirt. "He's never been anywhere like this before," the woman told Jane, as if day care centers were quite terrifying with their ladybird-shaped floor cushions and wicker baskets overflowing with toys. The woman glanced anxiously at a group of children who were engrossed in a vigorous game in which toy dinosaurs were being made to charge headlong into each other. There was a sharp *thwack,* a collision of prehistoric skulls.

"Joshua," Jane said gently, "would you and Mummy like to see our sandpit?"

The boy nodded uncertainly, yet remained unwilling to detach himself from his mother's clothing. He was gripping her tights now, tugging the nylon until it formed a semi-sheer tent. She waggled her leg in a feeble attempt to detach him. Jane had greeted hundreds of new children at Nippers. She excelled at coaxing them away from their mothers' hosiery, their fathers' neatly pressed trousers.

Sally had offered Jane shifts at Nippers when she and Hannah had moved to Albemarle Street. Although it was ideal—a mere five-minute walk from home—Jane had assumed it would just be a stopgap. Having a child of her own had felt so right, yet dealing with other people's kids and their perpetual emissions seemed quite alarming. Here she was, ten years on, now deputy manager and "a part of this place," as Sally was fond of putting it. It was well-meant but sometimes made Jane feel like an electrical appliance or a radiator.

Jane led Joshua, who was still clinging fiercely to his mother's limb, up the short flight of steps into the main play space. The woman's lips were pressed together in an anxious line. "This is our messy play area," Jane explained. "Do you like painting, Joshua?"

"Yuh," he muttered.

His mother scanned the chaotic array of paintings and collages tacked to the walls. "Josh has some allergies," she murmured, "and there's a piece of old blanket he really can't manage without, I hope you don't think it's silly—"

"That wouldn't be a problem," Jane said, accustomed to complex dietary intolerances and children who refused to be parted from some strip of damp satin that had once edged a baby blanket.

In the dining area children were guzzling milk from plastic cups. "Isn't this a lovely place, darling?" the woman asked.

Joshua gazed up at Jane. "Like nursery lady," he whispered.

Jane smiled, thinking, *if only fifteen-year-olds were as easy to win round*. She remembered Hannah the previous night, sounding outraged at being disturbed whilst on the loo. Yet for years, Jane had been unable to go to the bathroom without Hannah scuttling after her. Anytime she'd had the audacity to lock the door, Hannah had shoved madly scrawled notes through the gap beneath it—*Let me in!!! Wot are yoo doing?*—until Jane had abandoned any concept of privacy and allowed Hannah to play with her Tonka digger at her feet.

"If you ask Sally in the office," Jane told Joshua's mother, "she'll arrange a start date. The extension's nearly finished so we should have a place in a few weeks."

The boy's hot, damp fingers had curled around Jane's. He tugged hard on her hand, yanking her toward the face-painting table as he ordered, "Come *on*."

"So you're off to Max's new place?" Sally asked.

"Yes—going to see what the hell he's got himself into. According to Hannah, the place is a heap. It was infested with mice when he moved in."

"Really?" Sally was fearless when confronted by uninvited wildlife. She fed the savage-looking stray cats that prowled around her garden off Hackney Road, and had been known to lurk at her window at 2:00 a.m., hoping to photograph visiting foxes.

"He wants me to make him a stained glass window," Jane added.

"Oh, right. The place is about to fall down around his

ears, but he *must* have stained glass, designed by you, of course…."

Jane laughed as she pulled on her coat. "Who else would he ask? Anyway, he's probably sick of the boring practical stuff—the plumbing and electrics and all that. He wants something…indulgent."

Sally's mouth twitched as she suppressed a smirk. "Yes," she said brightly, "of course that's what Max wants."

Jane strode past St. Matthew's church. Its windows consisted of tiny, wizened panes, many of them cracked or missing. Jane yearned to get her hands on those windows. She'd restore them, carefully removing each damaged segment and cutting replacements in colors that virtually matched the original glass.

Hannah was in St. Matthew's right now, in the draughty back hall—home to her theater workshop, the only activity she'd stuck with over the years. She'd come home with rumpled scripts poking out of her bag, but rarely let Jane see them these days. Jane and Max had sat together, watching all the productions—*Calamity Jane*, *Grease*, *Bugsy Malone*—like any ordinary couple.

Soon the familiar streets around London Fields gave way to dingier terraces. There was a dilapidated dentist—its crude plastic sign read "entist"—and a junk shop, its jumbled contents threatening to escape through a half-open door. Jane paused, hating that she had to stop and consult her A-Z so close to home, despite Max's directions. Drizzle dampened the pages as she peered at the tangle of streets.

She memorized the next few turns, passing a dingy-looking Turkish restaurant, its window obscured by crooked Venetian blinds, and a huddled pub with a spiral staircase that coiled down to a sinister-looking club. And finally, here it was: Max's street, a curving terrace of once-proud houses, now weighed down by age and neglect. Jane stared up at Max's house. Its roof sagged gently in the middle, as if it had been sat on. The windows were grimy, their frames peeling, exposing blackened wood. This was the worst-looking house on the street. Why had he taken it on? He'd told her that he was planning to do most of the renovation work himself. He'd fitted out the cycle shop, all those years ago, transforming an unpromising kebab shop into a thriving business. Spokes had been voted Best London Cycle Shop in *Your Bike* magazine for its "nonelitist atmosphere" and "friendly, personal service." Max had done all that. He wasn't one of those DIY bodgers who severed electrical cables or pierced themselves with drills. Yet this was too much. How would he find the time to fix it all up?

Jane hurried up the stone steps and tried the old-fashioned brass doorbell, knowing it wouldn't work. She rapped on the glass, tried the handle and pushed the door open. "Max?" she called. "It's me."

Frantic hammering was coming from upstairs. Jane stepped into the hallway, breathing in chalky air. The walls were municipal green paint over woodchip. Now she understood. She remembered the excitement she'd felt when she and Max had found their perfect house. She'd hurried from room to room, ignoring hideous pansy-patterned wallpaper because she'd known it was right. Max had given her that raised-eyebrow look—code for, *this is it, isn't it?* Inside Jane's belly, their baby had flipped. She'd signalled back, *yes, this is it.*

"Where are you?" Jane shouted.

The hammering stopped, and someone called down, "Veronica?"

For a moment, Jane panicked that she'd marched into the wrong house. Someone else lived here—some stranger, with a woman called Veronica. She shrank back toward the front door.

Max appeared on the landing. "God…hi," he blustered. "Is it that time already?"

"Am I too early?" Jane asked stiffly.

"No, of course not." His dark hair was flecked with dust, his jeans ripped at the knees and splattered with paint. He never seemed to age, not really. He had a boyish face, was always laughing or chatting—*engaging* with people. Everyone liked him: his staff, his customers. And, Jane assumed, this *Veronica* person.

"Come up," he said. "I'll show you round—not that there's much to see." Max laughed uncomfortably. "Anyway, you found it."

"Easy," Jane fibbed, wondering if she should ask about Veronica—whether he was seeing anyone—and decided it wouldn't be right, interrogating him the minute she'd walked in. Max's love life was none of her business.

Jane climbed the bare wooden stairs and followed Max toward an open door at the far end of the landing. Through his thin gray T-shirt she could see the contours of his lean back and shoulders. His lithe body had stunned her the first time she'd seen him naked. She'd wanted to stop what they were doing with their hands and mouths and study him, tracing every muscle and bone. She'd had an urge to draw him, and later she had, although she'd destroyed her sketches soon after the thing had happened, ripping them into confetti scraps. She hadn't known then that cycling had made him taut and lean; that bikes consumed him. Later, after Hannah had been born, he'd spend hours disassembling gear systems amidst her toys on the living room floor. He'd finally come to bed, smelling of metal and oil, after Jane had drifted into half-sleep. Sometimes she'd wondered if he'd have been keener to come to bed if she'd possessed pedals and gears.

Jane followed him into a bedroom that overlooked the street. It was huge and airy, filled with light and possibilities. "It's lovely," she said, and it was, despite anaglypta walls and a ripped lampshade dangling cock-eyed from the center light.

Downstairs, in the shabby melamine kitchen, Max spooned instant coffee into chipped mugs bearing the Spokes logo. "It just felt right," he said, pulling up the chair opposite Jane. "I spotted it in the estate agent's window—the one at Limehouse station—and I couldn't believe the price...."

"Max," Jane said, "what really made you move? I mean, why now?"

He looked down at his mug. "Thought it was time I got on the ladder...."

Jane spluttered. "What, the property ladder? When did you ever care about stuff like that?"

He shrugged. "I told you, I couldn't let this place go."

"You wanted a project?"

"Yes, I suppose I did." He smiled sheepishly. "So, d'you think Hannah will like the big bedroom?"

"Won't you be sleeping there?" Jane asked.

Max stood up, strolled across the kitchen and swilled out his mug at the sink. "I tried sleeping there the first couple of nights. It felt too big, too—"

He turned from the sink, and looked at Jane. She studied his face; the deep brown of his eyes, the softness of his lips. It wasn't right, the way his eyes still drew her in. She tried to focus on the melamine cupboards.

"Too *empty*, Max?" came a voice from the doorway.

Jane swung round. A woman with great swathes of fair hair and red lips stood at the kitchen door, grinning broadly. "I can understand that," she added. "Single guy— must feel a bit lonely in there, eh, Max?" She strode toward Jane. "Veronica Fox, neighbor of Max's, three doors down. Been helping him out, making sure he's eating properly."

"Eating properly?" Jane spluttered.

Veronica frowned, then quickly corrected her face and lowered her dainty rear on to a kitchen chair. She was wearing a fitted suit in pinky-purply tweed—the colors of heather—that clashed rather nastily with the ageing tangerine cupboards. Over her shoulder was slung a burgundy mock-croc bag. "Terribly busy, isn't he," she ventured, "with the bike shop?"

"Yes, he is." Jane forced a smile.

"And so clever, building it up from scratch. That's dedication for you. I like a man who knows what he wants."

She smirked suggestively. Jane's smile had congealed. Max, who had gone rather pink around the cheeks, was fiddling with the kettle flex.

"Like some coffee, Veronica?" he asked.

"No thanks. You know I don't take it."

"Oh, of course." He dropped a tea bag into a mug but made no move to fill the kettle or switch it on. His teeth were jammed together; Jane could sense the tension in his neck. Clearly, Veronica was no stranger here. Max knew that she didn't "take" coffee.

An awkward silence settled around them, as if a teacher had marched in and caught them smoking. "So, do you like living around here?" Jane asked, floundering.

Veronica grimaced. "All I could afford after the divorce. It's lovely, though, isn't it, Max? My place?"

"Yes, um, it is," he muttered. Perspiration gleamed on his forehead.

"Had it gutted, soon as I bought it. *Threw* money at it, Jane, the way you have to in order to get the job done. You're down London Fields way, aren't you?"

"Yes, opposite the park." Jane glanced from Veronica to Max. Were they seeing each other or what? Surely he'd have told her? It wouldn't *bother* her—Max's private life was his business—but still, she felt hurt. He'd always told her about his dates, his short-lived relationships; they'd chortle over the women's eccentricities from the safety of distance once it was all over. Jane had especially enjoyed hearing about the woman who worked as a life model—spent the best part of her week stark naked in front of strangers—yet had insisted on wearing a button-up nightie to bed. "Well,"

Jane said, "nice to meet you Veronica, but I'd better get back. Hannah, my daughter—"

"Yes, I know about Hannah."

Jane felt a prickling sensation on the back of her neck. Max was pretending to examine the contents of a wall cupboard, even though it appeared to house only an iron.

"Yes, well, she's at a friend's, but she'll be home soon, and I really must—"

"Doesn't she have her own key?" Veronica asked.

"Yes, but I like to be there." Jane stood up and swiped her coat from the chair. She gripped it before her like a shield.

"You work at a day care, don't you?"

Christ, Jane thought, what other details did she know about her life? Why not rattle off her bra size while she was at it? *A 34C aren't you, Jane? Yes, thought so. Perhaps you could do with a bra that would offer a little more support, hmm?*

"Yes, that's right," she said.

"I'm in nutrition," Veronica announced, as if desperate to impart this vital nugget. "If you ever need any supplements… you are a bit pale, Jane, maybe a touch of iron deficiency? Not anemic, are you?" Veronica arched an overplucked eyebrow.

"Actually, I feel fine. I feel *great.*" Jane grinned ferociously.

"Ever get dizzy when you stand up?"

"Never," Jane blurted, even though she was, in fact, feeling dizzy right now; something to do with this blasted woman's overconcern with her mineral levels and Max's bodily sustenance.

A cell phone started trilling inside Veronica's bag. She marched out of the kitchen to take the call. Jane tried to make eye contact with Max but he'd turned to the counter and was stirring Veronica's tea with great vigor. "Want to show me where you'd like this window?" Jane asked quickly.

"Silly girl," Veronica snapped, clacking back into the kitchen and thrusting her phone back into her bag. "Zoë," she added, glancing at Jane, "my daughter. Brain of a flea. Trapped at the hairdressers, silly kitten."

"Trapped?" Jane pictured a child held hostage by fierce stylists brandishing hair dryers as weapons.

"Had enough to pay for the cut but not the color. I'll have to nip over to Upper Street, sort her out. Lovely to meet you, Jane. Heard lots about you. Max has filled me in on his past."

Has he? she wanted to ask, but Veronica had already swept out of the kitchen and was letting herself out of Max's house—a house that, clearly, she knew intimately—and clattering down the steps.

Jane looked at Max. "My neighbor," he murmured. "Come on, let me show you the window."

Max led her to the living room, which he'd omitted from his initial tour of the house. Tucked away at the back, it was shrouded in shadow. The graffiti—enormous aero-soled letters—shone like ghosts through thin white emulsion. "It's this one," Max said, indicating the smaller of two windows: a skinny rectangle overlooking an unloved garden.

They took measurements and talked colors and shapes.

Veronica's gleaming smile shimmered in Jane's mind, like a gaudy flower it was impossible to ignore. "You know it'll take me a few weeks," she said

"Yes, of course. There's no rush."

He kissed her goodbye at the door, his customary peck on the cheek. "Good to know she's making sure you're eating properly," Jane teased him.

Max frowned. "What's up with you?"

"Nothing!"

"She's just a neighbor…"

"I know, she said…three doors down." Jane bit her lip.

"All right," Max said, "she's weird, but what can I do? She shows up with these meals and cakes and some kind of flapjack with sunflower seeds in…"

Jane spluttered. "It's not normal behavior."

"What's normal, Jane?" Max sighed.

"Well," she said, aware of the words tumbling out before she could stop them, "no man's ever thought, 'Oh, look, poor single mother, better pop round with a roast chicken dinner…'"

He chuckled softly. "Maybe you don't look like you need feeding up."

"You're saying I'm fat," she teased him.

"Don't be ridiculous."

"Next time I come," she called back, heading down the front steps, "I'll bring you a casserole."

"You can't cook," he yelled down the street.

What was it, Jane thought as she strode home, about single men living alone that had women fretting about their nutritional intake? The rain had come on again, and was becoming steadily heavier. Veronica's darling daughter's new hairdo would be ruined, after all that expense and a mercy dash to Upper Street. Spotting the bus at the stop, Jane pelted toward it and clambered on, plopping herself in the only space available.

Beside her a man was coughing vigorously into a stained hankie. Trying to shut out the hacking noise, she figured that Max had moved barely two weeks ago. That woman was a bloody fast worker. A terrible image formed of her heather-colored suit cast onto the floor of Max's front bedroom. *I thought,* Veronica was saying—no, purring— *that if I pretended to leave—made up that crap about Zoë at the hairdressers—then we'd get rid of her quicker.* How they'd laugh as she ran those long elegant fingers all over his smooth chest and—

"Got a spare hankie?" the man asked, thrusting his bulbous face into Jane's airspace. He smelled of lager and cheese and onion crisps.

"No, I haven't," she replied quickly.

"Rotten day. Coming for a drink at the Blue Parrot— cheer yourself up? You don't half look pissed off if you don't mind me saying."

"I'm fine," Jane said firmly, rummaging through the chaotic assortment of receipts and scribbled notes to herself that crowded her bag. She was aware of the man's stare as she pulled out a pen and her notebook. She flicked to the page where she'd jotted down Max's window's dimensions and a jumble of notes:

north facing overlooking back garden large trees over-hanging shadowy colors strong not too dark room needs max light. curves, leaves, petals? reds & oranges plants stems curvy & loose.

"Curvy and loose?" the man read aloud. Jane snapped her notebook shut. "Just how I like my women," he leered. "Is that a camera you've got? Not a tourist, are you? If it's the Tower of London you want you're on the wrong—"

Jane stood up and lurched to the front of the bus. This was the breed of man she attracted these days: drunk with oniony breath and foul hankies. "Hey, love," he called after her, "I'll be in the Blue Parrot, seven o'clock. Write that down in your little black book."

Were women like Veronica hassled on buses? Of course not, Jane thought bitterly. They didn't "take" buses.

4

For several hours now, Max had been working like crazy to finish painting the smallest bedroom. He often worked like this—urgently, without thinking—and didn't mind when his arms ached and his shoulders hurt. He worked this way at the shop, switching to mundane jobs in the evening that he could tackle without engaging his brain. Stuff like fixing punctures or attempting to clear space in the workshop. Work was useful. It stopped his mind from wandering toward other, more troubling territories.

Now his energy had withered, leaving him stranded with a three-quarters-painted room and a throbbing callus on his thumb. At least Jane had approved of the house, which made him feel marginally better. He'd known she would. She loved bright, airy spaces; it saddened him that she'd gone from one tiny, dingy house to another, when her work—

at least her stained glass work, which Max considered to be her proper job—was all about light. The moment the estate agent had shown him into the house, Jane had popped right into Max's head. It was pathetic, after all this time, the way she invaded his thoughts. He'd have to get a grip on himself.

Max rested his roller in the paint tray and rubbed his hands across his jeans. What about Veronica, barging in and ranting on about Jane's iron levels? He wasn't accustomed to bargers. It had unnerved him at first, the way she'd invite herself in, presenting him with a carton of milk and a wholemeal loaf before he'd even started unpacking. She was attractive, of course. Model-attractive, if you liked that sort of thing. Why the interest in him—a skinny bloke with an overly large nose and decrepit house, not to mention an ex-wife and daughter? "We've all got baggage," Veronica had told him a few days after their first meeting. "They're part of your history, Max. Your past makes you what you are today."

It had amused him, her habit of talking in self-help soundbites. Of course, Jane wasn't history. She was anything but. "I guess you're right," Max had said. He'd thanked her for the bread and milk and wondered when she might leave. She'd arranged herself prettily on a kitchen chair. He hadn't fancied her exactly, but there was something about her inane chat and frequent bursts of sparkly laughter than made him feel lighter somehow. Which, after four hours of unpacking his sorry array of belongings, was precisely what he'd needed.

Max picked up the roller and dunked it into an old paint can which he'd half filled with turpentine. He couldn't face applying one more stroke of paint to the blasted wall. In fact, as he examined his handiwork, he wasn't sure that he even liked blue. Where colors were concerned he was beyond hopeless. He'd allowed that young salesguy with vinegar breath to convince him that Hazy Dawn was the perfect shade for a boxroom. "It's soothing and neutral," he'd insisted, but on the walls it looked bleak. It matched the way Max felt inside.

It was occasions like this—following casual meetings with Jane—that reminded him how dismally he'd failed as a human being. There wasn't even anything decent to eat in the house. He headed downstairs, grateful to escape from the paint smell, figuring that he'd toast the remains of some aging bread. He found himself wishing he had butter or even margarine to spread on it, which struck him as particularly tragic.

He opened the kitchen cupboard and grabbed a packet of biscuits. They were a brand he'd never heard of, purchased from the nearest corner shop where the depressed-looking owner had been smoking and scattering ash all over a word-search puzzle. Jane and Hannah never opened a cupboard to find only a sole packet of biscuits called 'Coffee Time.'

It pained him, as he ripped open the packet, to admit to himself that he'd bought this house fueled by some ridiculous notion that it might bring Jane back to him. As if these huge, light-filled rooms might draw her in like some homecoming bird. He must have been out of his mind. Now he was stuck with a walloping mortgage and three times more rooms than one person required, all requiring major repair.

A sharp rap on the front door gave Max a start. By the time he'd reached the hall Veronica had let herself in. "Hi," she said through her perfumed aura. "I'm back. Hope I'm not intruding, Max, but I ordered this Thai chicken salad from the new organic take-away and there's too much for me. I wondered—" she flashed a pearly smile "—if you'd like to share it."

He thought of his stale bread and Coffee Time biscuits. "Thanks," he said, "that's really thoughtful of you. Come in, have a seat—I'll find us a couple of plates."

She carried the foil tray to the kitchen. He placed two plates on the table and she divided the salad between them. She had changed from the suit, which had made her look rather scary, into a floral summery frock and pale blue cardi. Over her potent fragrance Max could smell chili and lime from the salad. His mouth watered. Veronica opened the cutlery drawer and took out two forks. "I hope I'm not imposing," she added.

He glimpsed the biscuits' cheap-looking red-and-yellow wrapper on the worktop. "Of course you're not. This looks great."

The first forkful tasted delicious. Veronica looked up at him across the table, widening her eyes as if to say, *isn't this good?* "Hey," Max said, "there's a bottle of wine in the fridge. Why don't I pour us a glass?"

"That would be lovely."

Max found two tumblers at the back of the cupboard, poured the wine and took a large gulp. Veronica sipped hers daintily.

He glanced at her, and a surge of warmth fluttered

through him. She wasn't remotely his type, and he had zero intention of getting involved on any intimate level. Yet sitting here, drinking wine and eating Thai salad, he'd begun to feel better. Better, in fact, than he'd felt in a long time. Max was sick of painting, sick of Hazy Dawn, and sick to the pit of his stomach of being alone.

5

*W*henever Ollie Tibbs was around, Hannah was aware of every cell of her body, every nerve ending and hair on her skin. It was as if she'd morphed into an incredibly lifelike android, and the most instinctive of acts—walking, blinking, sipping Coke from a can—now consisted of hundreds of separate, minutely connected movements. No wonder she hadn't been given the part of Audrey in *Little Shop of Horrors* when Beth had announced the leads at theater workshop tonight. She was ungainly, embarrassing—a robotic fake.

"It's not fair, Han," Ollie was telling her as they wandered along the towpath beside the murky canal. "You deserve a main part. You're really good, you know that? You should say something to Beth."

Hannah forced a laugh. "I'm not bothered. Anyway,

she's already decided—there's no point in arguing and making a fuss."

Ollie cast her a quick glance. "You really don't care?"

"It's just a crappy little club," Hannah murmured. Why had she said that? It sounded as if theater workshop was some dumb activity she involved herself with solely to while away Monday afternoons. In truth, she loved it; it was where she could lose herself, be whoever she wanted— though not Audrey in *Little Shop of Horrors,* obviously.

It had rained while they'd been inside the church, and their footsteps were mushing a thin layer of mud. Hannah was conscious of slowing down her natural pace. Ollie strolled, rather than walked. He had an angular, rich boy's face, and a rich boy's accent—faintly posh, but stopping short of the kind of laughable plumminess that made Hannah think of polo matches and shooting pheasants. He managed to sound confident, yet warm and interested.

Ollie's fair hair flopped around his finely sculpted face. He had pronounced cheekbones, gray-blue eyes fringed by long, curving eyelashes and full lips, which made Hannah think of them pressing against hers as she breathed in the scent of his skin. Despite the fact that they'd being hanging out after theater workshop for the past few weeks, he hadn't kissed her or even held her hand. All they'd done was talk.

Since Ollie had joined a couple of months ago, Hannah had found herself becoming ridiculously excited about Mondays. On Sunday nights she'd lie awake with her belly fizzling and her brain swishing with lurid thoughts. How could he possibly not know that she'd been thinking those things about his lips and his skin? In an effort to compose herself, Hannah fixed her gaze on a lone duck that was pecking at a floating milk carton on the canal.

"What I think," Ollie continued as they climbed the steps to the bridge, "is that the classes should be more structured, don't you think?"

"Um, yeah," Hannah said, even though the lack of structure was precisely what she enjoyed. Why did she feel the need to be so *agreeable?* "It helps though," she added, "because you feel more comfortable with yourself and get to know the others in the group. There are enough rules at school— 'Do this, stop that, is that eyeliner you're wearing, Hannah Deakin?'"

"*Is* that eyeliner you're wearing?" Ollie asked, making her laugh.

"No, I was born with these incredibly dark, smoky eyes...."

"Well," Ollie offered casually, "you look good to me." Hannah's earlobes singed. He'd never complimented her before. "And freezing," he added quickly, pulling off his coat and draping it around her shoulders, a gesture that felt kind and sweet but oddly old-fashioned.

"Thanks," she said, feeling the warmth of his body all around her. She wished she didn't feel so shy; that she was capable of asking pertinent questions about his life, his family, what he got up to when he wasn't at college or theater workshop. Trying to formulate coherent sentences felt like plunging her hand into a bag of Scrabble letters.

"Want to go to the park, see who's there?" she asked, even though she didn't fancy running into Emma or Georgia or any of the others who hung out at the bandstand after workshop. Those girls always seemed to have some boy-friend on the go. They'd often show up with their necks decorated with lovebites, which they'd make a big performance of trying to hide with pasty concealer. One snog was all Hannah had had, with Michael Linton, a horrible fuzzy-chinned boy who'd ground his chapped lips overenthusiastically against hers round the back of Angie's Bakery. It was an episode she'd rather forget. If the kissing hadn't been bad enough, the bakery boys had come out with their giant trays of loaves, and laughed uproariously as they'd loaded the van. Hannah couldn't smell baking bread without being haunted by the spectre of Michael's undulating mouth.

"It's too cold for the park," Ollie said. "I'm starving—fancy getting something to eat?"

"Okay," Hannah said. She checked her watch; just gone five thirty. Jane wouldn't expect her home from Amy's for another hour or so. They could get chips, or a sandwich from Bert's Bagels.

"Let's go to the Opal," Ollie said.

Hannah wanted to ask, "What's the Opal?" and, "How much does it cost to eat at the Opal?" but he'd already turned swiftly down a side street and was sauntering, more purposefully now, along the narrow lane that ran alongside the canal.

The Opal's sign swung idly from its spindly support. Hannah hadn't known this place existed, and why would she? She and her mother ate out around twice a decade. Ollie stopped outside the restaurant, fished out his cell phone from his pocket and read a text. As he tapped out a reply, Hannah glanced at the framed menu on the outside wall. Ollie probably came here all the time for grilled haloumi, whatever the heck that was. His mum, Hannah had decided, would be one of those women whose handbag toned with her shoes, tights and nails—every detail carefully thought out and matching. She wasn't sure that her own mother owned a single accessory. Jane stuffed her purse into the pocket of her jeans, her hair usually looked like she'd taken about one second to tie it back into a ponytail, and her nails were always clipped short. Despite her age—thirty-six, thirty-seven or thirty-eight—she could be quite decent-looking, if only she'd make something of herself. Ollie's mum would be groomed, Hannah was certain of that. Their house would have a massive flat-screen TV. There'd be a conservatory, one of those patio heater things in the garden, and no embarrassing shed. Not that Hannah cared what Ollie did or didn't have. She'd already decided, when he eventually invited her round to his house, that she'd manage to look totally *unimpressed*.

The Opal felt warm and smoky as Ollie pushed open the heavy glass door. *Café*Vins*Petit dejeuner*Diner* was etched across the pane in ornate writing, as if this were some tucked-away place in Paris—not that Hannah had ever been to Paris—and not a gloomy side street in Bethnal Green.

"Hope there's a table," Ollie muttered. Hannah glanced around at the gaggle of drinkers crowding the bar. The Opal seemed to be the kind of place where everyone fitted in. A man was perched on a bar stool—he looked about a hundred years old—reading a damp-looking newspaper. A bunch of studenty types were tightly packed around a table, picking at bread from a basket. Everyone seemed happy and relaxed. Even Ollie, who was just two years older than Hannah, knew how to *be*.

Hannah threaded her way between tables toward the bar. The music was jazzy, the air thick with garlicky smells. She caught sight of herself in a tarnished mirror, grinning inanely, like an idiot who'd stumbled in by mistake. Her bulging schoolbag, stuffed with the school uniform she'd changed out of before theater workshop, thudded like a boulder against her hip.

"Glass of wine?" Ollie asked from the space he'd miraculously discovered at the bar.

"I, um—"

"The house white's good, or there's a decent sauvignon or a sancerre…"

Did he have to refer to wines by their French names? Hannah had dropped it last year, incapable of grasping the concept of ordinary things like chairs or suitcases being a "he" or a "she." She blinked at the bar. The Opal's drinks menu depicted an elegant girl with ridiculously thin limbs perched on a stool. "Malibu and Coke please," she said quickly.

Amusement flickered across Ollie's face. Hannah silently cursed herself. She'd had alcohol plenty of times before—at Granny Nancy's sixtieth birthday do, and at Amy's when her mum had been out and they'd helped themselves to vodka and orange, which they'd sucked noisily through bendy straws.

This was different. She was in a bar—a place that sold *vins*—when she should have been immersed in biology homework at Amy's. While Ollie ordered, she found a space to stand by the cigarette machine where she willed herself to turn invisible. "Hi, Han!" someone called from the students' table. The girl had rod-straight hair, which was pulled back from her face by a confusing array of glittery clips.

"Hi," Hannah mouthed back. Panic rose in her like a fluttering fish. Who was that? Hannah was sweating; she could feel moisture pricking her forehead and upper lip, and—worse—her underarms. She felt trapped inside too many layers of clothing and feared that her face was blazing red. No one else had burning faces in the Opal. They were *normal*. At some point she'd have to take off Ollie's coat and her jacket, and there'd be stinking damp patches under her arms. Her sweat was probably soaking straight into Ollie's coat right now. She could smell something meaty, although that might have been coming from the kitchen.

The straight-haired girl beckoned Hannah toward her table. Hannah took a few tentative steps. "Here with some friends?" the girl asked. "Never seen you in here before, Han."

Hannah could place her now. She worked with her mum at Nippers. Christ. "Just some people from theater work-shop," she replied. She swung round to face the bar and cut that girl from her line of vision.

"Here you go," Ollie said, handing her a drink.

"Guess what," Hannah hissed. "I've just seen someone who works with my mum."

Ollie frowned. "Not going to be in trouble, are you?"

"No, of course not." She took a desperate swig of her

drink. It tasted like Coke with sweets dissolved in it; she could barely detect the Malibu at all.

"You don't look underage so maybe she won't think to mention it to your mom," he added. "Come on, let's see who's here."

She felt foolish, trotting behind Ollie like a puppy. The cigarette smoke was making her chest hurt and her breathing feel tight, but no way was she pulling her inhaler out. A waitress squeezed past her with some kind of towering open sandwich on a tray. Ollie had already joined a table at the far end of the restaurant. She checked her watch; just gone six. A wave of sadness came over her. Ollie was bantering with his friends as if he'd forgotten she existed. One of the girls threw back her head and laughed theatrically.

If she stayed to eat she'd be horribly late. Her mum would start calling her cell— "I'm not hassling you, love, just wondered when you'll be home" —and it would be so cringey and embarrassing and end up with Hannah withering inside. She couldn't have her mother phoning her at the Opal.

Ollie turned round from the table and smiled at her. Ollie, with those lips and those cheekbones, surrounded by rich boys and girls who looked gleaming and golden as if they'd all been on holiday together. More than anything, Hannah wanted to belong.

The girl from Nippers had turned back to her friends, seemingly forgetting that Hannah was there. *Stuff it,* she thought, fishing out her phone, switching it off and plunging it back into the murky depths of her schoolbag.

Taking a deep breath, and gripping her Malibu and Coke, Hannah sauntered over to join her vivacious new friends at the Opal.

6

$\mathcal{A}$rchie-someone, that was who Jane needed right now. She'd seen those colors—fiery shades to bring warmth into Max's dingy back room—at Archie-someone's exhibition at the Barbican. She flicked her gaze along the spines of books crammed onto the shelf in the studio. From a distance, Archie's panels had looked crazed, like stars exploding. Up close you could see the tiny fragments bonded snugly together.

Jane hadn't planned to see the exhibition or known the first thing about stained glass. Yet she'd found herself pacing the gallery, reluctant to leave, and had still been enthusing about Archie's work as she and Hannah had left the building. Hannah had fixed on her *yeah-yeah* face.

Unable to find any reference to an Archie in her books, Jane headed back into the house. There were three answer-phone messages: "Han? It's me, Amy. What are you up to at the weekend? Want to come over? I've tried your cell but it must be switched off." Weird, Jane thought: Hannah was at Amy's right now. Must be an earlier message.

"Jane," Sally gushed, "sorry to land this on you—meant to mention it but you were in such a rush to see Max…how was his house by the way? Anyway, could you cover for Lara on Wednesday, do the double shift? She's got some hospital appointment, so sorry…" Jane could hear the frenetic rustling of papers in the background.

"Jane, are you there?" There was a clang, and the sound of a tap being turned on full blast. Nancy, Jane's mother, was incapable of attempting one task at a time. She'd be slapping gloss paint on to a window frame while pouring industrial-strength coffee; brushing mud off her boots while squabbling on the phone with a council employee about trash collection. "Just checking," her mother boomed, "that you and Han are still coming on Tuesday, got some belly pork in, don't want it going to waste. There's enough waste in this world with all those food mountains." The phone was slammed down abruptly.

Jane smirked as she switched on the PC in the corner of the living room. She logged on and Googled Archie Stained Glass. Here it was: the exploding star, the colors melding together like cross-sectioned volcanoes in Hannah's geography books.

The phone rang again. Jane picked it up in the kitchen and brought it through to her seat at the PC. "Hi, Mum," she said, still focusing on Archie's website.

"So are you coming?" Nancy asked.

"Yes, of course—only no meat for Han, Mum. She's vegetarian, remember? Has been for seven years."

"It's only *belly pork*."

"Pork's pig, Mum. Pig's an animal."

"Oh, for goodness sake, how did everyone get to be so faddy?" Nancy's voice was swamped by a glooping noise.

"What are you doing?" Jane asked.

"Mixing concrete."

"In your kitchen?" Only her mother would argue that mixing concrete in a kitchen was a perfectly normal activity.

"It's *for* the kitchen, Jane. That cavity where the washing machine's bits went into the wall before the damn thing caught fire…you do remember?"

"Yes, Mum," Jane said resignedly, clicking the "about Archie" button. Here was the man himself: Archie Snail, with weaselly eyes, a fluff of unruly gray hair and a short, tufty beard. His eyebrows swooped down toward a magnificent nose, as if a stranger had burst into his studio and forced him to be photographed entirely against his wishes.

"See you Tuesday, then," Nancy said brusquely, "and tell Hannah she'll have to make do with side veggies."

"That's fine, Mum. I'm sure she'll *love* the veggies."

Jane logged off and pulled out a sketchpad from the shelf beneath the desk. Hannah would have eaten at Amy's, so she wouldn't have to cook. She stared at the blank sheet, waiting for ideas to form. She began scribbling, making sweeping lines, her elbow colliding with Hannah's birthday nail polish. It fell to the floor, the bottle smashing and forming a mossy-green pool. Damn, she'd wipe it up later, replace Hannah's nail polish tomorrow.

Jane's hand moved freely across the page. She'd make something special—something to bring that sad little room to life. All these years she'd tinkered away in her studio, kidding herself that this was a proper business she was running; she needed to rev up, to *push* herself, like her mother was always nagging her to. Nancy would, of course, conveniently forget that Jane had a full-time day job, and that Sally asking her to cover someone else's shift happened so frequently it no longer surprised her.

Jane stared at her sketches. This piece, she sensed, would be her turning point. She'd create the loveliest thing she'd ever made in her life. Hannah was growing up, pushing her away; fighting it made it hurt even more. Jane needed something else—a life beyond a sullen daughter who shrank away from her as they passed on the stairs as if she'd become surplus to requirements...or, worse, a downright irritation. Something that, given the chance, Hannah would get rid of as swiftly as possible, like a verruca.

Jane's heart was racing. She was a wart on the foot of her daughter; the person she'd made the focus of her entire world for the past fifteen years. Jane snatched another sheet from the pad and worked on and on, ideas swilling feverishly around her brain, not noticing that the room was shrouded in shadow and Hannah still hadn't come home.

7

By the time Hannah left the Opal, a fine mist had descended on the street, making everything look hazy and not quite real. Or was that all the drinks she'd had? One of Ollie's mates—Tara, or maybe Lara—had laughed at her Malibu and Coke, saying, "That's such a girlie drink, Han. You don't strike me as a girlie girl at all." Despite the teasing, Hannah had liked the way Ollie's friends had slipped so easily into calling her Han. Next round, she'd asked for wine like everyone else.

Hannah had never had undiluted wine before—only with fizzy water at Granny Nancy's when she'd barely been able to taste it. She could taste it now, raw in her throat, blending nicely with that heap of slimy mushrooms with garlic and bits of unidentifiable leaf.

What had made her order mushrooms? She detested mushrooms—a fact that her dad occasionally forgot. Why did everyone assume that vegetarians went crazy for mushrooms, and tomatoes, too, for that matter? She'd gawped at the menu, hoping desperately to spot something familiar—something unobtrusive like an omelette or pasta or plain bread and cheese. The stress of the whole choosing business had killed her appetite. Yet she hadn't wanted to sit there, twiddling the stem of her wineglass while Ollie and his posh mates stuffed their faces all around her.

Hannah glanced around the foggy street, aware of smoke and food smells clinging to her jacket and hair. She didn't know which way to go. Ollie and the others were still in there, having coffee now, spooning froth from their cappuccinos. If any of them were drunk, they were doing a brilliant job of hiding it. Hannah felt woozy, as if in a half sleep, and was unable to figure out her current location. She cupped her hands around her mouth and exhaled to check if her breath stank of alcohol. All she could smell was her skin.

She squinted at her watch. Its hands, and the tiny black dashes for numbers, looked fuzzy. In fact there were two sets of dashes, overlayed and slightly out of register. Hannah rubbed her watch's face in case it had steamed up or she'd got grease on it from the mushrooms. The dashes still hovered uncertainly.

Was this how it felt to be drunk? It wasn't as extreme as she'd imagined. Her limbs appeared to be functioning normally. She hadn't gone cartoon-wobbly, like Barnaby Lake acting drunk—very badly, she might add—in *Whisky Galore* at theater workshop. She wondered if she'd sound okay when she spoke. She needed to test her voice, to rehearse her excuse: "Hi, Mum, sorry I'm late. Was my phone off? Must've run out of juice. No, I didn't go to Amy's—change of plan. A few of us went out for a bite to eat. I know, Mum, you must've been worried. I'm really, really sorry." There—how simple was that? Too many sorrys, maybe, she'd have to watch out for that. Didn't want to overdo it. If lying came this easily when she'd had a Malibu and Coke and God knows how much wine, maybe she should drink alcohol more often.

Hannah strutted to the end of the street, confident that this was the corner she'd turned with Ollie. There was the canal, shimmering eerily beneath the low wall. A narrowboat swayed lazily. She was doing okay. She felt light all over, graceful and fluid, like a dancer. She wished she could dance right here on the pavement, and that she'd had the forethought to wear the lovely top her mum had bought for her birthday. It was mottled blue-green with tiny pearls stitched around its hem. Jane had good taste, Hannah granted her that. Shame she hadn't picked out a few new things for herself when she'd bought it.

Hannah trailed her hand along the square-cut railings as she walked, enjoying their metallic smell. The evening had gone well, she decided, even when the issue of money had come up. "I've only got three quid," she'd whispered to Ollie.

"Don't worry about it," he'd said with a casual flap of his hand. "Call it your late birthday treat." No one seemed concerned by the astronomical prices of the drinks, or how much they were racking up with the food, drinks and coffees. Next time—Hannah was sure there'd be a next time—she'd rake together some money from somewhere. She'd save her pocket money, ask her dad for a tenner, maybe do some jobs for her mum to earn extra. She could offer to clear out the studio. No, not the studio. She'd cut the grass. Did grass still need cutting at the end of September?

Hannah knew where she was now. She'd been less than a mile from home. She smiled, feeling proud at handling herself so well with all those strangers. "Come on, Han," Ollie had said when she'd finally forced herself up from her chair. "Stay a bit longer. We're going back to Felix's to watch a movie." Perhaps it was best that she'd been first to leave. Didn't those dumb girls' magazines always tell you to play it cool?

Although they were students—media studies appeared to be a common theme, apart from Ollie who was at sixth-form college—no one had made her feel like an idiot schoolgirl. Hannah wondered if she'd ever reach a point in her life when she'd be able to say, "I'm a student," while tucking into a salad that looked like a small unruly garden with a poached egg draped over it, and have it seem as if she was actually enjoying it.

Albemarle Street was in sight now. London Fields looked spooky beneath its thin veil of mist. Hannah could make out the yellowish light from her living room window and the bushy outlines of the plants in the window boxes. She walked briskly, feeling cool and elegant like Audrey from *Little Shop of Horrors*. Even her schoolbag felt lighter.

She pressed the catch on the rusting wrought-iron gate and pushed it open. Hannah no longer cared about her dad leaving the old house, and a bunch of strangers moving into it, including some kid who'd be sure to spot that loose floorboard and lift it and find her—

The door flew open. A woman stood there—her mother, silhouetted against the rectangle of creamy light from the hall. Hannah couldn't make out her face, but she could sense worry; it shivered in the air between them. She stepped forward, trying to muster a smile; a *bold* smile, like she'd practiced on the way home. "Hannah?" came Jane's voice. "Where on earth have you been?"

Hannah opened her mouth. Her mum didn't sound angry but scared—really scared. She could see now that her eyes were pink and sore-looking. "Why was your phone switched off?" Jane demanded.

"I—" Hannah began. No more words came out.

"I've been so worried. You can't imagine what it's been like." Jane's voice wavered. She sounded old—way older than usual. She swept her hands over her face, pushing back her hair distractedly. Hannah tried then, really tried to make words. She opened her mouth.

All that came out was a garlicky burp swiftly followed by white wine, Malibu and Coke and the mushrooms and little green herby bits, splattering the cracked paving slabs and the weeds that jutted between them.

8

"*A*re you *sure?*" Max asked.

"Of course I'm sure," Jane retorted. "She threw up all over the path! I've just cleared it up and poured disinfectant all over it. What else could it have been—food poisoning?" She clamped her mouth shut. She was ranting, as if any of this were Max's fault.

"Could it have been her school dinner?" he asked hesitantly.

"She doesn't have them. Takes a packed lunch. You think a cheese sandwich would've made her—"

"No, no," Max muttered.

"Anyway, I could smell drink on her breath. She *reeked*, Max. She'd been out after theater workshop, getting plastered with God knows who. Where d'you think she could have gone?"

Max paused. "Didn't you ask her?"

"Yes, but she was really vague. Said she'd gone to some place—that's all she'd tell me, a *place*—with a bunch of people I'd never heard of. Ally someone. Tara or Cara. I just helped her upstairs and put her to bed. Couldn't bring myself to keep on at her when she was feeling so awful."

"I'll have a talk with her," Max said gently.

"Don't worry. I'll do it."

"It's not fair, expecting you to deal with every little thing that comes up."

"I don't want you to *do* anything." She'd have to stop calling him, Jane decided, whenever some minor emergency occurred. She'd gone straight to the phone when Hannah had been balancing wet-footed on the bath's edge, fallen in and split her forehead on the tap; she'd needed him when Hannah had located a wasps' nest in a tree trunk and been stung countless times on the scalp, triggering an asthma attack and Ventolin treatment at Whitechapel hospital. The frequent accidents, an asthma attack during maths just six months ago—Jane had needed Max every time. Just spilling words down the phone would make her feel better.

But what could Max do at eleven at night with Hannah already in bed and snoring throatily? After helping her upstairs, sponging her face and hair and easing her out of her clothes, Jane had felt oddly alone. The house had seemed eerily still, as if the person she'd invited had failed to show up. It had made her feel desperately sad, the way Hannah had slumped on the edge of her bed, all pale and crumpled-looking, not caring about being naked in front of her. Usually, if Jane happened to catch her in bra and knickers, she'd fold her milky arms over herself as if her own mother was some unfamiliar male who'd barged into her room.

"I could come over," Max said. "I'd be there in ten minutes on my bike."

"Don't be silly. It's late and really foggy outside."

"I was working anyway, starting to rip the cupboards out of the kitchen."

Jane smiled. "Bet your neighbors love all that racket at this time of night."

"No one's complained so far," Max said.

They wouldn't, would they? Jane thought, picturing Veronica in her heather-colored suit, probably rapping on his door—no, swishing straight in—and insisting on helping with cupboard removal. "Are you on your own?" Jane asked.

"Of course I am," Max said softly. "Why wouldn't I be?"

"I just wondered."

"Shall I come now, see how you're getting on with the window designs?"

"Okay," she said with a smile, "come over and see my etchings."

Max had a knack for saying the right things. Solid and sensible Dad-type things that had the effect of shrinking one dramatic yet out-of-character event to something approaching its rightful proportions. "We've both been there, haven't we?" he said. "What about that time on the train back from Brighton when you threw up all over my shoes and—"

"I was eighteen!"

"What's the difference?"

"She's fifteen—only *just* fifteen—and it's not me who went out and got pissed. It's my daughter."

"*Our* daughter," Max corrected her. They were lounging on the living room floor with Jane's sketches spread out all around them. She'd roughly tinted the shapes with watercolors; the colors of nasturtiums and violent poppies. Max picked one up and cocked his head.

"Well," Jane said, "what d'you think?"

He traced a finger along the graceful curves. "They're fantastic, but I'm not going to choose one. I think you should do whatever feels right."

She threw him a glance. Working with clients was never this simple. Mr. Pemberton from the Golden Fry had deliberated over her sketches for weeks.

Of course, this wasn't a client. This was Max. He went through to the kitchen to make tea, and when he reappeared with two mugs he looked hesitant. "Can I ask you something?" he said.

"Sure."

"Remember that neighbor of mine, the one who—"

"Yes, of course I remember." Why wouldn't he say her name, Jane wondered?

He placed the mugs on the floor and stretched out on his side on the rug. "She's being...persistent."

"What kind of persistent?" Jane asked, trying to keep her voice light.

"She wants to go out for dinner on Friday."

"With *you?*"

"Don't look so shocked. It's weird, though—she'd booked a table for seven thirty before checking with me. I'm never home from the shop until at least eight, you know that…."

Jane wasn't sure if it was the too-early thing that was worrying him, or the whole dinner-with-Veronica thing. *Max has a date,* she told herself. *So what? Look pleased for him, dammit.* "Are you going to go?" she asked, some sort of smile on her face.

He frowned. "I don't know. I feel…kind of pushed into it."

"Poor, defenseless Max…" Jane smirked.

"What d'you think?"

"It doesn't matter what I think."

She was still telling herself that it really didn't matter—that Max's Friday night plans didn't relate to her life in any way whatsoever—as he wheeled out his bike into the cold, damp night.

Jane couldn't sleep. She was worried about Hannah being sick again and she was worried about worrying because it was keeping her awake and she'd be exhausted next day at Nippers. Each time she closed her eyes, her mind filled with pictures: of Max's window—before and after—and the awkward scene when Veronica had flounced into his kitchen. Max had behaved as if two separate sides of his life had been slammed together: the dazzling-new-neighbor side, and Jane. The ex-wife side.

What did it matter that they were having dinner and God knows what else? Beneath the pushy manner, the overdone face and obsession with strangers' iron levels, she was probably a perfectly decent person. Max would have some fun, if nothing else; they could laugh about it once it was all over. Jane tried to pictured them chuckling over Veronica's insistence on getting up at 5:00 a.m. in order to fashion her hair into those tumultuous waves. But she couldn't do it. She was incapable of imagining the "over" bit.

It was pathetic, the way she still thought of Max as somehow belonging to her. He'd been in her life for so long, that was the trouble. They'd met as eighteen-year-old students. She'd been drawn in by those dark eyes and perfect mouth; most boys' lips verged on the too-thin or bulbous or, thanks to a short-lived craze during their freshman year, were garnished with endless variations on the creative facial hair theme. Max didn't possess facial hair. He had a smile that made Jane want to kiss him, which she had, not caring who might saunter down the corridor and see them. Next morning, she'd woken up in his bedsit and spied her clothes bunched up on the floor. They looked as if they'd come off in one swoop.

Jane had been on the brink of leaving home, and it had made sense for her to move into Max's bedsit. A backpacking trip to India and severe stomach upset later—and, presumably, throwing up the Pill—and she was pregnant. Too fast, like Hannah's speedy delivery. Jane had barely known who she was. Yet, when Hannah was born, she'd felt as vital a part of Jane as her own heart.

Then one night, when Hannah was nearly five years old, Max had blundered home looking bewildered and poured it all out—that he'd slept with a woman who worked at the shop. He'd waited for Jane to start shouting and crying. She hadn't cried—not in front of him anyway. But she'd frozen inside, as if her blood and heart had stopped moving, and everything had changed.

Hannah was coughing now, crying, "Mum!" from her room.

Jane tumbled out of bed and hurried through. "What is it, Han?"

"Was Dad here?"

"Yes." Jane crouched beside Hannah's bed and touched her clammy forehead.

"Why?" Hannah asked hoarsely.

"He…he just came to see the drawings I'd done for his window."

"You weren't talking about me?" She sounded like a little girl.

"No, darling. Go to sleep." Jane bent to kiss her cheek. An acidic smell hung in the air.

Later, as dawn crept into her room, Jane wondered if it had really happened: Hannah throwing up, Max blurting out that Veronica stuff. It had been a night, she decided, for all kinds of stuff falling out of mouths.

Nancy's knife rapped against the chopping board like some manically pecking bird. While Jane had ploughed gallantly through her mother's dinner, Hannah had shunted tinned peas and boiled potatoes around her plate before excusing herself to watch TV in the living room. "How's the window business going?" Nancy asked, battering a nectarine with the rusting knife.

"Really well," Jane said, refusing to be riled by her

mother's refusal to use the term *stained glass. Window business* made Jane think of cold callers trying to hard sell double glazing.

"Had many commissions?" Nancy asked, swiveling round from the worktop to fix Jane with her beady gaze. Her eyes glimmered like sequins.

"It's been a good month," Jane said firmly. "I've done a window for a restaurant, I'm restoring a panel for a church in Stoke Newington and Max has this window—"

"You're working for *Max?*"

"Why wouldn't I, Mum?"

"And three jobs is a good month?" Nancy remarked, for once resisting the urge to comment on her curious relationship with Max. Jane had never told her mother why she'd left him. Throwing everything away over one silly one-night stand? Nancy would have thought she'd lost her mind.

"It's enough," she said, perching on the table's softly worn edge. "A panel takes me at least a couple of weeks— sometimes months." *Months,* Nancy would be thinking, *and I had that wall concreted in one afternoon?*

Nancy lived alone in an echoey house in a quietly fading tree-lined road in Muswell Hill. Her kitchen was of a 1950s vintage with the odd post-war toast crust poking out from under the oven. One afternoon, when Jane had been helping her mother prepare dinner, she'd opened the oven door and glimpsed the grisly remains of what appeared to be an antique shepherd's pie.

Nancy was short and stocky with wiry hair cut close to her face. Her hands were large and powerful, like a farmer's.

Since Jane's father had died five years ago, Nancy had appeared to be entirely self-sufficient. When a car had skidded into her front garden wall, Nancy had rebuilt it. She'd boycotted supermarkets with the advent of loyalty cards— "Do these people really think they can bribe me, Jane?"—shopping instead at local butchers and greengrocers and lugging her purchases home in numerous disintegrating shopping bags.

At sixty-seven years old, Nancy still maintained the clippings library that she'd run for over three decades. She'd come up with the idea the week Jane had started at primary school. Other mothers, giddy with freedom, had launched into a convivial round of coffee mornings and charity committee meetings. Nancy wasn't one for baking brownies or manning a Guess the Knitted Scarecrow's Birthday stall. She read voraciously, stored information in her brain like a primitive but remarkably effective filing system, and had put her talents to work. Articles about actors, musicians, artists, the royal family—anyone with the merest smidgeon of interest about them—were snipped from newspapers and magazines, filed and sent on request to journalists and researchers.

The smaller downstairs room—it had once been a dining room, Jane vaguely remembered—was lined with looming filing cabinets and tea chests piled high with dust-strewn files. On top of the cabinets were stacks of ancient jigsaws that Jane and her mother—then, later, Nancy and Hannah—had pieced together on the threadbare carpet. As a child Jane had tried to avoid going into the clippings room. She'd feared that, if she had so much as touched one file, the entire library—years' worth of painstaking work—would come crashing down all around her.

Nancy piled the fruit into three bowls and sploshed Rose's Lime Cordial over the top "to make juice." She and Jane carried the bowls into the living room where Nancy snatched the remote control from the sofa. "*Gran*," Hannah protested as Nancy flipped from the music show to a documentary about wildlife in the Scottish Highlands.

Jane squeezed on to the worn sofa and nibbled a chunk of brownish apple. On TV a stag was posing on a hillside while a doe emerged from a nearby forest. With its wide eyes and tremulous legs, it reminded Jane of Veronica. The doe stepped gingerly toward the stag and nuzzled around him.

"You might learn something, Han," Nancy teased. "I know what you girls are like with your heads full of boys."

"I'm not *you girls*," Hannah retorted. "I'm *me*."

Nancy's face softened. She slid a chunky arm around her granddaughter's shoulder and said, "I know you are. You're my wonderful girl and you're to tell your mother to give that business of hers a kick up the backside."

Jane glanced at her mother: an infuriating woman who wrecked perfectly acceptable fruit by dowsing it with cordial, refused to call in tradesmen and had stood by her husband—despite his perpetual philandering—just to prove that she was tough enough to handle that, too.

They left Nancy's road with the windscreen wipers flapping urgently. Nancy's was one of the few places Jane drove to. She'd bought a car only when it had become apparent that she'd need transport to bring equipment into the studio, to pick up supplies of glass and deliver finished panels. She drove a metallic green Škoda that Hannah had nicknamed "The Embarrassment", but otherwise she preferred to walk or cycle. Jane's bike was a lumpen no-frills model—a cart horse with crumbling joints compared to Max's nifty gazelle—and was currently nursing a puncture back in the hallway.

"Kate from work said she saw you last night," Jane said, casting Hannah a swift glance.

"Yeah?" Hannah murmured.

"She said you were in some bar-restaurant place near the canal, couldn't remember its name. Some new place."

"We just went for something to eat." Hannah released a small sigh.

"And drink," Jane added. "Did you have enough money?"

"Ollie—a *friend* paid. It wasn't much."

"Okay, Han. You know, don't you, that if you drink that much you're going to get sick?"

"Uh-huh."

"How did you manage to get served?"

"I don't know. Suppose I must look older."

"You don't," Jane insisted. "You look your age. You look *fifteen*. Were you with older people?"

"Yeah." Hannah gazed pointedly out of the window.

"Getting that drunk," Jane continued, "makes you vulnerable. God knows what could have happened. Don't feel you have to keep up with the kind of people who go to these places." She hadn't intended to lurch into a sermon, not with Hannah in a reasonably pleasant mood after visiting Granny Nancy. Now that she'd started, she couldn't stop. "There's plenty of time," she rattled on, "to go out drinking when you don't have school in the morning and you're old enough to—"

"All right!" Hannah's right ear was burning bright red.

"I rang Amy's mum, did I tell you? She said you haven't been to their place for weeks. You've been *lying* to me, Han."

"Can we forget it, please?" They'd stopped at a red light. Jane's chest was juddering with the effort of trying to sound controlled, and not lose her cool or carry on past the point at which Hannah would listen. So much of being a parent required one to be in control at all times; to talk calmly, as if you'd been programmed not to overreact, when what you really wanted to do was grab your kid by the shoulders and yell, "Who's this *Ollie?*"

The familiar streets snaked between row upon row of redbrick houses. Jane breathed deeply, remembering going to pubs when she wasn't much older than Hannah; it wouldn't have occurred to the jaded staff to ask for ID. Her father, a neurologist, would be too wrapped up in his work and extracurricular affairs to note where she went, and her mother would spend long days in the clippings room with the door firmly shut. Unlike Jane, Hannah wouldn't be allowed to touch alcohol again until she was twenty-seven.

"You would tell me," Jane added, "if something was worrying you?"

Hannah paused, biting her lip. "Actually, there is something."

Jane tightened her grip on the steering wheel. "What is it?"

"I only had a few of Gran's horrible peas. Can we stop for chips?"

Jane smiled, indicating left. "Of course we can." This was their secret pit stop after a visit to Nancy's: the Golden Fry, featuring Jane's sleek stained glass fish above its entrance.

As they ate in silence in the car, Jane replayed her talk with Max. He was right; some kids went out and got drunk all the time. They took drugs and had underage sex and got pregnant. They were lucky, Jane reflected, to have a daughter like Hannah. She and Max had a lot to be thankful for.

She piled in more chips, trying to erase the lime cordial taste from her tongue.

9

*W*hat was happening to Max's beautiful daughter? Getting drunk wasn't really the issue. Didn't all teenagers do that at some point? Barely a day had gone by in his late teens and twenties when he and Jane hadn't gone out for a few drinks or got stuck into the wine at home. Back then, he'd been able to get away with it. As a student, and later a cycle courier, he'd been able to lurch through the following day without having to properly engage his brain. When he'd started to take cycling more seriously, acquiring not one gleaming steel-framed model but also a training bike, touring bike and mountain bike, Max had realized he'd have to start taking care of himself, not to mention watching his cash. The shop had changed everything. Spokes required every ounce of his concentration and energy. A couple of glasses of wine were pretty much his limit these days.

"She was probably trying to keep up with her friends," Veronica told him over the restaurant table.

"I don't even know who her friends are," Max sighed. "She's changed so much these past few months. Some days she'd come to the shop after school. She'd hang about in the workshop, helping the guys with repairs and make tea and—" What the hell was he saying? He was having dinner with a woman. A woman who'd booked the table and asked him out—in that order—which surely indicated a certain degree of keenness. Veronica was, he decided, charming company: attractive, full of life and sparkle, a fine antidote to endless DIY.

Max wouldn't have chosen the restaurant. It was a little too prissy, too self-consciously smart for his taste. Yet they'd fallen into easy chat, and the food was magnificent. Now he was going to ruin the evening by babbling on about Hannah. What did Veronica care about his moody daughter or, worse, his business? "Don't talk about cycling," Andy had warned him in the workshop. "Women can detect this obsessive glint in your eye. It puts them off, believe me. You can mention races—especially races you've won—but *on no account* start on about tubular steeling or alloy wheels."

"So," Veronica murmured, "tell me more about your shop." She'd ordered sea bass—not with the roasted root vegetables that were supposed to accompany it, but a mixed salad and dressing on the side. It glimmered with virtue from its white plate.

Max shrugged. "It ticks along. Spokes isn't your flashy, showroomy kind of place. We manage, but it's pretty chaotic."

"And you're happy with that?" she asked. A piece of watercress wavered on the end of her fork.

"I'd love to expand, have more space. I've started looking for premises in Stoke Newington or Stamford Hill."

She leaned toward him eagerly. "The shop's won awards, hasn't it?"

"Yes, a couple."

"So why put yourself down, Max, by saying it just ticks along? It's amazing what you've done. Didn't you set it up when Hannah was a baby? Honestly, I don't know how you did it."

He didn't mention the fact that he'd hardly been there for Jane and their baby daughter. Although it pained him to admit it, he'd resented having to cut down on training and racing. Nothing could have prepared him for the sacrifices you were required to make as a parent. "I haven't done it on my own," he added. "I've got Andy, who manages the shop—at least the sales side of things. I'm not really a salesperson."

"What kind of person are you, Max?" Veronica's eyes gleamed in the candlelight.

He swallowed, wondering what kind of information was required at this stage. Max had never met anyone quite like Veronica; certainly no one who'd made their intentions so clear. He couldn't help admiring her. And now, as he sawed into his medium-rare steak, he was glad he'd come. "I suppose I'm quite obsessive," he said.

"About what kind of things?"

"Well, cycling, of course. The competitive aspect—the racing. You don't get anywhere unless you push yourself."

"That's what I feel," Veronica said. "My business keeps me

going but it's not enough for me, Max. I'm ambitious, like you. I need to throw myself into something one hundred per cent." She popped a morsel of fish the size of a fingernail clipping into her mouth. "Maybe," she added, "you could help me."

"How?" Max asked.

"By telling me how you've done it—built up a business from scratch."

Max shifted uncomfortably. "It's been hard. The shop has affected other parts of my life."

"Such as?" She stabbed a halved cherry tomato with her fork.

"My personal life, I suppose. My marriage."

"That can't have been all your fault."

If only you knew, he thought. "When I was setting up Spokes," he told her, "Hannah had just been born. She'd wake in the night and start crying and I'd shut my ears and will her to stop. Jane dealt with all of that."

"You were *working*," Veronica insisted, neatly aligning her cutlery on her plate.

Max looked at her, wondered how it was possible to have such perfectly shaped, symmetrical eyebrows. "Yes, but what's more important—work or family?"

"But you're a good dad."

"I don't know about that." He had no intention of telling Veronica what he'd done when Hannah was nearly five years old, when he hadn't been a good dad or a good husband or even a particularly good human being. Max and his staff had gone out to celebrate a glowing article about Spokes that had appeared in *Your Bike* magazine. They'd all been drinking, knocking it back. Max had, too, even though he hadn't had a drink for months. It had been a release: some fun and frivolity after years of slog.

A release that had screwed up his life.

"None for me, thanks," Veronica said, waving away the waiter with the dessert menus.

"Are you sure?" Max said. He was in no hurry to leave. His house was cluttered with stepladders and power tools and cans of paint. The Hazy Dawn bedroom still wasn't finished.

"I thought we could just…go home." Veronica smiled coquettishly.

Jesus, he'd never been propositioned so blatantly. He was blushing, for heaven's sake, at thirty-eight years old. His palms were sweaty. He met the gaze of the woman who'd stormed into his life with her fabulous meals and legs, which, if he wasn't careful, could turn him into a lecherous old man.

She was absolutely gorgeous. He'd met some lovely women over the years but no one who'd knocked him out with her piercing eyes and succulent lips. Earlier that evening, when he'd gone to the loo, he'd half expected her to have upped and left by the time he returned to their table.

They left the restaurant just after nine. Max's head milled with the possibilities of what the rest of the evening might offer. He hadn't slept with anyone for—how long was it? A year at least. He didn't like to dwell on it. The last one had been Michelle, the life model. Sex had felt like something they were obliged to get over and done with, like asking about each other's jobs. Afterward, she'd retrieved her nightie from somewhere under the duvet, stepped neatly into her clothes and politely asked him to order her a cab. After a few weeks she'd stopped calling, and Max couldn't find it in himself to care.

Veronica stepped on to the pavement and hailed a cab. She took Max's hand as it pulled up beside them. "You okay?" she asked as they settled into the backseat.

"Better than okay," Max replied.

"You don't mind going home this early?"

"No, of course not." Veronica had rested a hand on his knee. He felt warm, happy and about fifteen years old. The night was…Max almost laughed at the corniness of his thoughts. *The night was still young.*

10

*H*annah carefully fed each arm into a coat sleeve and pretended to hunt around the church cloakroom for her bag. Although she was fully aware that she'd stashed it beneath the slatted bench, she carefully checked every corner of the room. So thorough was her search, she was starting to believe that she really had lost her schoolbag and would have to find Beth, who ran theater workshop, to report it stolen.

Ollie had been here today but they'd been working in different groups and she hadn't had a chance to talk to him. In fact, he'd paid her no attention whatsoever. He hadn't even *looked* at her. She'd hoped that he might at least have asked what she was doing afterward, and had already decided to say that she was heading straight home. She'd think of some reason that didn't make her look too school-girlish to hang around drinking wine at the Opal. She wouldn't have him messing her around—being her friend one minute, blanking her the next. Now, it seemed, she wouldn't need to trot out any excuse because Ollie must have wandered off without saying goodbye.

Disappointment pooled in Hannah's stomach. Had she done something to annoy or upset him? She wished she could stop caring so much what other people thought of her; that she could acquire a slick of confidence like those girls at the Opal, or Emma and Georgia and the theater workshop elite. The whole session today, they'd been full of their parts in *Little Shop of Horrors*. Ollie was playing Orin, the crazy dentist. At least he deserved it. Whenever he was performing, you'd stop noticing the grumbling pipes or the cleaning lady who'd propped open the door with her mop, letting in cold air.

Everyone except Beth and the cleaner had left the church. Hannah felt stupid, hanging around in the vague hope that Ollie might come back to find her. She wished she had someone to walk home with—someone like Amy, who she could have a laugh with and maybe share some chips, but she'd stopped coming months ago.

Beth appeared at the cloakroom's entrance. She was wearing a gray felted sweater, skinny jeans and a string of brightly colored African beads. "Everything okay?" she asked, cocking her head.

"I've lost my bag," Hannah explained. "It must be here somewhere."

Beth scanned the hooks and benches, her gaze finally resting on Hannah's hiding place. "Is it that blue one under the bench?"

"Oh, yeah, thanks." She dived down to retrieve it.

Beth hovered, clearly wanting to chat. Her springy auburn hair looked as if wanted to escape from the plastic claw that gripped it on top of her head. "I hope you're not too disappointed with not getting a main part," she added.

Hannah came up to her feet, shaking her head vigorously. "Of course not."

"It's just…you've seemed a bit distracted lately. I was wondering if you're still committed to the group, if you're enjoying—"

"I *love* it," Hannah protested.

Beth smiled warmly. "Well, that's good. Just as long as you're not upset…and you'll be brilliant in the chorus."

"I'm fine," Hannah said, slinging her bag over her shoulder to signal: *I want to go now.*

"Have you seen Ollie?" Beth asked.

"No, I think he must've left."

"He was looking for you. Said he'd see you in the usual place." Beth crooked an eyebrow.

"Okay, thanks." Hannah flashed a quick smile, hoping that Beth wouldn't register the instant blush that was flaming her cheeks, and hurried out into the dusk.

She saw him smoking under the bridge on the towpath. "Hi," she said, trying to dampen the breathlessness in her voice. "Why didn't you wait?"

He took a quick puff of his cigarette. "Had a bit of trouble with my mum this morning. She'd threatened to come and pick me up from the church so I skipped off early."

Hannah wouldn't have imagined Ollie experiencing

Trouble With Parents. He was virtually an *adult,* for God's sake. "What happened?" she asked.

"Nothing much. She's just a bit…intense."

"Mine, too," Hannah murmured. Ollie rested his back against the pitted stone of the bridge. Hannah leaned against the spot beside him, even though her part was slimy and she was forced to stand with her feet unnaturally apart to avoid slipping in the sweet-and-sour something.

Ollie flicked his half-smoked cigarette into the canal, where it landed with a hiss. "Hope you didn't get into trouble last Monday night," he ventured.

"No, it was fine."

"You looked a bit tipsy when you left."

"I was okay," Hannah said firmly. Ollie looked at her as if he knew it hadn't been okay at all. She flinched as his hand touched hers. It was as if the warmth between them, and not their actual skin, was making contact. Hannah's entire body stiffened.

"Want to come over on Saturday?" Ollie asked. "I'm having some friends round, bit of a party. Mum works Saturday nights so I've got the place to myself."

Her heart was bounding like a wild thing, caged in her chest. "What about your dad?" she asked.

"I thought I'd told you. My dad's never been around—it's just me and Mum."

Hannah paused, then asked, "Did your dad die?"

"No, but he's never been part of my life." Ollie's voice was flat as a puddle.

"Why not?" Hannah asked, unable to help herself. She was just like her mother: eager, prying, unable to let go.

"I don't think him and my mum were really together. It just sort of…happened. I was an accident, Han." He laughed. "It's not a big deal. D'you see much of your dad?"

"It's meant to be every other weekend but it's never as organized as that. It works out okay. My parents are pretty friendly with each other."

"Weird," he said, squeezing her hand. "So, Saturday. Think you can come?"

"Sure." She'd figure out some way of spending Saturday evening at a seventeen-year-old boy's house with no adults present. Granny Nancy was always reminding her how smart she was. She'd come up with something.

They stood there, with the bridge arcing over their heads like a giant arm, and the traffic rumbling above them. It felt safe: dark, damp and secret. Ollie raised a hand and stroked Hannah's cheek. Then his lips were on hers, and it wasn't remotely like horrible Michael Linton, who'd tried to crumple her face with his mouth. You read all that crap in the girls' magazines—the ones Amy and Rachel bought religiously—and it was all about eyes closing, lips meeting and learning how to relax. Kissing wasn't something you *learned,* Hannah realized now, or wrote to some patronizing agony aunt about in the hope of gleaning tips. It just happened.

Kissing Ollie felt natural, as if the billions of cells in her body had suddenly figured out how to behave. She kissed him and kissed him, not caring that she was probably standing in a puddle of sweet-and-sour sauce.

She wanted to kiss him forever.

11

"*H*ello?" chirped the female voice on the phone.

"Sorry, I think I've called a wrong—"

"Is that you, Jane?" the woman asked. "It's Veronica. Max just stepped into a bath. Shall I ask him to call you later?"

Jane was conscious of a numbness spreading up her body. It was how she'd imagined an epidural might feel: rattling toward her head, unstoppable. "There's no hurry," she blustered. "I'll talk to him when he's, um, out of the bath."

"Okay, take care now," Veronica said.

Jane replaced the receiver and glared at it. So Max was wallowing in a warm bubble bath, sipping a glass of wine, perhaps, that Veronica had kindly brought in for him. She'd be perched on the side of the bath, chatting away as he soaped himself. Maybe *helping* him soap himself. Jane shuddered, and tried to shoo the thought away.

Did he have a pet name for her yet? How would you shorten Veronica—to Ronnie? Or Nonnie? She was, Jane was certain, wearing some saucy negligee/robe-thing with nothing underneath. That voice—slow, drawly, with a husky edge—definitely had a tinge of the postcoital about it. Max seemed to have made the transition from lonesome singleton requiring meals-on-wheels to part of a couple, half of *Max-and-Veronica,* in the space of a month. Jane was shocked by the speed at which he'd slipped in to we-speak. Sure, there'd been evidence of the odd girlfriend at the old house: an unfamiliar lemon dressing gown hanging from a hook in the bathroom, a tub of moisturizer looking abandoned on the windowsill. No one, as far as she knew, had swanned around his bathroom, checking the water temperature for him: *ready for a little more hot, sweetheart?*

Jane wasn't wearing anything remotely robe-like. She was dressed in her oldest jeans, which were ripped at the knees, and a sweater she reserved for working in the studio during the colder months. Leaving Hannah playing music in her room, she marched across the back garden to the studio.

She pulled up a stool at the workbench where she'd spread out her watercolor sketches. Although she'd taken photos of Max's back room, she'd lost any sense of its dimensions and space. Her sketches looked crude and amateurish. Some of the Nippers kids could have produced better.

Hannah's golden star panel caught her eye. She'd made it when she was nine or ten and had been so proud that she'd insisted on taking it to school cocooned in thick layers of newspaper. Now it was propped against a wooden wall with no light coming through it. Hannah must have taken it down from the bathroom and dumped it here.

She wouldn't ask her daughter why she'd moved it, just as she'd forbid herself from mentioning Max's nudie wine waitress next time she saw him. He'd assume she was jealous, that she had a *problem* or something, which was so ridiculous as to be laughable. Did *she* need someone to answer her phone while she took a bath? Or to take *her* to dinner without being asked? No, she most certainly did not.

"Veronica's not what you think," Max said, levering the back tire from Jane's bike. The workshop at Spokes was jammed with wheels and dismembered frames heaped up like discarded scaffolding. Jane could barely squeeze in without fear of elbowing a tin of spanners from a shelf.

"I'm not thinking *anything*," she protested. "I don't have any preconceived ideas about her. She seemed really, really—" She scrabbled for words.

Max glanced up from his crouched position. In his new, coupled-up state, he even looked different. Kind of sleepy, more wrinkled around the eye region. His eyes looked different, too. They were glinting, Jane noticed. She'd never realized that eyes were actually capable of acquiring *glints*. He gave her a quizzical look, then turned back to her bike and fitted the new inner tube. He replaced the tire and flipped the bike the right way up. Jane pulled her purse from her bag.

"Don't be silly," Max said. "When have I ever charged you?"

"Well, thanks for fixing it."

"You know what?" he added. "I really think you'd like Veronica. She's managed all on her own for years with two kids. It hasn't been easy. Her son Dylan's a bit weird—quiet, withdrawn—but Zoë seems fine. She's a year older than Han. Maybe they'd get on."

What was this: some teenagers' matchmaking service? Jane pictured a younger version of Veronica minus the overglossed lips, weeping at the hairdressers. "You really think so?" she asked.

Max wheeled Jane's bike from the workshop through to the shop. "Might be good for her to broaden her circle. Stop her going out and drinking with those losers from theater workshop."

"She only did that once—"

"Just an idea," Max said. "I'm having a party, a kind of housewarming thing. You'll come, won't you? Hannah and Zoë could get to know each other."

"Your place can't be finished already."

"Nowhere near," he said, laughing. "It was Veronica's idea. She's been helping me paint downstairs and offered to dress the house for the party."

"*Dress* the house?" Jane blurted. "What will it be wearing?"

Exasperation clouded Max's eyes. "Why are you being like this?"

"I'm not being like anything!"

"Yes, you are. You're being…Jane."

"Sorry," she muttered, taking her bike from Max and gripping its handlebars fiercely. "Maybe I'm just feeling weird about being thirty-seven."

Max's hand shot to his mouth. "Shit, Jane—your birthday. I totally forgot."

"That's okay," she said, thinking: *you never forget*.

"Well, happy birthday."

"Thank you."

He held the door open as she wheeled out her bike, adding, "You will come on Saturday, won't you? It's just a casual get-together thing."

"Sure," she said, even though the prospect of Hannah be-friending this Zoë girl seemed as viable as jamming together pieces from different jigsaws and expecting them to fit.

12

*H*annah perched on the blue canvas sofa in the foyer of Nippers Nursery—"Quality Day Care From Three Months To Five Years"—trying to blot out the incessant whooping that was coming from the main play area. Someone was squawking about her picture not drying fast enough. A nursery song tape struggled tinnily in the background.

Hannah had never been a nursery song kind of kid. Like the fairy stories her dad had chosen for her, with their tales of princesses with shattered glass hearts, they'd made her yearn to run out of her nursery class and pull on her elastic eye patch and do some cutlass-waving. Now it sounded like every kid in the nursery was running on the spot. Imagine, she thought, spending seven hours a day here, as her mum did. Imagine coming home from work with face paint smeared on your trousers, glitter in your hair and your voice hoarse from all that storytelling and singing. Hannah couldn't help pitying her.

Would she ever reach a point when she'd want a child of her own? Hannah doubted it. Anyway, to get pregnant you had to have sex, a concept that she found faintly intriguing, yet represented a potential minefield of blundering embarrassment. Unlike Amy's mother, Jane had never subjected her to "the big talk." She'd merely dispensed little nuggets of info over the years; enough for Hannah to decide that, even if some boy ever wanted to do it with her, she'd be sure to use at least five methods of contraception at once.

A couple of mothers had wandered into the foyer and squished their blubbery bums on to the sofa on either side of Hannah. One had a mole on her chin with a wiry hair poking out of it. Hannah's thoughts of sex had brought her neatly round to Ollie Tibbs. At seventeen, surely he'd done it. He certainly looked like he had. He had this air about him—an ease with himself. Hannah imagined him kissing her and touching her. The two of them, all lips and limbs on his bed this Saturday night, with his friends all gone home and his mum not back for hours.

One of the mothers bent to prize a drawing pin from the sole of her clumpy shoe. The other was using a matchstick to gouge dirt from under her fingernails. They were sitting so close to Hannah they could probably tell she was daydreaming about a boy. They'd be having those *young people today* kind of thoughts. Hannah tried to focus on more mundane matters, like the process of osmosis that they were doing in biology. One substance absorbing another. Even that made her think of sex. Hannah blinked at the door to the play area, willing her mother to come through it.

They were singing now, a great swell of kids' voices:
Happy birthday to you,
Happy birthday to you,
Happy birthday dear Jay-ayne…
Christ, her mum's birthday. How could Hannah have forgotten? "Come to work after school," Jane had said that morning, "and we'll go somewhere nice for dinner."

Hannah had thought it was weird, this dinner-out-of-the-blue. Then she'd figured: end of the month. Jane would have just been paid. What hadn't registered was that September 30th was her birthday. She was thirty-six or thirty-seven or thirty-eight. Bloody hell.

Hannah checked her watch. Jane would be out any minute. She scanned the foyer hoping that, by some miracle, she might spy something to pass off as a lovingly chosen present. Her eyes flitted across multi-colored backpacks that hung from pegs like scrunched kites. A jumble of slippers and elastic-fronted plimsolls were heaped under a bench. The two mothers' kids were ferried out by a whey-faced day care nurse who looked about fourteen and was busily swamping them with coats and hats. They all clattered out, letting in an icy gust and leaving Hannah alone on the sofa.

She delved into her jacket pockets, the crumby remains of some long-forgotten Kit Kat embedding itself under her nails. She rifled through the schoolbag that lay at her feet. Nothing remotely giftlike in there: just a dog-eared biology homework jotter, a leaking green gel pen and a half-eaten packet of Starbursts. To her embarrassment, she realized she must have absent-mindedly combined her name and Ollie's in Biro on the inside of her schoolbag: *Hannah Tibbs.* It was time she grew up, got a grip on herself. She made a mental note to erase it—with bleach, maybe, or Wite-Out.

Hannah's entire body was rigid with panic. She had about ninety seconds to concoct some kind of excuse. Any old lie would do. She'd bought a present ages ago and lost it—or had left it at Amy's because it was too big to hide at their house. When had Hannah ever bought her mother anything *big?* Last birthday it had been a turquoise leather purse from Camden Market. She couldn't remember the present before that, but recalled the childish junk she'd bestowed upon her over the years. A coffee jar covered with ripped sticky paper—"for your pens, Mum!"—and a beaded bracelet made from self-hardening clay. Hardly the most alluring of gifts, but Jane had always seemed ridiculously pleased. She'd worn the clay bracelet for months until the elastic had snapped on the Roman Road and the beads had bounced down a drain.

"Hi, Han," Sally said, bundling a little girl toward the toilets.

"Hi," Hannah said dully. A string of snot was dangling from the child's nostril. The sight of it caused bile to rise in Hannah's throat. How could Jane deal with these kids and all their bodily fluids without puking? Sally had paused by the loo door and was studying her intently. "Looking forward to your night out?" she asked.

"Yes, thanks." Hannah forced herself to produce the

expected smile. There was something faintly comforting about Sally's round, cheery face with its flushed cheeks and cherry-colored lips. She looked like the kind of friendly auntie who'd always have something delicious baking in the oven. "Do me a favor," Sally added. "Remind your mum to use her present before it runs out."

"What is it?"

"A voucher for an aromatherapy massage at Serene. She could do with a treat, don't you think? It's got a three-month use-by date, so make sure—"

"Need *toilet*," the child protested, jerking Sally's arm.

Shit, thought Hannah. A massage. Her best friend had arranged for her to be slathered with exotic oils and Hannah hadn't even got it together to buy her a fifty pence nail buffer. Her gaze rested upon a pile of cards on the front desk. It was probably intended for some art project or other. The cards were pale blue and an off-putting lobster color and looked as if they'd spent years slowly fading on a windowsill. Just one: that was all Hannah would need to make a card. She hadn't made one since primary school. Jane would be so surprised and delighted, it might detract from the absence of gift. Hannah watched her own arm slide forward, as if mechanically controlled, her fingers pluck at the top sheet—a lobster one, as bad luck would have it—and jab it into her bag.

By the time Sally and the child had emerged from the loo, Hannah felt reasonably confident that she looked normal. Moments later, Jane was saying her goodbyes and hurrying in the reception area. "Hi, darling," she said, kissing Hannah's cheek. She pulled out her ponytail band and dragged her fingers through her hair like some primitive comb. "So," she said, "all set?"

Hannah rose awkwardly to her feet. "Happy birthday, Mum."

"Thanks, love. Where shall we eat? I haven't booked anywhere. Didn't think I'd need to this early."

"I don't mind," Hannah said, wondering when she should bring up the lack-of-present issue.

"Shall we just walk, see where looks good?" Jane swiped her coat from its hook.

"Okay."

After the heat and squall of Nippers, the outside world felt pleasantly cool. They walked without talking, passing a noodle bar with black-and-white portraits evenly spaced along its white walls. Trees were shedding their leaves. In the window of a Russian restaurant sat an enormous gilded tureen. "I think your dad's seeing someone," Jane ventured.

"Who?"

"That neighbor of his, the one I told you about? She brings round meals, is worried he can't take care of himself."

Hannah giggled. "God, how pathetic."

"She answered the phone last time I called," Jane added.

"Not living with him, is she?"

"Of course not," Jane said quickly. *I hope not,* was what she meant. Hannah could tell that she really minded this woman answering the phone. Her mother's eyes and voice revealed her every thought; she was virtually transparent.

"Let's try down here," Jane said, turning down a side street. The blue-and-white lettering of the Opal's sign came into view. *Please, no,* Hannah thought.

They stopped outside, and Jane perused the menu on the wall. Under the 'light suppers and snacks' section a dish caught Hannah's eye: pan-fried mushrooms with garlic and parsley on toasted ciabatta. She was aware of a staggering sensation in her stomach.

Through the frosted glass door she could see and hear people chatting and laughing: people like Ollie and those rhyming-name girls—Lara/Cara—who could negotiate wine lists and never threw up. "I don't like the look of it," Hannah murmured.

"Why not? It looks cosy—"

"I just…" Fragments of excuses jerked around her head. "It'll be smoky," she said firmly. "I can smell it out here." She felt lousy, playing her asthma card.

"Oh," Jane said, "sorry, Han, I didn't think. Anyway—" she glanced at the menu again "—it looks a bit poncey. Let's go for a blow-out Indian."

"That sounds great," Hannah said, trying to keep the swell of relief from her voice as they wandered off down the street.

In the restaurant Jane squinted at the menu. She was taking an age to decide, as if this were some Michelin-starred place and she was revving herself up to savor every bite. After much deliberation— "Ooh, this sounds lovely, what are you having, Han?" —she'd always go for the same viciously hot lamb dish with pilau rice and a naan bread filled with almondy stuff. To Hannah, that tasted all wrong—like a marzipan sandwich.

She stole glances at her mother as she tore into her meal. She really could pack it away—even that horrible belly pork at Granny Nancy's with a thick slab of fat round its edge. It was a wonder she wasn't twenty stone. She had a lovely figure, Hannah reflected, at least for someone of nearly forty: a narrow waist, a slightly rounded bum and perky breasts. In double art last week, Ritchy Harrison had leaned over and growled, "Hey, Han, I saw your mum the other day. She looked hot." Hannah had refused to respond to a crass comment like that. She'd scowled at his sagging lips and turned back to her Still Life With Trainer.

Watching Jane shovel in rice, Hannah felt a stab of guilt. She burrowed in her bag for the card. "Oh, Han," Jane enthused, taking it from her, "that's lovely. You haven't made me a card since you were—"

"Yeah, Mum, I know."

"Remember the last one you made? You'd cut out all these tissue paper shapes and stuck them on a—"

Hannah fazed off, wondering why parents were so fond of reminiscing about their children's younger days. It was if they wanted to keep you that way, frozen in time, still clutching Biffa and driving your pedal car.

"Han," Jane was saying, "did you hear what I said?"

"Sorry, what?"

Jane smiled uncomfortably. "Your dad's having a house-warming party. That new girlfriend's helping with the food and stuff."

"When?" Hannah asked.

"Saturday, around seven."

The announcement rolled over Hannah like a horrible wave. "But I can't," she stumbled, "it's—"

"Not busy, are you?"

Hannah's head milled with excuses. She'd arranged to go shopping with Amy...no, extra rehearsals for *Little Shop of Horrors*... Damn, she didn't even have a proper part. "Just a couple of hours," Jane added. "Veronica has a daughter around your age. Dad seems to think you'd get on."

This was getting worse, if that were possible. Instead of spending a long, virtually endless Saturday night at Ollie's house, Hannah would be forced to make friends with some spoiled-princess-stranger. She glared down at her rice. She usually loved it—the grains colored orange, yellow and green—but now it looked fake and unappetizing. "Do I have to?" she asked weakly.

Jane nodded firmly. "We'll escape early if it's awful. We'll have a code."

Poor Mum, Hannah thought; this can't be much fun for her either—feeling obliged to show up at a party arranged by her ex-husband's new woman. She knew she still had feelings for Max. Her parents weren't exactly how you'd expect a divorced couple to be. They weren't even legally divorced. "We haven't got around to it," Jane had said casually when Hannah had asked, as if she was referring to having the front door repainted.

Jane ripped off a hunk of naan the size of a mitten. She looked pretty with her lovely clear skin and peppery freckles across her nose and cheeks. She deserved more than a crappy card scrawled in the restaurant's toilet cubicle. Hannah was seized by an urge to tell her about Ollie: how she could hardly sleep for thinking about him, and even when she'd finally drifted off she'd wake at weird times like 5:37 a.m. with eerie light creeping into her room. Yet telling her would change everything. It felt too fragile to share.

Jane asked for the bill and re-read the message in her birthday card: *To my wonderful mum, all my love, Han xxx.* She looked up; their eyes met. Hannah detected a flicker of knowing, as if Jane was fully aware that the card had been hurriedly scrawled on the Bengal Star toilet.

As they left, Hannah could feel shame weighing her down, like a scratchy blanket she couldn't shrug off.

B

"*J*ane!" gushed Veronica in the hallway—formerly *Max's* hallway, now seemingly *Max-and-Veronica's* hallway—as if they were long-lost friends who'd been reunited on some cheesy TV show.

"Veronica!" Jane said, her entire body tensing with the effort of trying to exude warmth.

"You look wonderful," the hostess announced. Veronica's eyes made the journey from Jane's strappy suede shoes through long, purple skirt and black velvet top at astonishing speed.

"Thanks, so do you. Your dress is gorgeous."

She gave a little shrug. "Just a little old thing I found at the back of the wardrobe. Anyway, don't just stand there. Come in, join the throng. You must be Hannah. Gosh, aren't you like your father? Those astonishing dark eyes, an absolute beauty. There's a fruit punch in the kitchen, Han.

Come through and I'll pour you a glass. Now, Jane, what are you drinking?"

"I'll just have a—" Jane began, but Veronica had already swished into a kitchen populated by glossy strangers. Most of the women had backs and shoulders on display. No one appeared to weigh more than eight stone. The guests were chatting enthusiastically as if they'd known each other since babyhood; despite all these people, Jane noted with surprise that the kitchen had been refurbished with glossy white units, granite worktops and twinkling spotlights sunk into the ceiling.

Hannah hovered behind her like an anxious cloud. Max, who looked especially handsome in rumpled linen trousers and a pale blue cashmere sweater—Max in *cashmere?*—was engaged in an animated conversation with a man wearing domino-shaped specs. Jane tried to catch Max's eye. He turned away to open a curvaceous silver fridge and hand the bespectacled man a beer.

A cluster of women with gym-toned arms and deep tans were cackling throatily by the island unit. A couple of girls of around Hannah's age were sipping mysterious puddle-colored drinks. Who on earth were these people? Max wasn't party man. He wasn't a *cashmere* man. He was a biffing-around-the-shop-until-all-hours man, a man who'd cycle down to Kent—as if Kent were at the end of the street—and come home with a coating of mud and dead insects. Jane knew most of his friends, obsessive biking types who kept their hair cropped and their legs shaved. These party guests looked as if they'd need emergency counseling if they happened to encounter an oil can.

"Here you go," Veronica said, emerging from the throng to hand Jane a champagne flute and Hannah a glass of the puddly stuff.

"Thanks." Jane grinned fiercely at her, hoping it didn't look like a snarl.

Fixing on a wistful smile, Veronica gazed around the kitchen with a pride that suggested she'd refitted it all by herself. She was wearing a silver halter-necked dress and had somehow piled up all that tumbling hair on top of her head, although no clips or alternative holding devices were visible. Her skin was light brown and utterly smooth. She looked like she'd been molded out of toffee.

"Han," she murmured, leaning conspiratorially toward her, "my daughter Zoë's dying to meet you. Be a darling and pop over. She's the blond one in the pink top." Throwing Jane an uncertain glance, Hannah obediently threaded her way across the kitchen.

Veronica turned away to chat to a man with dense ginger hair and most of his shirt buttons undone. Jane made her way toward Max, but by the time she'd journeyed to the fridge he'd moved on. "Suzie Dellaware?" asked the domino-specs man enthusiastically.

"No, I'm Jane. Jane Deakin, a, um, friend of—"

"Ah, wrong person." Despite her not being Suzie, he mustered the energy to give her hand a halfhearted shake. "Simon Hatterstone. Old friend of Veronica's. We're looking into production opportunities, hoping to strike up a deal. We're pretty confident in the product. What we're looking for now is a manufacturer with the same passion and energy."

Jesus, did he always talk like a machine? She took a huge gulp of champagne, which crackled down her throat. "What's the product?" she asked.

"Snack range, top-quality ingredients sourced from all over the world—Chile, Peru, West Indies. Aphrodisiac qualities. Did you know that pine nuts are supposed to revive the, um, libido, Janet?"

"No, I must get some."

"You'll notice a big difference." His luxuriant eyebrows did a mini-dance.

"I hadn't realized Veronica made snacks," Jane added, focusing on a fragment of crisp that dangled from his bottom lip. "I thought she treated people with mineral deficiencies."

"She's expanding," Simon explained. "Aiming for a major aphrodisiac line in leading health food stores by the end of next year. It's a big leap—" his hand bounded from the worktop toward the newly quarry-tiled floor "—but she's a gutsy woman."

"I'm sure she is," Jane managed to say, but Simon had already turned away and was exclaiming, "Ronald!" with livid enthusiasm, as if this might be the manufacturer with passion and energy that he'd been looking for.

Jane drained her glass, swiped another from a tray on the island unit and headed for the living room. This, too, had been spruced up with remarkable speed. Sofas were festooned with oatmeal throws and furry oatmeal cushions—everything, Jane realized, was a slight variation on the oatmeal theme. She felt as if she was drowning in porridge.

An oval tray drifted toward her as if carried on some mysterious air current. It took her a moment to register than the tray was being carried by a boy; an embarrassed-looking boy with doleful brown eyes and a blunt, heavy fringe. He slumped to a halt next to Jane. "Oh, thank you, um…sorry, I don't know your name—"

"Dylan," the boy said flatly.

"Hi, Dylan." Jane peered at the canapé tray. On closer inspection these revealed themselves to be miniature versions of ordinary foods: tiny chips and slivers of fish wrapped in doll-sized newspaper cones; sausages like sections of earthworm emerging from mashed potato mounds. There were pizzas the size of milk-bottle tops, teeny twirls of spaghetti piled on to some kind of biscuit base. All this Lilliputian food was making Jane feel enormous and unwieldy and suddenly not hungry at all. "I might have something later," she said. The boy showed no sign of continuing his journey.

Max was doing the rounds, refilling glasses. He greeted Jane with a fleeting kiss on the cheek before being swiftly redirected by Veronica to talk to the ginger-haired man. Hannah had sidled off somewhere; the loo, probably, and Jane didn't blame her. They shouldn't have come. It had seemed important to Max, but what did it matter whether she was here or not? Veronica's hand was clamped firmly upon his right shoulder. Jane decided to track down Hannah and escape; it was her only hope of feeling normal again.

"The packaging will be crucial," Veronica was saying. "It's a lifestyle we're selling—a *dream*." And Jane got it, finally: this wasn't Max's housewarming party but one enormous, mingling business deal. Max probably hadn't realized it himself.

"So," Dylan murmured, giving Jane a start, "what d'you think?"

She'd forgotten he was there. "Think of what?" she asked.

He narrowed his eyes and indicated Veronica. She was laughing heartily now, her entire body aquiver beneath its flimsy silver covering. "Mum," he said.

"That's your mum? I didn't realize. I'm Jane, Hannah's mum—you've probably met her…" Dylan nodded. "I can't find her anywhere," Jane added. "She must've sloped off on her own."

"I'll look out for her." Dylan picked up a minuscule pizza, nibbled its edge and dropped it back onto the tray.

Max had worked his way to the window, where he was standing alone. He looked tense, Jane decided, as if interior designers had forced entry while he was at work and filled his home with things he'd neither chosen nor wanted. Out of the corner of her eye Jane watched Veronica creep up behind him. Her thin, bronzed arms snaked around his waist from behind, the hands clasping at his middle like a buckle. "Come on, babe," she chastized him, "you're being unsociable."

Simon with the domino-specs sidled up next to Jane. By now the champagne had surged to her head. "Veronica," he mused, "has astounding vision, doing this place up…."

"It's actually Max's house," Jane said before she could stop herself.

"Max?" The man frowned.

"You know—Max who's standing by the fireplace. You were talking to him by the fridge."

"Oh, *that* Max." He laughed heartily, as if the party was stuffed with several hundred interchangeable Maxes, and Jane had foolishly omitted to specify which one she meant. He frowned at her. "I forgot to ask. What do you do?"

"I work in a nursery."

"Ah, horticulturist?"

"No, it's a day care. You know—for little children and babies."

For a moment he looked as if he were struggling to clear a blockage in his throat. "Right," he muttered. Then, clearly registering that nursery workers didn't feature in his realm—and were unlikely to be bristling with passion and energy—he adjusted his specs, brushed the crisp crumb from his lip and lurched to the safety of Veronica's glittering entourage.

14

*T*he girl was wearing jeans and a tight pink T-shirt with the words You're Only Jealous emblazoned across the chest. From her seated position on the back step, Hannah gave the T-shirt a fleeting smile. She'd seen the girl in the kitchen—been ordered by Veronica to talk to her—but had chosen to duck out to the back garden instead. The girl loomed over her now, hands firmly planted on hips. "D'you smoke?" she asked.

Hannah shifted position. "No thanks," she said.

The girl bobbed down to sit beside her. "I'm not offering you one. I *need* one, absolutely choking for a smoke. You out here for some fresh air or what?"

"It was just…really crowded in there." Hannah was un-accustomed to some brazen stranger invading her territory and demanding fags. Despite the cold, damp air, she'd felt quite content on the step that overlooked the dead-looking plants and half-collapsed fence at the bottom of her dad's new garden. It looked as if no one had bothered with it for decades. A split traffic cone lay on its side in a tangle of weeds. Hannah had been imagining the nighttime creatures that might emerge and start prowling about if she was patient enough.

The girl rummaged in a sparkly purse, which dangled from a fine plaited cord from her shoulder. Her arms were bare and goose-pimpled. "Hey," she announced, "the cig fairy's been." She extracted a single squashed cigarette from her bag. "Got a lighter? No, course you don't. Shit. I'm Zoë, by the way. You must be Hannah."

"That's right."

"You've met Veronica? That's my mum. Complete embarrassment, forcing your poor dad to host this party only…what is it? Six weeks since they met? She'd have had it at ours only we've got the builders in, fitting a wet room, which Mum's decided is an absolute must-have. Must've read about it in one of her stupid magazines."

Hannah laughed, even though she didn't know what a wet room was. It sounded like something you'd have *fixed,* not fitted. "How old are you?" Hannah asked.

"Sixteen."

"Does your mum know you smoke?" Damn, why had she asked such a juvenile question? So many aspects of being young involved trying to act older than you really were—being cool and knowing when you were floundering inside. It was hugely stressful.

"Yeah, she gets on at me a bit," Zoë said, twirling the unlit cigarette between her fingers, "but she's not really bothered. Doesn't get that involved. Especially now she's going out with your dad."

Hannah cringed inwardly. "Is it…serious, d'you think?"

"Reckon so. It's all, 'Max this, Max that.' God, it's freezing out here—want to come round to my place?" Zoë swiveled round to face her. She had vibrant blue eyes, plump, glossy lips and a husky voice that hinted at mischief. Her fair hair fell around her face from a messy centre parting.

"Won't they worry—" Hannah began.

"Mum'll figure out where we've gone. She'll be cool. You coming or what?" Zoë sprang up from the step. A strip of perfectly flat, tanned tummy appeared between her T-shirt and jeans.

"What, just us?" Hannah asked.

"Why not?"

"I saw you in the kitchen. I thought you were with a friend."

Zoë rolled her eyes dramatically. "Oh, her," she muttered. "Some tedious girl my Mum lined up for me to be friends with. I choose my own friends, okay? Come on, let's go."

Hannah had never seen a bedroom like Zoë's. The walls were cream, the enormous bed shrouded by a fluffy white throw and a neat line of cushions in varying shades of putty and plum. One of the pillows was a sausage shape and looked hard as a rock. Hannah wondered if Zoë used it for sleeping—it would crick her neck, surely?—or if it was just for decoration. "It's gorgeous," she said, gazing around her. Zoë smiled but said nothing, as if not wishing to distract her new companion from her appraisal of the décor.

The walls were bare apart from three gold-painted capital letters which spelt "ZOË". Where had she got an *e* with the dots, Hannah wondered? Perhaps it been carved especially for her. She did strike Hannah as the sort of girl to whom people gave specially made things. The floorboards were painted off-white, and three shelves housed perfectly aligned CDs. There were no books that Hannah could see. She realized she was trying to breathe in a quiet, tidy manner.

"Is it always as neat as this?" she asked, picturing her own room with clothes strewn all over the floor and drawings pinned haphazardly onto the grubby walls.

"Mum does it," Zoë said, flopping on to the bed. "She's a perfectionist. Tidiness freak. Bleaches coffee cups, disinfects the phone, that kind of mental behavior. Sick really. We have a cleaner of course, but she only comes three times a week and lounges about reading Mum's mags. I've caught her." A smile zapped across Zoë's face. "Here, sit on the bed, get comfy. You're making me nervous."

Hannah perched next to Zoë, wondering what to do next. "I like this color," she ventured, indicating the walls. "It's kind of peaceful."

"Thanks. I chose it—it's called calico."

Hannah didn't know what to say about calico. She focused her gaze on a *Cosmo* magazine on the floor. It was still wrapped in cellophane with a free polka-dot makeup bag. "Don't you think they're crap?" Zoë asked.

"What?"

"Those mags. All these free gifts—just bribes, aren't they? It's the same old shit inside—how to be orgasmic, make him *die* for you. Stuff you've read a million times over."

"Yeah," agreed Hannah, although she'd only ever managed one hasty flip through *Cosmo*. Amy's mum had left a bedraggled copy on the side of the bath, that night of the vodka and orange. Hannah had managed to read roughly one third of an article entitled "The Only Sex Advice You'll Ever Need," her eyes skidding over phrases like *deep satisfaction* and *erogenous hotspots* before Amy had started banging on the door, saying she was desperate and if Hannah didn't hurry up she'd have to pee in the garden.

"It's Mum's," Zoë added. "She buys every magazine known to woman—files them in her office. They're like her gods. 'Oh, I worship thee at the altar of *Cosmopolitan*…'" She laughed throatily and unbuckled her sandals, kicking them off the edge of the bed.

Hannah had never met anyone of her age who wore high sandals with jeans. Their straps looked like orange spaghetti. "Where's her office?" she asked.

"Upstairs. She pretends she's doing paperwork but really she's hiding from me and Dylan. Did you meet my weirdo creep little brother yet?"

"No, I—"

"Well, you will. Take no notice of him. Want to try my new body oil?" Zoë bounded off the bed. "It's grapefruit and lime flower. Meant to awaken your inner temptress or something. Here, roll up your sleeve."

Zoë snatched a curvaceous glass bottle from the dressing table. Obediently, Hannah pushed up her sleeve. The oil felt expensive as Zoë rubbed it in; almost precious. "Got a boyfriend?" Zoë asked.

"No," Hannah said, then heard herself adding, "There's this boy, he's a bit older than me. Ollie, goes to theater workshop. We're just friends really—nothing happened for ages—but last time I saw him he kissed me."

"So, are you going out?"

Hannah glanced down at *Cosmo* as if it might throw up some kind of answer. "I think I've blown it. I was supposed to see him tonight—he's having a party—but Mum forced me to come here and I don't have his number or address and I only ever see him at theater—"

"Hey," Zoë said gently, "things could be worse. If you'd gone to his party you'd never have met *me*."

Hannah mustered a smile. "Now he'll think I've stood him up."

"When d'you see him usually?"

"Mondays after school."

"Only two days 'til Monday. There are loads of other Mondays, Han. You've probably got, um, about eight million more Mondays in your life. It's good not to make yourself too available." Put that way, it made perfect sense. Why hadn't Hannah thought of it like that? He'd be waiting for her, wondering why she hadn't shown up, which would make him want her even more.

And so the hours passed, with Hannah feeling so right in the calico room with Zoë and her Stila makeup and knack for saying the right thing. She found herself spilling out all the Ollie stuff. She even told Zoë how gutted she'd been when her dad had moved out of the old house, leaving her worry dolls trapped under the floor. She wasn't even embarrassed when her bag fell off Zoë's bed and her inhaler rolled out. All Zoë said was, "Better put it back in your bag, 'cause you don't want to lose that, do you?"

Hannah was opening up to this exotic stranger who wore orange sandals with jeans, and it felt so good.

15

*V*eronica stood in Max's bedroom doorway. "Don't you think it went well?" she asked.

She was naked. Her entire body looked oiled, or possibly varnished. What kind of stuff did she slather all over herself? Max wondered. He shifted position in bed. "It was okay," he said.

"Only *okay?*" She sashayed toward him, tugged back the duvet playfully and slithered in beside him. It was roasting in here. Sweat was prickling Max's entire body; he'd have to adjust the central heating. He hoped she wouldn't notice how clammy he was. "Well?" Veronica prompted him.

"It's weird, hosting a party," Max said, tugging the duvet back up. "You can't relax when you're worried about everyone having a good time."

"Aren't you silly?" she teased him. "Of course everyone

had a good time. They're not strangers, are they? They're our friends."

They lay on their sides, facing each other but not touching. Max glanced up at the ripped paper shade. It was crazy, really. He'd spent thousands on the kitchen—way more than he'd intended, with Veronica helping him to choose units; he had to admit she had impeccable taste. All that expense and effort and he hadn't got around to replacing a lampshade. He hadn't even intended for this big room to be his bedroom until Veronica had waltzed in and insisted that he couldn't let it "go to waste," as she'd put it. "They're *your* friends," he said. "It's not as if I really know them."

"Don't you like meeting new people?" She reached out and whirled a finger across his chest.

"Of course I do. I'd just have liked some of my friends to be there. Andy, Pete, Gary—friends from the shop and my cycling club."

"I don't believe in mixing different groups," Veronica said. "It can be awkward, you know? Throwing people together from different, um, backgrounds."

"You mean my friends are common?" Max felt irked, although he couldn't fully pinpoint why.

The chest-whirling stopped. "Of course not. I'm sure they're absolutely lovely. I'd love to meet them—why don't we ask them round for a little drinks party sometime?"

"Maybe," Max said warily. Housewarming parties, drinks parties: these social gatherings weren't his scene at all. As for that food—the miniature sausage and mash and all that—what was that all about? What had he been thinking, blowing all that money on caterers and their stupid miniature food? What was wrong with crisps, for God's sake? He'd liked to know what the guys from the club would have made of those mounds of spaghetti.

Yet maybe this was what people expected at parties. Max was out of touch; he couldn't remember the last time he'd been to one. He'd certainly never been to a do with Jane and his new girlfriend in the same room. He'd wanted Jane to come, yet when she'd arrived in that lovely purple skirt and those sexy high shoes, he knew he'd made a mistake. He wasn't used to seeing her dressed up like that. The whole scenario had unnerved him.

"You know it's important to me," Veronica murmured, "to network and find an investor. It's not just my job, Max. It's my *life*."

He nodded and reached out to stroke her hair. "I know it is." He'd been wrong to dismiss her as a flaky airhead. These past few weeks she'd worked into the night, sourcing suppliers and researching obscure aphrodisiacs. He'd popped round to see her one evening. Zoë had sent him upstairs to her office. There'd been a little jar of reddish powder on her desk; its label had read Yohimbe Bark. "Try it," Veronica had said, dipping her finger into the jar and offering it for him to lick. He'd felt ludicrous, sucking her finger like that. The powder had tasted like soil.

"Anyway," Veronica added, "Jane and Hannah were there."

And I barely spoke to them, Max thought. An image of Jane looking marooned in his living room flashed into his mind. "Perhaps," he said, "I'm not a party person."

"*I* think you are," she murmured, her hand traveling

south now, sending ripples right through him. "You were fantastic, Max. Everyone had fun. I'm sure Simon or Tony will be able to tie down an investor." She flashed her teeth at him. "That is, if I want them to."

"What do you mean?"

Her hand hovered between his legs. "I've been mulling things over. You're thinking of opening another shop, aren't you? Looking at premises and whatnot?"

"Uh-huh…"

"Why not save yourself all the hassle and stress?"

"I don't follow," Max said.

"Invest in my range instead. I've come up with a name, did I tell you? I'd been thinking Veronica Fox Loving Foods but it hardly trips off the tongue, does it?"

Her fingers fluttered around his groin. "No," Max croaked.

"So I've come up with FoxLove. Capital L in the middle. Don't you think it's perfect?"

Max swallowed and nodded.

"You could be part of it," she continued. "We could be partners—as well as other things of course." She giggled. "You could invest in *me*."

With that, she started kissing his chest, her soft lips traveling down and down until she'd slithered right under the duvet and the only word Max could utter was, "Yes."

16

Jane was astounded at how seamlessly Zoë had slotted into Hannah's life. She had never known her to fling herself into a friendship with such abandon; at least not since she'd been scooped up by Amy and Rachel at five years old. The two of them were upstairs in Hannah's room now, snorting with laughter. Jane was relieved that she'd remembered how to enjoy herself. It was almost like having the old Hannah back.

Three weeks had passed since the party when she'd finally returned from Veronica's house with startling blue shadow smeared over her lids and smelling distinctly of grapefruit. Jane had been perturbed about the two of them arranging to meet again—it felt too close, too entwined—but had given herself a stern, silent talking to. What did it matter that Zoë happened to be Veronica's daughter? It was time

Jane accepted that she and Max had moved on. Look at his life now: granite worktops, cashmere knitwear, not to mention new girlfriend. These were extremely adult, moving-on things. Being cool about Hannah and Zoë's friendship would, Jane felt, prove her to be equally grown-up, even if she didn't own a curvaceous fridge.

Since that night, Zoë had given Hannah several gifts: a bottle of chocolate truffle bath deluxe bath foam, a Bourjois blusher, a packet of powdery leaves to sweep over her face and blot shine. Hannah had started to look very matte. She had also—encouraged, Jane suspected, by Zoë—allowed her plum wash-in color to fade out.

Zoë appeared to be the font of all knowledge in terms of maintaining one's appearance. "You really should use toe separators," Jane had heard her announce in the bathroom that morning, in the way that a doctor might retort, "You really must stop smoking." Jane had stifled a laugh. Of course she was ridiculous—Jane had never met anyone so desperately shallow—but the girl was likeable and charming beyond her years. "Thanks, Jane, that was a delicious lunch," she'd said that day, when it had been hastily assembled from odds and sods from the fridge.

Zoë had stayed over last night. Jane had become accustomed to her trotting around in her jean-and-sandal ensembles, and those flimsy tops that looked like they'd been constructed from scarves tacked loosely together. She had warmed to the girl, in the way that you might become fond of a friend's exotic pet that you were looking after while they were on holiday. You might not want one for yourself, but would enjoy its novelty value for a limited period.

★ ★ ★

"God," Sally exclaimed. "That girl sounds awful. Completely vacuous and self-obsessed. What the hell does Hannah see in her?"

"Zoë's just a normal sixteen year-old," Jane insisted. "It sounds as if her mum's loaded. I'm sure most girls would blow loads of money on clothes and makeup given the chance." When the girls had headed out to the shops, Jane met Sally at a new branch of Bella Pizza in the Roman Road. Their pizzas weren't remotely *bella*. Jane's was heaped with fibrous tinned tuna and Sally's appeared to have been smeared with a thin layer of ketchup.

"Hannah's not like that," Sally pointed out.

"I'm not trying to stick up for Zoë and put down Hannah…."

"I know you're not," Sally interrupted. "It just sounds unhealthy, the amount of time they're spending together. It's almost as if Hannah's been *seduced*."

Jane hacked at her unyielding pizza. "If she didn't like Zoë she wouldn't hang out with her. Anyway, as least she's cheered up. You know, she actually talks to me these days? A few weeks ago she'd hardly look at me. Max was right—it's been good for her to find a new friend."

Sally sighed, apparently deciding to change tack. "So it's still on with Max and that Vanessa?"

"Veronica."

"Think it's serious?" Sally asked.

"It's looking that way." Jane avoided Sally's penetrating gaze.

"And what about Hannah's other friends? She hasn't ditched them for this bimbo idiot, has she?"

Jane paused. She'd already been accosted by Donna, Amy's mum, in the Indian grocer's. "How's Hannah these days?" she'd asked tersely. Jane had felt her neck go hot as she'd babbled that Hannah had been terribly busy. She'd realized, as she'd escaped from the shop, that Hannah had subtly let Amy go even before Zoë—a process that had been no more significant than a tree shedding a leaf.

"Girls' friendships are fickle," Jane told Sally. "I've asked her to call Amy but I can't keep nagging. She'll get in touch when she feels like it."

Sally frowned as she reached for her purse. "And you don't mind Zoë hanging about at your house?"

"Honestly," Jane insisted, "she keeps Hannah occupied. She's really no trouble at all."

17

$\mathcal{H}$annah and Zoë stepped out of the chemists and into the bright winter sun. The sky was an impossible blue smudged with flimsy clouds, and their breath came out in pale puffs. Across the street, two men who'd been washing the deli's windows started waving and whistling. Despite her burning face, Hannah felt a whirl of delight in her stomach. Before she'd met Zoë, men had never acknowledged her presence. They weren't looking at *her*, of course—Zoë was the stunning one, the one strangers gawped at—but she was still registering on the periphery.

Hannah strode away from the shop, stopping when Zoë failed to follow her. "Come on," she said, "let's get something to drink."

Zoë smiled. She pulled her hand from her pocket and uncoiled the fingers. "Look," she said.

"What is it?" Hannah frowned at the golden tube.

"A lipstick, dummy." Zoë removed its lid. It was an expensive brand: a slick column of candy pink.

"Did you just buy it?"

"No." Zoë's voice dropped to a whisper. "I took it."

"You mean stole it? From in there?"

"Shhh!"

"You *shoplifted* it?" Hannah glanced anxiously back at the shop. Its windows were crammed with Christmas trees and tinsel; a gaudy, festive mess.

"Uh-huh," Zoë said.

"What if somebody saw? God, Zoë!" Hannah started to march away, pushing between harassed-looking shoppers laden with bulging carrier bags.

"No one saw," Zoë insisted, hurrying after her. "They never do. It's easy, Han. I can't understand why everyone doesn't do it."

They ducked into a bakery, bought Cokes and sat at a tiny speckled Formica table in the café area at the back. It felt warm and safe with its comforting cake smells and the raucous hiss from the coffee machine. Hannah stared at Zoë across the table. "How long have you been doing this?" she asked.

"Long as I can remember. Started with tiny things—the odd blusher, eye shadow—then bigger stuff."

"Like what?"

"You know that makeup set I've got with all the drawers and the twenty-four eye shadows and magnifying mirror?"

Hannah's hand shot to her mouth. "Bloody hell."

"*And* my ceramic straightening irons," Zoë added smugly.

Hannah started to snigger. She thought she'd really got to know Zoë over these past few weeks. She'd told Hannah about the pathetic, pimply boys at her school, and how rumor had spread that she was easy—"only because of my looks, Han"—when she was really anything but. She wasn't intending to let any of those acne-faced twerps anywhere near her. "You've got to respect yourself," she'd asserted, "or no one else will."

Now Zoë was telling her that she habitually nicked makeup and God knows what else. "One time," she carried on merrily, "I nicked this life-sized plastic head with its own makeup. You know the ones that little girls put lipstick on and style the hair? I didn't know what to do with it so I went to Vicky Park and left it on a bench. Some little kid would've come along and taken it home. It would've made someone's day." Put like that, shoplifting seemed almost like a charitable act.

"Don't you think it's wrong?" Hannah asked. "I mean, don't you ever feel guilty?"

"Why would I?" Zoë scoffed. "I'm not stealing from *people*. I'm only taking stuff from massive corporations that won't miss the odd little thing. They budget for it, Han. Natural wastage, they call it. When you think about the terrible crimes that go on, no one's bothered about someone nicking the odd tester bottle of perfume."

Hannah couldn't help feeling a tweak of admiration. Zoë just kept on surprising her. "What about those powder leaf things you gave me?" she asked, swigging her Coke.

"Stolen goods, my dear," Zoë drawled.

"And the chocolate bubbles?"

"Ditto."

"God. I'll feel weird every time I have a bath."

Zoë laughed and fished her phone from her bag to read an incoming text. "Just Mum," she muttered, "wanting me to pick up her precious silver dress from the dry cleaners on my way home."

Hannah rolled her eyes dramatically, as if her own mother was equally prone to asking her to collect designer attire. "Want me to show you how it's done sometime?" Zoë asked.

"What, nicking stuff?"

"Keep your voice down. Yeah, if you want to. I'm not forcing you though. Not pressurizing you."

"You'd better not," Hannah said. She finished her Coke and linked arms with Zoë as they sauntered out of the bakery. "I'll do something for you though," she added.

"What?" Zoë grinned.

"I'll visit you in jail."

18

*N*ancy's right foot was propped on a chair in her kitchen. Beneath a hideous, ribbed knee-high, the big toe was thickly bandaged, the result of being crushed by a shopping bag. "You were trying to carry too much," Jane scolded her. "Why don't you get a taxi back from the shops, or call me and I'll pick stuff up for you?"

"It was only *tins,*" Nancy retorted. "A few cans of Ambrosia creamed rice. Doctor says it's healing nicely, not that I'll be going back to him—he was barely more than a child, Jane, and I don't need some whippersnapper telling me what I can and can't do." As if to demonstrate the digit's remarkable healing power, she bumped her foot on to the floor and hobbled toward the nerve center of the clippings library.

Jane followed her in, breathing in the smell of aging

newsprint. "There's something I want to show you," Nancy said, extracting a faded green file from a drawer. She pulled out a rumpled newspaper cutting and offered it to Jane. "I thought of you when I found this," Nancy added. "Didn't you see his exhibition years ago? I have to say, this really is art—a world away from the kind of work you produce. Thought you might pick up some tips."

You've never seen anything I've produced, Jane thought. She examined the cutting: Archie Snail. "Well," Nancy said, "is that him?"

"Yes. I can't believe you remember."

"You know me," she said, cackling. "I forget nothing. Have you read much about him?"

"Not really. He's American, and doesn't seem to have produced much since—"

"He works in Scotland," Nancy interrupted. "He's just started running courses, workshops, whatever you call them. Something about being ruined financially, having to keep himself afloat. Why not nip up there, sharpen up your skills?"

"I can't just *nip* up to Scotland," Jane protested. "I've got Hannah and my job…."

"Doesn't that nursery give you holidays? Couldn't Hannah stay with Max, if he's not too tied up with that fancy woman?"

Jane winced. "It's too far, Mum."

"Glasgow's not that far. It's hardly Madagascar. Get on a train at King's Cross and bingo."

Jane peered at the cutting. The newspaper had used the same photo as the website; same weaselly eyes and vexed demeanor. She scanned the text, picking out phrases: *out-standing craftsman…most gifted artist in the stained glass medium…financial hardship after a fire that destroyed his studio and virtually all of his work…runs five-day courses on a remote Hebridean island…* "It's nowhere near Glasgow," Jane murmured. "His studio's on some tiny island off the west coast."

Nancy lowered herself on to the room's sole chair and hoisted her bad foot on to the opposite thigh. "You've traveled, haven't you? What about that summer you and Max took off, went to India before—"

"Yes, Mum, I got pregnant."

"Well, I'm sure a reasonably intelligent thirty-eight-year-old woman like you is capable of getting herself from London to some Scottish island. Hannah won't mind. I assume she's still besotted with that ridiculous Zoë girl? Too busy, is she, to come and see me?"

"She's got extra theater rehearsals," Jane fibbed, feeling a twist in her stomach. Hannah hadn't wanted to come to Granny Nancy's; she and Zoë were going to study together, which could be roughly translated as *We're going shopping, using Zoe's limitless funds, then coming home to beautify ourselves. Pity us our hectic lives.*

"On a Saturday?" Nancy huffed. "You don't need to humor me. If Hannah doesn't want to come anymore, that's absolutely fine."

"Of course she does," Jane said, knowing that her mother was right; between hanging out with Princess Zoë or being told what to watch on TV in cabbage-smelling living room, there really was no contest.

Jane slipped the Archie cutting into her jeans pocket and kissed her mother's papery cheek. "And Mum," she added, "I'm only thirty-seven."

"What shall I do about Mum?" came Hannah's voice.

Jane tensed in the water. She'd poured herself a shoulder-deep bath, sloshing in a liberal helping of Hannah's chocolate truffle bath deluxe foam. It looked far too expensive to be poured, least of all into a bath; its golden top and metallic label made it look like some exotic sweet drink, though its label read Do Not Drink. Jane lay as still as possible, but couldn't make out Zoë's reply. It sounded like, "Your mum's all right." *Well, thank you kindly,* Jane thought angrily. *You're sleeping over yet again; you drift around our house, doing whatever you like, and I'm deemed as "all right."*

"She was going on about those nail varnishes," Hannah continued, her voice clearly audible from her room. "Said I should politely ask you not to keep giving me stuff." An outburst of giggles. "Please, Zoë," Hannah continued, affecting a ridiculous cut-glass accent, "would you be so kind as to not keep showering me with presents, there's a love?"

Zoë was laughing openly now. Both of them were. Hadn't it occurred to them that Jane might hear them? Didn't they care? "God, Han," Zoë said, "you're so funny, you know that? You're not like anyone I've ever met. The girls at school are all so superficial and up themselves."

"That's what you get for going to a posh school."

"Wish I went to *your* school."

Jane glanced over the side of the bath. One of Zoë's

sandals was lying on its side by the loo. Emma Hope Shoes read the oval-shaped label on the sandal's inside. Regalia for Feet. Jane and Hannah's shoes weren't "by" anyone. They were from Dolcis or Shelleys or Roman Road market. They weren't Regalia.

Hannah's beaten-up trainers lay beside Zoë's pink embroidered confection. The ends of the laces were grubby and frayed; they looked like the footwear of a different species. Jane wondered when Hannah would start asking for Emma Hope shoes. She'd already acquired a new habit of applying full makeup before school. It was subtle enough to sidestep the no-makeup rule; what concerned Jane was the time it took. Most mornings Hannah was running late, often with homework not done.

"What d'you think I should do?" Hannah asked.

"About what?"

"Mum getting on at me."

Christ, Jane thought, is that how she sees me? She glared down at the bubbles. They weren't chocolate-colored—not the luscious molten Aero she'd expected—but disappointingly white. "She's probably going through the menopause," Zoë ventured.

"You think so? What happens then?"

"You go completely weird. Mum told me all about it."

"Is your mum having it?" Hannah asked.

"God no. She's *way* younger than your mum. But she told me what happens, about your bones going brittle and—" pause for stifled snort "—how you shrivel up *down there*."

Jane's heart was thudding urgently. She could see it—the

agitated pulsing of her chest. She glared down at her long, slender legs and tried to imagine the noncrumbly, virtually *indestructible* bones inside them. "You start piling on weight around your middle," Zoë continued, "and your face gets hairy. You know how old women have hairs poking out of their chin? Like, they have to get them electrolocized? And you get sweaty at night and don't want sex anymore but—" she sounded as if she were choking on her own tongue now "—that's okay 'cause no one wants to do it with you anyway!" They erupted in laughter.

Ha-di-bloody-ha, thought Jane, poking a toe—a rather gnarled toe, she realized now—through the thin layer of foam. Not that she had a sex life to lose. Her last encounter with the male species had been over a year ago. She and Daniel Banks—a thin, shy surveyor who'd commissioned a bathroom window—had spent several nights together when Hannah had been staying with Max. He'd been so well-meaning—so eager to please—that Jane had felt wretched for not fancying him back. Pretty soon, she'd realized that she was hiding him from Hannah as if he were an embarrassing stain. There was nothing wrong with him exactly. Nothing she could put a finger on. Yet if the prospect of introducing him to her daughter was beyond remote, what was the point in continuing?

Jane grabbed the bottle and sloshed in more chocolate foam. She shut her eyes, breathing it in, this evidently near-menopausal woman who was due to shrivel up into a tight little ball at any moment—or go off, like a malfunctioning burglar alarm. The bath had gone tepid and there was no more hot water in the tank. Jane hauled herself out and wrapped herself tightly in a clammy towel, trying to dampen the pounding in her chest. How dare they discuss her like that? She gave Hannah acres of leeway. What about the puking incident? Jane hadn't made a fuss. She'd even washed the goddam path! And hadn't she been justified in questioning all the makeup Hannah was acquiring? How many nail polishes did a girl need? Max, or maybe Veronica, must be doling out money to the girls. It would have to stop. They wouldn't be beholden to some woman who developed a formula for aphrodisiac cookies. Swathed in her towel Jane stomped to her room, shutting the door firmly behind her.

Even in bed there was no chance of sleeping. Jane's brain whirled, fueled by marauding hormones signalling her impending withering up. She thought about her own mother who, at sixty-seven, paid no heed to her age and, damaged toe aside, could tackle any task you could throw at her. She swiveled out of bed, retrieved her jeans from the floor and pulled out the Archie cutting from the pocket.

She could read it properly now, without Nancy breathing coarsely down her neck:

> Unleash your creativity in the unspoilt and stimulating environment of Croft Crafts. An advanced course, aiming to encourage students to explore color and form within a stimulating natural environment…other courses are available including mosaic, natural dyeing and dry stone walling…course program starts February 18…contact Croft Crafts on 01764 458765 or visit www.croft-crafts.co.uk

for details of fees, accommodation and availability. Small groups ensure personal attention.

Jane figured out the dates. Hannah would be on half-term break. She'd give her the option of coming but sensed that she'd prefer to stay with Max, Zoë and Non-Menopausal-In-Her-Sexual-Prime Veronica. Fine: they could do with a break from each other. Jane examined the mischievous curl of Archie's mouth, the challenging spark in those narrowed eyes. She slipped the article into the drawer of her bedside table.

Pulling the towel around her, she crept downstairs and logged on to her PC. She tapped in Archie's Web address. The "accommodation" button threw up an image of a stately home called Hope House. That couldn't be right. It was all turrets and bay windows in formidable gray stone, backed by extravagantly sweeping hills.

She fired off an e-mail:

I would like to enquire if places are available on Archie Snail's Advanced Stain Glass Workshop, commencing February 18. Could you also please advise me of availability and cost of accommodation at Hope House for one/possibly two people.

With many thanks, Jane Deakin.

On her way back upstairs, Jane heard Hannah's voice. She paused, holding her breath. "Will that happen to us?" Hannah asked.

"What?" Zoë said.

"The fat, hairy-faced thing. The *menopause* thing."

"Fuck, no," Zoë exclaimed. "By the time we're that old, there'll be some kind of pill we can take to stop all that happening."

"Well," Hannah said, "thank God for that."

19

*O*llie's house wasn't remotely as Hannah had imagined. There was no garden, no conservatory, no patio heater; in fact it wasn't even a house, but a flat in a stark concrete block with a rusting radiator lying on its side by the front entrance. "Which one's yours?" she asked.

"Top floor," Ollie said. He smiled at her, and his eyes said: *See? There's stuff you don't know about me.*

Hannah felt her preconceptions fall away. Ollie wasn't posh. He might have a posh voice, and be studying at a posh sixth form college—not to mention have the means to drink wine and nibble salad with poached egg draped on top at the Opal—but he didn't live a posh *life*. He flicked his cigarette on to the puddled ground. "Come on," he said, "I'll show you my palace."

The stairwell smelled of fierce disinfectant. In an attempt

to spruce up the entrance someone had placed a wicker basket filled with grimy plastic tulips on a windowsill. Hannah felt a swill of nerves as they climbed the stairs. Ollie had already said that his mum would be working at the restaurant. Before she'd seen where they lived, Hannah had pictured her gliding around some exclusive place—being the person who showed you to your table, but didn't have to deal with the horrible remains of people's dinners. Now she wondered if Ollie's mum did something more ordinary, like washing up, or peeling potatoes.

They reached Ollie's front door, and he rummaged in jacket pockets for keys. Hannah studied the back of his neck; the way his hair curled, asking to be touched and kissed. His skin was so soft—virtually edible. As he opened the door, she realized she was gnawing noisily on her gum. She swallowed, and the gum skidded down her throat.

"Hey," Ollie said, "are you okay?"

"Fine," Hannah said brightly as she followed him in.

A pair of black tights was draped over a radiator. The living room was sparsely furnished, but not in a minimalist way—not like Zoë's room with its golden letters and calico walls—but in a manner that suggested that Ollie and his mum didn't own much stuff. The walls were an unsettling shade of red, as if painted by someone in the throes of emotional trauma. The whole place smelled of damp washing.

It was dark outside. Through a glass door, which led from the living room onto a balcony, Hannah could see blurred headlamps inching along Cambridge Heath Road. "Have a seat," Ollie said, sounding shyer than usual—almost awkward.

She perched on the sofa's edge, feeling as if they were strangers who'd found themselves in the same room and were obliged to make conversation. Her tongue had shriveled up. She was aware of a vein pulsating on the side of her neck. On the wall above the tiled fireplace were black-and-white photos in clipframes. Each photo was of the same woman. Her enormous eyes were heavily rimmed with black liner, her mouth forming a pensive smile. Although pretty, she looked kind of folorn—almost scared.

Ollie sat beside Hannah. "So," he said, "you're in the show after all."

"Yeah, as a plant."

He laughed and said, "You'll make a lovely Venus flytrap. It's a good idea of Beth's—having a person play Audrey Junior instead of that papier-mâché disaster they were building…."

"I'll be *wearing* the papier-mâché disaster," she retorted, pulling up her legs and trying to nestle into the unyielding sofa. She glanced at the overdressed Christmas tree in the corner of the room. An ungainly angel, its features crudely drawn in felt tip, was perched on the top.

"That's Mum's contribution," Ollie explained. "She's like a little girl when it comes to Christmas." He indicated the clip-framed pictures. "That's Celia, my mum."

"She looks so young!" Hannah exclaimed.

Ollie smiled. "She doesn't look like that now. They were taken years ago, when I was a baby."

"Why are there so many pictures of her?"

"She was a model until—well, she couldn't work anymore. Stuff happened to Mum. She hasn't modeled since I was a kid."

Hannah frowned, wanting to know more. "Was she famous?"

"No, she didn't do designer shows or any of that. She was more your thermal underwear catalogue kind of girl. You want something to drink?"

"Just tea please," she said, hoping that didn't sound feeble. She'd told her mother that she'd be home after costume fittings. She had no intention of overstepping the mark by going home with boozy breath.

Ollie ambled through to the kitchen. Alone in the red room, Hannah got up to examine the photos. Celia. The name was familiar. Unusual, old-fashioned, matching her makeup and hair. There'd been some Celia mentioned at home: maybe a day care worker at Nippers, or a friend of her mum's who'd drifted away. "Celia Tibbs," she murmured.

Hannah glimpsed her reflection in the mirror above the fireplace. She was wearing her own jeans, Zoë's floaty top and a beaded bracelet that she'd nicked from a hippy shop on Bethnal Green Road. Her face was made up with stolen eye shadow (in "Pewter"), lipstick ("Candy Girl") and mascara ("Cocoa"). She'd painted her nails Very Cherry but had decided it looked too goth and quickly covered it with Mauve Kiss. No wonder she'd been late for theater workshop. Getting changed after school used to take her five minutes max.

The phone rang, and Hannah heard Ollie taking the call in the kitchen. "Hey," he said gently, "it's okay. Yeah, just got a friend here. Of course I will."

Hannah examined her nails. Zoë had been right: nicking stuff wasn't that difficult. Plenty of shops didn't put security stickers on their goods, and Zoë knew which ones were "safe," as she put it. You could use one hand to pick up something and examine it, while your other hand closed around a small item and casually slipped it into your pocket. Or you could pick up two of the same thing, put one back and leave the other concealed in your loosely clenched fist; a white-knuckle grip was a giveaway. Bigger items were trickier, but not beyond the well-practised lifter. Last week Zoë had gleefully showed her the chocolate leather jewelry box she'd pinched for Veronica's Christmas present. You just had to be calm, brave and know exactly what you wanted, and, Hannah surmised, those were pretty smart rules for life.

Ollie said, "Love you, too." Hannah frowned. It was a *girl* he was talking to. Did Ollie have some girlfriend on the go? Surely he wouldn't speak to her with Hannah sitting a few feet away. "We'll talk later," he added, then emerged from the kitchen with two mugs of tea.

As he set them on the floor, Hannah tried to bring up the issue of him crooning, "I love you" without sounding weird or possessive. Where was Zoë's *Cosmo* when she needed it? "Ollie," she started, "I just wondered…"

He looked at her, then his lips were on hers, and he was kissing her more forcefully than on the towpath; it was dizzying. Hannah's foot collided with her mug, but she didn't stop to worry about the spillage and mess because her head was full of kissing and wanting him. "Let's go to my room," Ollie murmured.

Hannah's heart lurched. "Can't we stay here?" she managed to say. Her mother would know if she went to bed with him, even if they did nothing more than lie there kissing. She'd come home supposedly from an extremely innocent theater workshop costume fitting with *I've been to bed with Ollie Tibbs* scrawled all over her face. Anyway, he didn't just want to kiss in his bedroom; he was seventeen and a boy and he wanted to do it. "Hey," he said, taking her hand, "it's okay. Hang on a minute...."

Stepping over the puddle of tea, he sauntered across the living room, straightening his T-shirt and jeans, and started rummaging through the drawer of a pine unit. What was he looking for? God, thought Hannah: he's getting a condom. Is that where he kept them, in a drawer in the living room for his mum to find? He was going to get his thing out and expect her to put the condom on for him. They'd had a go at rolling them on to bananas in sex ed at school. Mrs. Finch had rolled on her own rather enthusiastically, then whipped it off with a flick of her wrist and pinged it across the room into the bin. It had been screamingly embarrassing.

Hannah's heart was walloping in her chest. She wanted to be at home, lying in a chocolatey bath, merely *thinking* about doing all kinds of delicious things with Ollie. "Here it is," he announced, pulling something from the drawer and stuffing it into his pocket.

"What is it?" Her voice sounded strangled.

"Come out to the balcony and I'll show you. I'm desperate for a cig. Mum goes mad if I smoke in here."

He took a key from its hook, unlocked the door and they stepped outside. The balcony was dominated by a collapsible plastic washstand, which was heavily laden with underwear. Bras and knickers glittered with a fine covering of frost. Ollie didn't seem to notice, or at least didn't comment. Maybe, thought Hannah, his mum left her underwear out here all the time. She felt safer here. Nothing scary or dramatic was going to happen on a balcony with traffic crawling about all around them.

Ollie fished out a battered packet of cigarettes and a box of matches from his jeans pocket. He lit a cigarette and pulled out the other, slightly larger box. Hannah's lips still tingled from the kiss. "Here," Ollie said, handing her the box. "Sorry I didn't have time to wrap it."

"What is it?"

"Early Christmas present, nothing much."

She opened the box and lifted the silver chain from its velvet nest. It was so delicate, with tiny pink crystals spaced along the chain, that she feared she might snap it by breathing on it. "I had no idea…you didn't need—"

"I wanted to buy you something." Ollie stared at his feet.

She looked at him. The gaudy colors of Christmas lights flitted across his lovely face. He'd chosen and bought this for her; this pool of silver in her palm. "Ollie," she said, "who were you talking to on the phone?"

"My mum, why?"

"I just wondered." She stared at the necklace, then placed it carefully back in its box. "It's gorgeous," she said.

Ollie kissed her again, in full view of his mother's red lacy knickers and said, "So are you."

20

*J*ane stood on Max's doorstep, fluffing her hair to erase an imprint caused by the Santa hat she'd worn all day. She'd come straight from Nippers' Christmas party; her entire body felt coated by a fine layer of sugar. She raised a hand, about to knock. "I just want a holiday," came Veronica's voice, "a bloody *holiday*, Max, like normal people have."

Jane had come to show Max glass samples for his window, and to take Hannah home. She couldn't decipher Max's response, didn't want to hear it. She'd turned into a snoop: first Hannah and Zoë, gleefully speculating on her crumbling bones and withering vagina. And now this. She could picture Max, his mouth set firm, his eyes gone cloudy—his I'm-not-really-here face.

"I work hard," Veronica charged on, "and I deserve some little treats. D'you know how much effort I've put in to get this range off the ground? I'm exhausted, Max. Look at me. I'm completely shredded."

It must be exhausting, Jane thought, *blending aphrodisiacs all day.* "You go," Max snapped, "with Dylan and Zoë."

"Are you kidding? I'm not taking *them*. I'm meeting up with Hettie and Jasper in Chamonix like I always do, I—"

"So why d'you need me?"

A pause. "Of course I need you," Veronica declared.

Jane gripped the handle of her sample box. If she hurried away they'd hear her and think—and *know*—she'd been listening. How humiliating would it be to be caught creeping back down the steps? Hannah was in there, hearing all this—or maybe the girls were beautifying themselves at Veronica's. They seemed to drift between Max's house and Veronica Villas. Perhaps Max should build a bloody tunnel.

Jane felt stranded on the step, hating the bitterness that was flooding her veins. This was where Hannah preferred to be these days. Jane was aware that teenagers push their parents away; what she hadn't been prepared for was the ragged hole they left behind.

A slight figure with heavy fringe had stopped on the pavement. Dylan, the canapé server, cocked his head and gazed up at her. "What's the matter?" he asked.

"I've come to collect Hannah." Max and Veronica's voices had faded. Jane clattered quickly down the steps.

"Why didn't you knock?" Dylan enquired.

"They sounded…busy."

Dylan smirked. "Having one of their *moments?* Thought

they might. She wants a holiday—not with us, of course. She never takes us." He sounded resigned.

"Have you seen Hannah?" Jane asked, not wishing to be drawn into criticizing his mother.

"They're at our place. Come on, I'll show you. They're just back from one of their little…sprees."

All Veronica had been able to afford after the divorce was an immaculate three-story town house with vast bay windows and what looked from outside like a loft conversion. "Better take off your shoes," Dylan said, showing Jane into the faintly perfumed hall.

"Really?"

He grinned, indicating three small chrome cages on the floor. They looked like little prison cells for shoes. "One of Mum's rules."

Obediently, Jane pulled off her boots. She noticed that Dylan's trainers remained on his feet, and wondered if he was having her on. "Zoë, Han, you up there?" he yelled upstairs.

Jane peered into the living room. It was immaculate, almost a replica of Max's porridgy room. There was no evidence that human beings actually engaged in activities or even breathed in there. Shrugging at the girls' lack of response, Dylan led her into the room. In his scruffy black T-shirt and jeans, he looked like he'd wandered into the wrong house. He had pale, gangly arms, a flicker of mischief about him, and looked about fourteen. "Sit down," he said. It sounded like an order, so she did.

"Dylan," she said, "do Max and your mum, do they usually—"

"What, argue like that? Yeah, sometimes. Mum likes her own way."

She glanced at her stockinged feet. "Max isn't really the skiing sort."

"She reckons that if he's the cycling sort, then skiing shouldn't be a problem...."

Jane laughed. "They're kind of...different."

"Mum and Max?"

"Skiing and cycling," she said, thinking, *yes, that too.* A ripple of laughter came from upstairs, and Dylan went up to fetch the girls. A typed sheet of A4 lay on the coffee table. Jane speed-read the text:

> FoxLove. A tantalising new snack range to enhance your libido and entire well-being.

There was a picture of her at the top—the fox herself—with her hair mussed forward and lips hanging ajar in a half-pout.

> With my new range, I aim to bring you good health, maximum vitality and an enhanced love life beyond your wildest dreams....

"Hi, Mum."

Jane sprang up. "Oh, Han, I didn't hear—"

Hannah's mouth was set firm. She glanced from her mother to the leaflet. Zoë appeared beside her, quickly re-arranging her features to appear marginally less hostile. "Hi, Jane," she said with fake brightness.

Jane smiled tightly. "Han, are you ready? I'd like to get back." She snatched the box of glass samples at her feet.

"Okay." Hannah sighed.

They would leave, Jane realized, without her seeing Max or showing him the samples; she had no intention of interrupting the skiing row. She wouldn't see him now until after Christmas, a thought that made her feel hollow, and which she tried to banish. Hannah slung her bag over her shoulder. There was something different about her; something around the eye region. Jane frowned. "Have you plucked your eyebrows?"

"Yes."

Behind the girls, Dylan shuffled uncomfortably. "They look…different," Jane hedged. Hannah's dark, dramatic eyebrows—her former eyebrows—had been mercilessly plucked into cotton-thin curves. The entire brow area was puffy and pink.

Don't flip out, Jane warned herself as they left Veronica's house. It wasn't as if her fifteen-year-old daughter had gotten a tattoo or had a bolt put through her tongue.

It was only *eyebrows*.

Dear Jane,

Thank you for your enquiry about my courses. I am pleased to inform you that places are available in February, as is accommodation at Hope House, which is within walking distance of my studio. I attach details of prices and arrangements regarding meals, etc. If you're still interested please book accommodation with Mrs. McFarlane on 01797 345678. I look for-

ward to confirming your booking at your earliest con-
venience.

Sincerely yours,
Archie Snail

Jane hadn't expected a reply from Archie himself. She'd
imagined that several assistants would run the admin side.
Those swooped-down eyebrows—then Hannah's, plucked
to near-invisibility—flashed into her mind.

Heck, she'd book a place. Hannah regarded her with
such disdain—and was it any wonder when she lived her
life so cautiously? With anticipation fizzling in her stomach,
Jane tapped out her reply.

21

*H*annah glanced around the small, cramped shop. Strings of sequinned felt birds hung from the ceiling. Among the usual selection of jewelry, photo frames and trinkets someone had managed to squeeze in a Christmas tree festooned with glittering baubles. It was Christmas Eve. Hannah's breath felt tight in her throat. The salesgirl was tapping on a laptop on the counter. "Looking for something?" she asked, glancing up.

"Just browsing, thanks," Hannah said. There was a tremor in her voice. Now she was here—on the verge of doing it—she was feeling less sure of herself. She'd never done it without Zoë lurking nearby, projecting silent support.

Zoë had begun to feel like a big sister to her. Hannah had always wanted a sister, but even an annoying, grubby-nosed brother would have been better than the big fat nothing her parents had produced. That's how she'd thought of the worry dolls. Not as bickering sisters but the kind who'd be happy to listen and always knew how you were feeling. Like little Zoës, come to think of it. She glanced at a heap of multicolored glass beads and coils of silver wire on the counter beside the laptop. So the girl made her own jewelry. Zoë had nicked a bracelet from here but had somehow managed to lose it by they time they'd got back to Hannah's. "What's it matter?" Zoë had said. "It's not like it cost me anything."

It didn't seem right, stealing something that someone had made with their own hands. It could have been one of her mum's glass panels, and Hannah knew how much care went into making those. Of course, everything was made *somewhere*—yet stealing was easier to justify if the trinket had been mass-produced by the billion in some factory in China.

A hippyish elderly woman was putting on clip-on earrings and asking the salesgirl if they suited her. *They're lovely, really bring out of the blue of your eyes.* At the back of the shop a dad and his bored-looking son were deliberating over packs of Christmas cards. This time, Hannah hadn't asked Zoë to come with her. She'd wanted to do this alone, to pick a present for Ollie in exchange for the pink crystal necklace. Zoë would have taken over, picking something horribly expensive, which wasn't what Hannah wanted at all.

She scanned carved wooden boxes and a selection of silver-colored lighters in a wicker basket. That was it: a lighter. Small, understated, kind of grown-up. She picked one up, enjoying its cold weight in her hand. It was curved, almost kidney-bean shaped. It felt classy.

Her fingers curled around it. She imagined giving it to Ollie that evening. She'd just turn up, and if he wasn't in she'd leave it with his mum—she wanted to meet this Celia Tibbs in the flesh—or tuck it in the corner of the landing by the door to his flat. She felt that familiar surge of excitement. Shoplifting wasn't about needing things; look at Zoë and the plastic doll's head. It was about being daring—experiencing that heady rush the moment before you did it. It was about feeling *alive*.

Hannah glanced up at a shelf laden with hand-painted vases, and moved her hand clutching the lighter to the open zip of her bag. She uncoiled her fingers. Drop—in it went. That would do it. Unlike Zoë, she knew when to stop. She wouldn't be greedy; she'd just have the lighter and leave. Then, to make her excursion worthwhile, she nicked a tan leather purse, a pen encrusted with fuchsia sequins and a tiny mirrored photo frame.

The salesgirl was threading beads on to wire and didn't acknowledge Hannah leaving the shop. The bell dinged as she opened the door. After the warmth and the incense smells, the air felt cool on her face.

Hannah checked her watch, surprised by how long she'd been in there. A good twenty minutes. She'd have to be quicker next time—more efficient. She glanced around the bustling street. It was almost dusk; the street glinted with Christmas lights, which usually looked tacky but today seemed oddly beautiful.

Hannah started to walk, feeling carefree and happy until it landed—a hand, the fingers spread—on her upper arm. Hannah tried to speak but no sound came out. The Christmas lights blurred before her eyes. And a voice said, "Excuse me, I think there's something in your bag you haven't paid for. Could you come back into the shop?"

22

Jane sat beside Hannah at a fake wood desk in an interview room at the police station. On the chair beside her, Hannah was hunched with her hands flopped on to her knees. The windowless room smelt faintly of armpit. It was slightly less grim than the detention room where Hannah had been waiting when Jane had arrived, flustered and breathless, at the station. More than anything, she'd yearned to rewind to the point just before Hannah went into that damn shop. Why couldn't you manipulate time like that?

"So," she said flatly, "why did you do it?"

"I don't know." Hannah voice was tiny, virtually lost in the room.

"Is this anything to do with Zoë? Do you feel you have to keep up with her, have as much stuff as she—"

"No!" Hannah protested. She rubbed a fist into an eye.

"Not copying her, are you? Does she shoplift? She's always wearing new clothes, God knows how her mother—"

"Veronica buys her stuff. She gets whatever she wants."

"Lucky Zoë," Jane snapped.

Tears were rolling down Hannah's cheeks. "Mum, it was just…stupid. I wasn't thinking." Max had said much the same thing after the night with that woman; he hadn't been thinking. *Just a little mistake,* he'd said.

"Jesus, Han, you'll have a criminal record, you know that? Are you trying to ruin your life?"

"Of course not!"

"Who were those things for?" Jane demanded.

"Me," Hannah whispered.

"What—a lighter? Started smoking now, have you?" Jane didn't care about making a spectacle of herself; things could hardly get any worse.

Han shook her head. "That was for…a friend."

"What friend?"

"Just…a friend."

Jane rubbed her hands across her own face, cutting Hannah from her line of vision. This wouldn't have happened if she'd been out shopping with her instead of holing herself up in the studio. Did Hannah feel neglected? Perhaps she and Max were too mean with her. Look at the clothes and makeup Zoë managed to acquire. What you had or didn't have really mattered to girls of Hannah's age. Their home was a mess; Hannah was probably ashamed of it. Jane visualized Veronica's pristine hallway, and Max taking off his shoes obediently to slip into one of the cages.

Hannah's eyes had acquired a vivid pink tinge. Her hands looked pale and fragile on her lap. Maybe, Jane thought, it had been a mistake. She'd genuinely forgotten to pay. She wasn't a thief—not someone who should have been brought to the station in a police van. She'd been photographed and fingerprinted. She'd been treated like someone who robbed old ladies or mugged joggers in parks. She was on record, on police computers: Hannah Deakin the criminal.

An inspector with cropped graying hair and a vein-covered nose entered the room. He cleared his throat and sat in the vacant chair across the table. "Now, Hannah," he said, "because you admitted your offence and haven't offended before, I'm going to issue a reprimand. That's a formal verbal warning. Your file will be sent to the youth offending team."

He sounded as if he was recovering from a cold. Hannah's eyes gleamed with fear; Jane put an arm around her shoulders and pulled her close, as if she were a little girl again. "What's the youth offending team?" she asked.

"They're part of social services and set up voluntary programs to help with offending behavior. But in this instance," he added, "I'll mark Hannah's report as no further action."

Jane nodded, feeling sick in this horrible room with its stained beige walls and the man's coffee breath. "So is this the end of it?" she asked.

"Yes," the inspector said, "this time." He studied Hannah across the desk. He's just a man, Jane told herself; just an ordinary man doing his job. "Before you go," he added, "I want you to be quite clear that shoplifting is a serous offence. If you're caught again you could be placed in a young offenders' institute. Do you understand that, Hannah?"

"Yes," she whispered.

"Can we leave now?" Jane asked.

The inspector nodded. "You're free to go."

Jane stood up and gripped Hannah's hand. For once, she didn't pull it away.

"Well," came the voice just outside the police station, "look at you two with your long faces!" Donna, Amy's mother, had ground to a halt in front of them. She dumped a shopping bag at her feet and narrowed her eyes at Hannah. Amy lurked awkwardly behind her.

"Hello, Donna," said Jane.

"Last-minute Christmas shopping?" Donna asked, widening her eyes.

"Just a few bits and pieces," Jane replied.

"Hi, Han," said Amy. "How's Zoë these days?"

"She's fine," Hannah murmured.

Donna faked a smile. "Mind you, I don't blame you for looking pissed off. Nightmare, isn't it? So busy at this time of year. A load of commercial nonsense. I'll be glad when it's all over."

Jane nodded. "Me, too."

"Anyway, we'd better get on. We've still got crackers and stuffing to buy. Enjoy your Christmas—if you don't mind me saying, Jane, you look worn-out. Make sure you have a rest over the holiday."

Jane forced a smile. "Yes, I will."

As they parted she heard Donna muttering, "God, Amy, did you see the state of Hannah's face?"

23

*M*ax couldn't believe his daughter was a thief. He just couldn't take it in. When Jane had phoned, a ridiculous part of him had clung on to the hope that she was joking. Then Jane had blurted it all out—about the woman whom Hannah had seen trying on earrings really being store security. How this woman had stopped her in the street and led her back through the shop to a little back room.

He couldn't understand why she'd done it. Had she desperately wanted those things—a lighter, for God's sake— or stolen them just for the thrill?

"Max, honey?" Veronica cut into his thoughts. He'd been painting the skirting board in her study, trying to calm his racing thoughts while she tapped on her keyboard. Although it still involved painting, Max was grateful for a change of scene from his own house.

"Hmm?" he said.

"Come here, have a look. There's a stunning ski collection and it's all thirty per cent off." Max had surmised that the January sales were more enticing than Christmas to Veronica. While Christmas Day had been okay—Hannah had joined him, Veronica and her kids after lunch—there'd been something missing. It hadn't helped, of course, that he'd had to give Hannah a stern talking to about shoplifting. On Christmas Day, of all days. Not that there was ever a good time to deal with stuff like that.

Max rested the brush on the paint can and peered at the screen over Veronica's shoulder. Salopettes, jackets and something called a combi set—did she really think he'd be kitting himself out in proper skiing gear? "I thought I'd wear my jeans," he said.

Veronica chuckled. "You *are* joking, Max. Jeans aren't suitable for snow. You'll get soaked and freezing. What you need is—"

"Listen." Max rested a hand on her arm. "I'm not buying new stuff. The holiday's costing enough, okay? My head's full of the shop at the moment. If premises come up I want to put in an offer without worrying about—"

"It's only *clothes,* Max. Buying a cute little beanie hat will hardly bankrupt you."

"I don't want a cute little beanie hat!"

With a dismissive shake of her head, she clicked onto a page depicting 'base layers'—they looked like long johns to Max—and something called 'buffs.' Loosely resembling balaclavas, they were pattered with snowflakes and psychedelic swirls. Max knew, with absolute certainty, that he didn't require a buff.

"Well," Veronica teased him, "you can be an old scruff-monkey on the slopes. I'm treating myself to a few bits and bobs. What d'you think of these jackets, honey—shall I go for the lilac or baby blue?"

Max blinked at the images of skiers whipping down slopes. He'd felt warm and cosy, quietly painting in the corner. Now his entire body had chilled. "You choose," he said dully.

Veronica tore her eyes away from the screen and frowned at him. "You are silly, Max. These are real bargains. Kit yourself out and you'll actually be *saving* money."

He looked at her, expecting to detect a glimmer of irony. Her smile was pure, uncomplicated. Perhaps, he reasoned, uncomplicated was what he needed at this stage of his life. Someone who didn't rate his daughter's shoplifting spree as particularly significant, because there were more crucial matters to consider—like base layers.

Was he really making such a sacrifice by agreeing to go on this holiday when, clearly, it mattered so much to Veronica? "Maybe," he said, peering at her PC, "I'll order those socks with the spandex bit at the instep."

The smile illuminated her face. "Pervert," she whispered back.

24

"*Y*ou're going *where?*" Zoë spluttered.

"Scotland," Hannah said. "At least, some island in Scotland. Some teeny little place no one's heard of."

"Bloody hell." Zoë was struggling through a tray of Prêt à Manger sushi, which Hannah suspected she'd chosen for effect and not because she particularly relished raw fish. "Half term as well," Zoë added. "Waste of a school holiday, getting dragged off to the middle of nowhere. What is there to do?"

Hannah shrugged. "Nothing much, according to Mum. The house where we're staying looks really posh. Apart from that it's just sheep and mountains and stuff."

"Ugh," Zoë said, shuddering. "You could've stayed with me, if I wasn't being farmed out to God knows who while Mum and your dad go skiing. Don't know why me and

Dyl can't stay at home by ourselves. It's not like we're kids...."

"Where are you going to stay?" Hannah asked.

Zoë peeled off the fish and popped a lump of sticky rice into her mouth. "Not sure yet. Mum's desperately ringing round her friends but no one's that keen to have me." She giggled.

"Where's Dylan going?"

"Oh, he'll be fine. He's staying with one of his mates. They can sit up all night drawing their horrible weirdo comic strips."

"I didn't know he did that," Hannah said.

"He tries." Zoë licked her fingers and shut the lid of her sushi box.

"Don't you mind not going skiing?"

"I'm used to it. Mum's never taken me. Anyway, I wouldn't want to get between the loved-up couple."

The chocolate brownie felt like sawdust in Hannah's throat. She hadn't told Zoë about being caught shoplifting; she'd have felt idiotic, as if she'd somehow let her down by failing to follow her instructions properly. She hadn't even told Ollie during their snogging sessions at his flat on Monday evenings. They didn't seem to talk as much as they used to. Kissing or talking: it seemed there wasn't room for both.

"I can't believe you're going," Zoë declared suddenly, "without kicking up a fuss. You're fifteen, for God's sake. She's treating you like a baby."

Hannah scrunched the cellophane wrapper from her brownie. Although three weeks had passed since police station day, which she could hardly bring herself to think about, she was in no position to be difficult. In acquiring a reprimand she'd kissed goodbye to any bargaining power. "Actually," she murmured, "it might be a laugh."

"What, being stuck on a miserable island with no shops?"

"There'll be *some* shops."

"Yeah," Zoë sniggered, "like a Gap and Zara? What do they wear up there anyway?"

"Same as us, I suppose," Hannah said.

"I thought they wore kilts."

"That's just for special occasions, idiot." God, Zoë really knew nothing. Although Hannah was hardly a seasoned traveler, she'd been all over Britain with her mum or dad to various holiday cottages. She doubted if Zoë even knew where Scotland was.

"Tell you what," Zoë announced. "I could come, too. *Then* it'd be fun."

Hannah sniggered. The idea was ridiculous: Zoë plonked on an island God knows how many hundred miles from her hairdresser, and Jane agreeing to take her in the first place. "You're mad," she said.

"How long are you going for?"

"Five days I think."

"That's not so bad. Mum wouldn't have to stress out trying to find some place to dump me." There was a catch in Zoë's voice, and her eyes gleamed. *She does mind,* Hannah thought, as Zoë pretended to fiddle with the strap of her shoe. *She hates being left behind when her mum goes away. She thinks nobody cares.* "I'm not sure Mum would go for it," she murmured.

"Why not? Doesn't she like me?"

"Yes but—"

"I'll keep you company. Mum'll pay part of the petrol and food and my share of staying in that posh house. It'll be great, Han. Go on—ask her if I can come. Tell her I'm about to be abandoned by my uncaring mother and have nowhere to go. Say I'm practically *homeless*." Zoë managed a hollow laugh.

Hannah wanted to fling her arms around her and pull her close. She couldn't help admiring Zoë's knack of twisting the facts so the maddest thing—stealing a plastic doll's head, spending half term on some bleak, remote island— seemed like absolutely the right thing to do. Hannah looked at the face that still looked sunny and golden, even in January. She had to admit, the prospect of Zoë tagging along made the trip seem a little less awful.

"She'll let me come, won't she?" Zoë asked, pushing the glass door open. "We'll be stuck on an island with sod all to do. It's not as if we can get into any trouble."

25

"Are we nearly there yet?"

Jane gripped the steering wheel and tried to shut off her ears. Zoë had fired this question several times and they'd only just passed the turnoff for Hemel Hempstead. Weren't kids meant to grow out of asking such brain-jarring questions at around seven years old?

Hannah, who was installed beside Zoë in the backseat, was on charming form. Her urgent requirement for the loo had coincided with their joining the M1, so they'd already had to make a service station stop.

"So, are we?" Zoë asked.

"A few hours to go yet," Jane said.

"How many miles?"

"Hundreds. Thousands. It'll take us *weeks*."

Zoë groaned. This wasn't the deal, thought Jane: this

perpetual whining when they'd been on the road for an hour and a half. Had Zoë forgotten her impassioned speech when she'd begged to come? *Please, Jane, Mum's going to France and I've got nowhere to go. I'll be no trouble at all.*

Nancy, with arms firmly folded in the passenger seat, was crunching a licorice ball. It cracked noisily; Jane feared for her mother's teeth. Nancy's contribution to motoring pleasure had been the paper bag of boiled sweets, a flask of watery coffee and a package of ham sandwiches tightly wrapped in wrinkled foil. "Find out if there's space for me at that Hope House," she'd demanded.

"You're not interested in stained glass," Jane had protested. "You don't even call it stained glass. You call it my window business."

Nancy had chuckled and said, "It's the dry stone walling I'm keen on. It's a skill I've always wanted to learn." Jane had pointed out that there was little call for dry stone walling in Muswell Hill, but Nancy had insisted, adding that she'd take care of the cooking, which was done on a rota system at Hope House. So here they were: Jane, Hannah, Zoë and Nancy. Only four people, yet the car felt stiflingly overcrowded.

"Why's it all talking on the radio?" Zoë asked.

"It's a *play*," Nancy snapped. "Just listen to it and enjoy it."

Jane glimpsed Zoë's morose expression in the rearview mirror. Nancy had already assumed the role of Radio Boss and had twiddled the ancient dial, muttering to herself, finally settling on Radio 4. The play wasn't convincing. The actors sounded as if they were desperate to fling down their scripts and be normal. "This is boring," Zoë declared. "Can't you put on a CD?"

"No," Jane snapped.

"Our car doesn't have a CD player," Hannah retorted. "There was a tape player but it chewed up Mum's tape and broke."

"Oh," Zoë said flatly. "When are we stopping?"

"I was hoping to get past Manchester," Jane said, trying to keep her voice level, "then we'll have lunch."

Zoë slumped into silence, clearly finding Manchester's location as mysterious and unfathomable as planet Neptune. Several minutes passed. Nancy offered around licorice balls, but no one wanted any. Hannah was staring through the window at the lifeless sky.

Jane reminded herself that they weren't undertaking this journey for the hell of it—not just to make everyone miserable and have to endure Nancy's endless crunching—but because she'd meet Archie Snail, and learn from him, which would change her entire approach to her work. Nancy would throw herself into her course, and the girls...well, they could do whatever the heck they wanted. They could grumble from dawn to dusk and Jane couldn't give a flying fig.

It was dark by the time they reached the concrete block of a hotel that squatted bleakly at the side of the motorway. They'd already had one vile service station meal, and now they'd be faced with another. In the restaurant Jane eyed the sausages that lay like coiled snakes. Nancy, who had filled up on her own sandwiches, retorted, "The speed you drive, Jane, it'll take us six months to get there. I'm sure we could have done the journey in a day."

"I've been driving for nine hours," Jane muttered. As they sat at the table she studied the map. Such a rugged coastline. Islands like pastry crumbs fallen off the edge of a pie. It hardly seemed possible that people actually lived on them.

Later, in the hotel room, she stared through the gloom at the other single bed. Her mother was muttering in her sleep. The room was sparsely furnished; basic accommodation for people passing through. The radiator whined and grunted. She slipped out of bed and peered though the small window. Outside a rectangular pool glimmered beneath silvery streetlamps. Nancy, annoyed that her offerings hadn't been fully appreciated, had tipped the remaining ham sandwiches into the water. Jane watched them floating, a scattering of Hovis rafts.

The ferry departure point turned out not to be the bustling port that Jane had imagined, but a prefab hut manned by a gruff-looking man behind a glass partition. "We're booked on the eleven-fifteen," Jane said, rummaging through her bag for the e-mailed confirmation. The man took the printout from her and pulled in his lips. "Is there a problem?" she asked.

"Not with your booking," came the surprisingly soft voice. "But with the weather. Last ferry was canceled. And this one…" He shrugged, as if it might or might not be sailing, depending on a whim.

Jane glanced through the open door where wind was whipping up litter. "When will you know?" she asked.

The man shrugged again. "Hard to tell."

Hannah was shivering, forcing her arms up opposite sleeves of her sweater. They'd left Nancy in the car. After complaining that her hotel mattress had felt like a ruddy blancmange, she'd fallen into a heavy sleep with her mouth lolling open for the remaining journey.

Zoë was tapping at her phone by a revolving stand, which held a few dog-eared ferry timetables. "Can't get a signal," she announced.

"There's no signal here," said the man behind his partition.

"What about on the island?" she asked.

"Not a chance."

"So where *can* I get a signal?"

"Fort William," the man said with a chuckle.

"Oh," she said softly. "I just wanted to tell Mum we're nearly there."

Your mum's on her way to France, Jane thought. *She won't be thinking about you.* She glanced at Zoë's feet, which were prettily encased in turquoise wedge sandals. Why hadn't Veronica suggested that Zoë brought winter clothing? She saw it then: determination flickering across her perfectly made-up face as she thrust her cell back into her bag.

A girl trying to be brave, a million miles from a Prêt à Manger, and even farther from her mother's consideration.

Sunshine broke through, as the ferry docked at the island, and Hope House seemed to sparkle. Jane drove along the gravel driveway, which bisected an undulating lawn. The lawn, she realized now, was more of a meadow and clearly hadn't been mown for several years. And the house—she was close enough to see clearly now—wasn't quite as it had appeared on the website. Its stone facade was badly crumbling. A porcelain washbasin lay on its side in the long grass, and behind grimy windows there appeared only darkness. "It looks perfectly fine," Nancy announced, as if reading her thoughts. "Won't be spending much time here anyway, will we?"

"What *will* we be doing?" Zoë piped up.

"Jane and I will be doing our courses," Nancy replied. "You and Hannah can go for long, bracing walks."

"Oh," Zoë said weakly.

"I'm sure it's lovely inside," Jane added. In fact, as she pulled up on the graveled arc in front of the house, she decided she preferred it this way. Crumbling and unintimidating. She wasn't sure how she'd have conducted herself in some grand stately home.

Leaving Zoë and Hannah staring sullenly through the windows, she and Nancy stepped out of the car. "It's quite a place," Nancy said.

"Yes, Mum, it is." Jane inhaled crisp, cold air. Turrets soared upward, spearing downy white clouds. It's full of secrets, she thought. That, and promise.

26

*H*annah had been intrigued by the idea of staying in a mansion or castle, whatever it was. She'd imagined chairs with gilt arms and polished dining tables big enough to seat twenty-eight people. She'd envisaged butlers and servants, sumptuous meals kept piping hot under silver domes, perhaps a grand piano or two. "Good journey?" asked Mrs. McFarlane.

The group clustered around the front desk. While Jane said it had been fine—she'd clearly chosen to forget about Zoë's seasickness on the ferry, not to mention thirteen hours of unadulterated hell in the car—Hannah glanced around the foyer. She skimmed the cheap-looking desk, a stack of metal-legged chairs and a fire extinguisher attached to the scuffed wall. A pinned-up message read: *Meals can be prepared in small kitchen please ask Jean if no milk in fridge.*

Hannah wondered who Jean was. Could it be this small, narrow woman with pursed lips and a wrinkly neck? Mrs. McFarlane, her mother and Granny Nancy were having a rare old time discussing the weather. "I hope it improves for you," Mrs. McFarlane said, "because it's been awful dreicht."

Driecht? What did that mean? Mrs. MacFarlane's accent was thick, virtually unintelligible. Yet her mother and Granny Nancy seemed to be having no trouble deciphering it. Could they just be pretending to understand, nodding like puppets while having no clue what the woman was talking about? Hannah tried to catch Zoë's eye to send a signal. She was too busy checking her reflection in the chrome bracket that clamped the fire extinguisher to the wall.

At least they were here now, liberated from that stinking car. Hannah had spent most of journey gazing at signs for places like Penrith and Carlisle—places that sounded cold and Northern. Zoë had been no comfort. Sulking over having forgotten her iPod, she'd responded to conversation openers in monosyllables and turned back to *Cosmo* or *Glamour*. For someone who scoffed at women's magazines, she always seemed to have an extensive supply.

As for her mother's driving—was she trying to kill them or what? They'd been stuck in a jam near Manchester, barely inching along, but that was no reason to start doodling in a notepad when you were responsible for four people's lives. Hannah despaired of her mother's habit of drawing while driving, the way she'd jab the pen between her thighs when the traffic started moving again. What would happen if she had to brake suddenly? She'd be speared in the belly.

"Hannah?" Her mother frowned at her. "You okay, love?"

She snapped back to reality. "Just a bit tired."

Mrs. McFarlane gave her a tight smile. "You *look* tired, dear. Pale as a ghost. Come on, let me show you your rooms."

Hannah watched her clomping ahead in dumpy brown shoes. Hope House felt more like a youth hostel than a hotel: acres of gloss paint in bleary browns and greens, threadbare carpets and handwritten notices stuck all over the place. Mrs. McFarlane showed Jane and Nancy to their room, then journeyed onward with Hannah and Zoë trailing behind. At the far end of a corridor she opened a door. "Here you go," she said brightly. "I'll leave you girls to settle in."

As Mrs. McFarlane clopped away, Hannah stepped into the room and looked around her. Granny Nancy and Jane at least had a view over the garden and sea. Hannah and Zoë's room—a dingy cell in the bowels of the house—overlooked a yard furnished with a plastic water barrel. As Hannah peered out, a dollop of bird poo splatted the window.

Beside the window the embossed peach wallpaper was mottled with damp. Hannah read a notice aloud: "'Loo paper only down toilet please we have septic tank if blocked someone has to clean it out.' God, Zoë, how d'you reckon they clean out a septic tank?"

"No idea."

"Will *we* have to do it?"

Zoë had dropped to her hands and knees and was crawling around at skirting board level. "Aren't there any plugs?" she muttered.

"You mean a socket?"

"Yeah. You know, to plug my hair irons in."

Hannah spluttered with laughter. "Who's going to care about your hair?"

"*I* care." Zoë pulled herself up, claiming the larger of the two beds by dumping her case on it and yanking out her clothes. She was in one almighty huff, as if any of this was Hannah's fault. She stared at the clothes that Zoë was flinging out of the case. Jeans—fine. Pink top, aqua strapless dress, extensive array of delicate footwear—less fine. Hannah had packed thick sweaters and ancient jeans that barely saw the light of day in London. Her mother had bought her fleecy gloves, a scarf and a pull-on wooly hat. She'd die a painful death if Ollie ever saw her in them.

Grumbling, Zoë let her head and upper body drop over the bed while she delved into her bag. Now she was tipping out a great mound of creams and oils and makeup. The deep conditioning nourishing masque caught Hannah's eye. Zoë was the only person Hannah knew whose hair required a 'masque'.

"What are you looking for?" Hannah asked.

"Earplugs. Mum always gives me them when she's been on a plane."

"Why d'you need earplugs? We're in the middle of—"

"Don't tell me you can't hear them, Han—the sheep and that whooshing noise, the sea or the wind…"

"You live in London," Hannah laughed, pulling on jeans and sweater. "How can you say it's noisy here? There's just…silence."

Locating her earplugs and stuffing them in, Zoë flopped her head back onto her pillow. "Yeah," she murmured, "There's that, too."

"Hey," Hannah said gently, "cheer up."

"It's all right for you," Zoë muttered.

"Why? What makes it any easier for me?"

Zoë blinked at her. "You wanted to come."

"I had no choice! Not after I'd been caught—"

"Caught what?" Zoë narrowed her eyes.

She couldn't tell her. *Only idiots get caught,* Zoë had said. "Me and Mum had a fight," Hannah said quickly. "It was nothing really. Anyway, look, there's a plug—a socket—under the bedside table."

Zoë's face softened. "Thank God for that."

Hannah smiled. Even when she was acting spoiled and annoying, Zoë couldn't help being funny. Hannah wondered sometimes if this was a good thing; whether she was laughing at Zoë rather than with her, which implied that she thought of herself as somehow superior. "So," she added, "think you can cope, now you can plug your irons in?"

Zoë rubbed her goose-pimpled arms and glanced around the room. "It'll be better when the heating comes on."

Hannah touched an ancient radiator. "It *is* on."

"Shit," Zoë said.

27

$\mathcal{A}$rchie's studio was a proud, stone outbuilding with an end wall replaced by glass. Jane stepped inside, where mass introductions were taking place. There was a young, fresh-faced girl with cropped reddish hair and dangly feather earrings named Paula. A woman with a rich laugh and pregnant bump who spelled her name each time she introduced herself: *D-o-r-i-n-a*. There was an elderly man, whose pinched eyes and pulled-in lips gave him an air of general discontent, and a younger man in a checked flannel shirt with meaty forearms. "So you've come all the way from London?" he asked.

"I'm looking on it as a holiday," Jane explained, then, fearing that she'd sounded too flippant added, "It was Archie's work that got me interested in stained glass."

"Really?" Archie Snail stood in the doorway. He was

shorter—way shorter—than Jane had imagined: five foot
two at a guess, with a paunchy middle and a round, hot-
looking face that made Jane think of a pink balloon. His
mouth formed a terse smile as he strode toward her.

"This was years ago," she added quickly, "at the Barbican.
You were showing those pieces with the tiny segments, all
the fiery colors—"

Amusement flickered across his face. "Ah, yes. The good
days." He glanced quizzically around the studio as if trying
to figure why these random strangers with expectant expres-
sions had clustered around his table. He marched across the
room and lowered himself on to a seat behind a small desk
in the corner, clutching its edge like some wooden security
blanket.

An awkward silence descended on the room. The check-
shirted man winked at Jane. "Okay," Archie muttered,
"what I'm hoping to do is show you folks some influences
and techniques, arr…" He drifted off, as if suddenly remembering that he had something vital to attend to at
home: a leg of lamb in the oven, or a pan of milk on the
stove. "So, um," he continued, "what I'll do is get started
and, er, do something."

His mouth clamped shut, and he checked his watch.
Surely he hadn't run out of things to say already? Jane was
overcome by a wave of foolishness. What had she been
thinking, dragging Hannah and Zoë and Nancy all the way
here? Archie had picked up a pencil and was scribbling
urgently on a pad: making notes, perhaps, on how he might
possibly struggle though the next five days.

The door opened and another man strode in. He was tall

and angular, with finely sculpted cheekbones and intense blue-gray eyes that hinted at mischief. "Hi, everyone," he said, "I'm Conor, Archie's assistant. I'll show you round the studio, and if anyone needs anything, just ask me, okay?" Jane saw Archie throwing him a relieved look. All the women, she noticed, were gazing at him intently. "If you can't find me," Conor added, "I live down at Seal Bay. Just drop by anytime." Through the window he indicated a tiny white cottage perched at the point where fields met cream colored sand.

"Aren't you lucky?" Paula enthused. "The island's gorgeous."

Jane didn't register Conor's reply. She was transfixed by the way his mouth curled as he spoke, drawn in by the softness of his voice. To distract herself, she delved into her bag and pulled out her sketches for Max's window. By the time she looked up, the check-shirted man was bounding toward her. "I'm George," he said, shaking her hand firmly and planting himself on the next stool. He snatched her wodge of sketches, licking his thumb in order to flick through them as speedily as possible. "Nice work," he murmured. "You're a very talented lady."

Jane recoiled in her seat. "Thanks," she said, wishing he'd leave her drawings alone and put them back on the workbench.

"So, some dump we're staying in," he declared. "What d'you make of the place?"

"Actually, I like it. It's fine."

"You would—got the best room, haven't you? You and that older woman—"

"My mother."

"Hey," George said, nudging her, "check out those two." Jane turned to the glass wall to see Hannah and Zoë plodding across the undulating field, their faces set in grim determination. "Blond one's wearing high heels!" George spluttered.

"That's my daughter's—" Jane started.

"You're kidding! You're not old enough, surely…."

"Friend," she added, watching Zoë cupping her hands around her face as she tried to light a cigarette.

George made a *ffrrr* noise. "Jailbait." He grinned leeringly. Conor, who was sliding sheets of colored glass into pigeonholes, threw Jane a sympathetic glance. She smiled, feeling warmth in the pit of her stomach. "Look like they'd rather be at the pub," George added. "Hey, Conor, any pubs around here?"

"Yes, there's a couple in the village."

"Great. Up for a drink later, Jane?"

"Um, maybe," she said, glimpsing Hannah striding purposefully, Zoë tottering unsteadily behind her still trying to light her ciggie in the buffeting wind.

"Well, Jane," George announced, shifting his stool to be as close as possible without actually clambering onto her lap, "let's do that. Find a cosy pub, warm our cockles and all that." He beamed at her. "I think I'm going to like it around here."

She caught Conor's glance across the studio. It didn't unnerve her, the way he kept looking as if he could read her thoughts. She wasn't in Albemarle Street, being Hannah's mum or deputy manager at Nippers. Here on this island, with its wildly changing skies, she could be anyone, do anything she wanted.

You're right, George, she thought, returning Conor's smile. *I think I'm going to like it here, too.*

28

$\mathcal{T}$he mountains that loomed before Max were such a familiar image, he could think only of Alpen cereal. He could picture its box in his kitchen cupboard: snow-dusted peaks, impossibly blue sky, 100 percent natural ingredients.

"Isn't it awesome?" Veronica said.

Max turned from the bedroom window. It was 8:00 a.m. and she was already kitted out in a jaunty mint-colored zip-up top and salopette ensemble. He wondered if she was wearing a base layer underneath. She hadn't worn a base layer last night; Max had been taken aback by the complicated lingerie she'd swiftly changed into while he'd been brushing his teeth in the bathroom. He'd been looking forward to snuggling against the luscious curves of her body. Instead, he'd been confronted by an abundance of complex fastening devices and dangly bits to which sheer stockings had been attached.

"It's breathtaking," he said now, and it was. These were the Alps, for Christ's sake. Why couldn't he appreciate them? Veronica had a rosy flush to her cheeks, and her makeup—which she usually troweled on rather too enthusiastically for Max's taste—looked natural and fresh. She looked lovely, standing there in the white-and-pine bedroom, yet Max seemed to be having difficulty appreciating beauty.

He glanced back at the mountains, trying to figure out how he might describe them to Hannah. They were huge. They had snow on them. He wondered how Jane and the girls had settled into that grand stately home in Scotland, and quickly shooed the thought away.

"Aren't you getting ready?" Veronica asked. "The lifts will be open already. We don't want to waste good skiing time."

"I am ready," he said, throwing a *ta-da* pose in his stretchy gray boxer shorts.

Veronica smirked. "Very nice, Max. Not bad for an old man. Come on, though—Jasper and Hettie are keen to get out."

Max eyed the jacket and waterproof trousers that lay on the bed. They were yellow. He couldn't understand why he'd picked such a color when he'd collected his kit from the ski shop yesterday. The others had rushed him, that had been the problem; slow-coach Max, the only one who didn't possess his own gear. He'd gawped at rows of padded clothing and snatched the brightest and ugliest.

Sighing, he pulled on his clothes. Jasper's voice bounded

through the thin walls of their top-floor apartment. *Only a week,* Max reminded himself, *then everything will be normal again.*

"So, Maxy," Jasper boomed over breakfast in the pine-paneled kitchen. "I assume you'll be spending the first couple of days on the nursery slopes?"

Jasper and Hettie were tucking into great hunks of cheese, fruit and *saucisson,* which they'd had the forethought to pick up as soon as they'd arrived at Chamonix. Jasper had a thick neck, thick arms; thick everything, Max suspected. A silver wedding band pinched his thick, hairy finger.

"I, um—" Max floundered.

"Don't be silly," Veronica cut in. "Max paid for a lift pass like the rest of us. He might as well make use of it. You'll be okay on the green runs, won't you, darling? I'll be with you. We'll take it slowly. You don't want to be stuck on the boring nursery slopes with a load of screaming children."

Max bit into a slice of Emmenthal. Green runs, red runs, what was the difference? He wondered if Jasper was intending to call him Maxy for the entire holiday.

"I'm sure I'll be fine," he insisted.

"Haven't you booked lessons?" Hettie asked. She had a little snub nose and subtly highlighted hair that crinkled around her face. She was around Veronica's age—thirty-five-ish—but looked younger. Must be having all that staff, Max decided; a life unencumbered by stress. During the entire flight he'd had to listen to Jasper prattling away to some poor stranger beside him: about "our" cleaner, "our" gardener, even "our" cobbler, which made Max think of a tiny person, an elf dressed in rags, stitching pieces of leather in the night. "Our" imbecile cleaner, Max learned, had shrunk Jasper's Thomas Pink lambswool sweater in the washing machine. The arsehole had docked the poor girl's wages. When Jasper hadn't been boasting about their *people,* he'd spouted mysterious skiing terms: "moguls," "free-riding," "carving a turn." He might as well have been speaking another language.

"You know what lessons are like," Veronica declared, plucking a slice of kiwi from an artful arrangement in the centre of the table. "It's days before you're properly skiing. I'll teach Max the basics. If he gets tired we can always pop off for a hot chocolate and a little relax."

They were talking about Max as if he were four years old—or, worse, not present at all. As if wishing to high-light his insignificance, Hettie, Jasper and Veronica pushed back their chairs and started piling on hats and jackets.

Veronica opened the door and stepped outside. Biting air gusted into the kitchen, hitting Max's face. "Let's get going," Jasper said, virtually filling the doorway as he strode through it.

"Can I just finish breakfast?" Max protested.

Jasper pulled out mirrored wraparound shades from a pocket and popped them on. "Seems a pity to waste good skiing time."

Max popped a dog-end of *saucisson* into his mouth. "Okay, Jaspy," he said.

Max hadn't realized he was scared of heights. Subconsciously, he must have spent his entire life avoiding being high, at least from a geographical point of view. Veronica leaned toward him and kissed his cheek, causing the chair-lift to wobble uneasily. "Are you okay?" she asked.

Max nodded, focusing on the ragged tops of the mountains. He was troubled by the fact that he couldn't stop or climb off the lift. Max preferred modes of transport that he could control. You knew where you were with bikes. They didn't swing thirty feet off the ground or judder to a halt for no apparent reason. He felt ridiculously ungainly in ski boots and rented banana-colored clothing. His skis—Max glanced down briefly at their jaunty lime zigzag design—were alien structures that seemed to function perfectly well for other people but, he was certain, took a good decade or two to master.

As they neared the top of the lift, Max realized with alarm that it wouldn't come to a polite stop, allowing skiers to clamber off in their own time, but would keep on going, requiring one to lurch off from a significant height on to compacted snow.

Max lurched. "You did it!" Veronica enthused. "See, Max, you're a natural."

"Thanks," he said, shuffling uneasily toward her.

"I knew you'd get into it, babes. Just try to relax, keep your knees bent and the fronts of your skis together, like this." She wedged them into a snowplow position.

Max tramped behind her to the start of the run. His legs were aching and he hadn't even done any skiing yet. "How many times have you been skiing?" he asked.

"Maybe sixteen, seventeen times. I've lost count."

"Won't you get bored hanging around with me?"

She pulled down her shades into position. "Max, honey, I don't think I'll ever get bored hanging around with you. Look, I know it seems daunting. Years ago, when I was about fourteen and having lessons, my instructor said something I've never forgotten. It's like falling in love, he told me. You have to let yourself go, take a risk in the hope that something amazing will come from it." She squeezed his gloved hand. "Think you can do that?"

Max looked at her. He wanted to see her eyes, but all that looked back at him was his own anxious reflection. "I'll try," he murmured.

"Remember, just let yourself go." With that, Veronica swiveled her skis to point down the slope, gave a dramatic push with her poles and was gone.

Max looked down. This was only a green run—the easiest kind. Jasper and Hettie would be tearing down sheer rockfaces by now. A kid of around four years old whipped past him. Hettie had been right; he should have booked lessons, not expected to grasp the basics from Veronica. What had he been thinking? His heart rattled in his chest. Although the air was bitingly cold, his body felt clammy beneath its layers of padding.

Max was standing side-on to the slope. He had an awful suspicion that, as soon as he started to swivel around and point his skis downward, he'd zoom off with no way of braking. How did skiers stop? Veronica had missed out that vital nugget of info. Yet he'd have to get down somehow. He glanced anxiously at the chairlift in the distance. People were sitting in pairs on the swinging seats, chatting happily; one guy was even smoking a cigarette. No one used the lift to come down. The only way down was to *ski*.

"Need some help?" A tall, slender woman in a red one-piece had come to halt beside him.

"I think I'll be okay," Max said, in a voice that he hoped conveyed cast-iron confidence.

The woman smiled encouragingly. She was wearing oval-shaped goggles and a streak of white sunblock on her nose. Some kind of polka-dotted tubular thing—could this be a buff?—was bunched around her neck. "Max, it's *me*," the woman said, laughing.

"Oh, Hettie—I didn't realize."

"Can you get down, do you think? You look a bit… unsure."

He cleared his throat. Tiny, multicolored specs were milling about at the bottom. One of those specs was Veronica. *Like falling in love,* she'd said, as if that was ever simple. By now, she'd have reached the conclusion that Max was a complete incompetent. "I'm just taking my time," he muttered.

"If you're sure—"

He nodded. *Just go away,* he thought. While he appreciated Hattie's concern, he wished she'd bloody zoom off and leave him to deal with this situation in his own time. She grinned at him. "You set off," he answered. "I don't want to waste your skiing time."

"Oh, you're not. Jasper's found the gang he meets up with every year. They're all going off piste. I'm happy to mess around on the green runs for the rest of the morning. I'll keep you company if you like."

If he weren't trapped on a mountain, Max might have been able to enjoy Hettie's presence. "I don't want to be rude," he said, "but I'd rather ski down on my own. I feel a bit self-conscious."

Hettie smiled kindly. "Okay, Max, if you're sure."

With a nod, he shuffled around to face down the slope. "Remember to—" Hettie called out.

"Bend my knees, yes." Max gripped his poles, digging their points into the snow for some feeling of stability. He felt Hettie's eyes on him. He was vaguely aware of shouts and cheers and faraway chatter; people having a fun winter holiday. To calm his racing mind, he tried to conjure up pleasing images of what might follow his first day on the slopes: hot chocolate, warm bath, Veronica massaging his sore feet and legs and other sensitive areas.

Then he couldn't think, because he was careering downward with parallel skis, and an awful feeling that they shouldn't be parallel—that he was doing it all wrong—though there was nothing he could do about that now. He was gathering speed, utterly out of control on some terrible fairground ride where you'd scream for the man to stop the machinery and let you off, but he'd be too busy smoking and reading the paper. He thought he heard someone yell, "Max!" then was aware only of colors: flashes of green and searing blue, a dash of orange—that was his beanie hat flying off, Veronica had bought it at Geneva airport, what would she—

All he could see now was white: not powdery white or the white tops of mountains but the hard, sharp *thwack* of a snow-covered rock—

Then everything went black.

29

"Think I'll join your drama thingie when we get back," Zoë declared as they strode through sodden grass toward the bay.

Hannah's breath caught in her throat. Mondays were the only time she saw Ollie—not that things would stay that way when they got home. She intended to tell him, in no uncertain terms, that she wouldn't be going back to his flat after workshop unless he saw her at other times too. Unless they started *going out*, like a normal girlfriend and boyfriend. "There's a waiting list," she fibbed. "I'll put your name down if you like."

"Come on," Zoë scoffed. "Surely they can fit me in. Maybe that's what I'll be—an actress. What d'you think?"

"I thought you wanted to be a model." An unsettling

image of Zoë and Ollie sizing each other up flashed into Hannah's mind. She felt quite nauseous.

"Oh, I don't know. Anyway, where are we going? It's bloody freezing out here."

"I thought we'd go down to the bay," Hannah said.

"What's there?"

"What d'you mean, what's there? It's a beach. There'll be sea, sand, a few rocks. I thought we might see some seals."

Zoë frowned. "Can't we get a bus to the village?"

The thought of Zoë shoplifting on the island filled Hannah with dread. She wanted to be outside with billowing clouds all around her. Since coming here, her breathing had felt free, virtually *normal*. "I haven't seen any buses from here," Hannah said, "and it's too far to walk."

"Would your mum drive us?"

"She's busy in the studio."

"Can't we call a taxi?"

"No, Zoë, I just want to—"

"Han!" The scream flew out as Zoë toppled sideways. One of her feet had plunged into mud. Hannah froze, her head flooding with a terrible image of Zoë being sucked under and trying to pull her out and—

"Don't just stand there!" Zoë screamed. Hannah ran toward her and grasped both hands, pulling hard until the foot plopped free. The girls stared down at it. It was bare and slathered with mud, after all Zoë's efforts with the toe separators and Dior Rouge Noir polish. Zoë gawped at it as if waiting for it to miraculously self-cleanse. "My shoe," she whispered.

They stared at the dip in the ground that Zoë had slipped into. An invisible hole, with sinking mud underneath. No shoe was visible. In the distance a black-faced sheep gazed at them dolefully. "I think you've lost it," Hannah murmured. "Good job you brought plenty of other pairs."

"No, Han, I've got to get it." Zoë rubbed her hands over her face.

Hannah sighed. "We could go back to the house, see if we can find a stick or a shovel and try and dig it out…."

"Okay," Zoë whispered. "Maybe someone'll help us."

Hannah touched her arm. "It's only a shoe…."

"It's not mine, Han. It's Mum's. I took them without asking."

"She won't mind, will she?" *She must have at least thirty-seven other pairs,* Hannah thought.

"Of course she'll—" Zoë choked on a sob.

"God, Zoë, don't cry…."

Tears were sliding down her cheeks now. Her nose was running and her face had gone blotchy and pink.

Hannah put her arms around her. "What is it?" she asked softly.

"They're Mum's favorites. They're really old so I can't buy another pair, I bet they don't make them like that any—"

"Hey," Hannah said, "I didn't think your mum wore old things."

Zoë pushed back her hair distractedly. "They're not *ordinary* old. Those shoes—they're the ones she wore when she married my dad."

"Oh, Zoë." Hannah stared at the ground. Some friend I

am, she thought, lying about a waiting list at theater work-shop. Zoë might have everything, and act like she knew it all, but underneath she was just an ordinary girl who was scared of her mum. "Let's go back to the house," she said gently.

"Okay." Zoë wiped her nose on the back of her hand.

Lifting a finger to her face, Hannah brushed the tears away.

30

*J*ane washed her hands at the Belfast sink in the studio. It was late afternoon; everyone else had wandered off to Hope House or driven into the village. The workbench was strewn with drawings and pieces of glass. After Conor had left, Archie had descended into semislumber, signaling the end of the working day. Jane wondered why Conor had dashed off at 3:00 p.m. The island didn't strike her as a dashing kind of place.

The darkening sky hung heavily over the bay. Through the window Jane could see a glimmer of light from Conor's house. He'd been friendly enough so far, but then he'd been friendly with everyone. Any questions of a technical nature—like how Archie managed to keep lightness to his work when he'd fused so many tiny pieces together—had been answered by Conor. Archie appeared to want as little contact with his students as possible. "Waste of time and money," Dorina had muttered to Jane earlier. "Pay your fee and what do you get? A drunk idiot in the corner."

"It's only our first day. Let's give him a chance," Jane had replied, glancing at the sleeping Archie. A scrap of bread roll had embedded itself in his wiry beard.

No wonder he needed Conor, Jane reflected, switching off the studio lights and stepping outside. She suspected that the promised one-to-one tuition with Archie would be unforthcoming. She should feel disappointed—even angry— yet had enjoyed the day and lost herself in her work.

She strolled across the lumpen ground toward Hope House, hoping to find the girls. Zoë had been right; they hadn't been any trouble so far. In fact, apart from the communal lunch, when everyone crammed around a long table in dining room, Jane had hardly seen them. Hannah, she'd noticed, looked healthier already and her eyebrows had almost resumed their natural shape. Zoë had acquired a flat expression of resignation, but at least she'd stopped prattling on about her iPod.

Mrs. McFarlane looked up from the desk as Jane strode into the foyer. "I'm not sure if it'll come out the carpet," she announced.

"What?" Jane asked.

A pair of glasses hung on a cord around her neck. Her gaze was firmly fixed upon a dark smudge on the faded blue carpet. "The mud," she said. "I've let it dry but it still won't brush up."

Jane glanced at the offending mark. "It doesn't look too bad," she said.

"In a terrible state, your daughter was, the blonde one with her bare foot and—"

"What happened?" Jane asked, too startled to correct her wrong-daughter mistake.

"Fell into the mud out the front—don't they realize there's a path they should stick to? Blonde one lost a shoe, asked me if I'd go help her dig it out…." Mrs. McFarlane emited a withering laugh. "Kept on about Emma Hope, whoever that is. We don't have an Emma Hope staying here."

"Where are they now?" Jane asked anxiously.

Mrs. McFarlane shrugged. "Try their room. I'll have another go at this mud."

Jane stepped into the girls' room. It wasn't locked; no one seemed to bother with keys at Hope House.

Zoë's clothes were spewed all over her bed. Her hair irons had been left on, and were blazing hot. Jane unplugged them, winding their flex around the handle. She spotted some drawings on the dressing table. They were charcoal sketches of the Hope House. Some were verging on abstract: great swirls of cloud, and the ragged outline of the Fang, the island's highest mountain. So this was how Hannah had been filling her time. Jane couldn't remember the last time she'd drawn. Leafing through them felt like prying, but she couldn't stop herself.

Jane left their bedroom and toured the various stale-smelling communal rooms of Hope House. As she passed through the foyer, both Mrs. McFarlane and the muddy patch had gone. Jane suspected that she'd left it there just to show her—to make a point.

Heading outside, she cut across the field toward a crumbling barn. "I want you to pick up the stone," a man was enthusing inside, "and feel its texture, make *friends* with it." Jane peered in. The barn was lit with oil laps nestling in indentations in the stone walls, each producing a weak glow. There were five or six people: all men apart from Nancy, who, like the others, was perched on a bale of straw. She was craning forward, as if drinking in the man's every word. He was probably sixty-something, but had the lanky frame of a teenage boy. A gray ponytail fell like a wolf's tail down his back. "Can I help you?" he asked, squinting at Jane.

"I'm looking for my daughter and her friend. I didn't mean to interrupt—"

Nancy swooped down her eyebrows as if to say: you *are* interrupting.

"Perhaps they've gone to the beach," the man said. "I saw two girls heading that way. One was pretty upset...."

"That ridiculous Zoë girl lost her shoe," Nancy interjected. "Honestly, Jane, she expected me to spend the best part of my afternoon digging through mud to find it. A silly old shoe! What possessed you to bring her?" She exhaled noisily, then picked up the lump of stone at her feet and caressed it, making it her friend.

Jane found the girls hunched on a rock at Seal Bay and got Zoë's frantic retelling. Armed with a knobbly length of driftwood, they headed back across the fields. "I think it's here," Zoë announced.

"You *think?*" Jane snapped.

"No. Yeah. It looks kind of familiar…." Zoë stepped back, as if to distance herself from a potentially messy procedure. Jane delved through the mud, but each time she managed to work a solid object to the surface, it would be nothing more precious than a stone. It was almost dark, and the moon cast an eerie silver glow.

"Dad," came a small voice, "what's that lady doing?"

Jane looked up and peered toward the house. Two figures were approaching; it was Conor, with a boy by his side. The reason, she surmised, for his disappearance at 3:00 p.m. today. "We're looking for something," Jane said, feeling foolish; island people didn't lose shoes in bogs.

"What?" the boy asked. Up close she saw a distinct resemblance: Conor's pale eyes and mischievous mouth, but a shock of reddish hair instead of the brown.

"Zoë lost a shoe," she explained.

Conor glanced at the girls, and looked as if he was trying to affect a concerned look, but a smile escaped. "Can I help?"

"*I'll* find it," the boy announced, stumbling forward.

"Jane," Conor said, "I haven't introduced you. This is Lewis, my son."

"Hi, Lewis—"

"Dad, let me dig! I'm really good at finding stuff. It's like a treasure hunt…."

"It's okay, Lewis," Jane said, "I know where I've already looked. I'm trying to be…"

"Systematic." Conor chuckled. "Must be a very special shoe."

Jane wished they'd stop watching. She'd hoped to run in

to Conor outside the studio, but not like this: ankle-deep in bog, her boots and jeans splattered with mud. She felt ridiculously city-ish.

"Dad told me about you," Lewis added with a smirk.

"Did he?"

"Yeah. He said your drawings are the best."

Jane stopped stirring and felt herself blushing. "Really? Thanks."

Conor smiled and took his son's hand. "Come on, Lewis. I thought we were going to the beach for sticks."

"I want to watch her."

Jane met the boy's gaze. "Tell you what. You have one dig around, and if you can't find it we'll give up, okay?"

"We *can't* give up," Zoë lamented.

Lewis rejected Jane's stick. Instead, he plunged his arms up to the elbows into the bog, clearly relishing the feel of cold mud squelching up his coat sleeves, and laughing a minute later as he plucked out one solitary, mud-plastered shoe.

"He's found it!" Zoë yelped, pelting toward him and snatching it.

They all peered at it as if it were some priceless artifact. Conor unwound a woolen scarf from his neck and used it first to wipe as much mud as he could from Lewis's hands and coat, then took the shoe from Zoë and rubbed at it. "Will it be all right?" she asked anxiously.

"It's a bit storm-damaged," Conor said. "You'd better take it to the house for a proper cleanup job." He held out the shoe. Clearly visible now, its label read: *Regalia for Feet*.

Jane rested a hand on Lewis's shoulder. "You're a clever kid," she said.

He grinned up at her. "I know. C'mon—me and Dad are going to get some sticks from the beach for my costume. You can help."

"The tide's nearly in," Conor contradicted, "we've left it too—"

"I'd love to," Jane said. "Come on, I'm sure there'll be some driftwood lying about."

"Well, okay." Conor smiled shyly.

As the girls headed to the house, and Jane strolled with Conor and Lewis to the bay, she silently thanked Zoë for bringing her here at precisely the right moment. Perhaps, she thought, dumb high heels were pretty useful on an island after all.

"D'you watch *Doctor Who?*" Lewis asked as his father pushed open the unlocked door of their cottage.

"I did, a long time ago," Jane replied. "Me and Hannah used to watch it together."

Lewis hovered at her side as they entered the low-ceilinged living room. "Did she get scared?"

"No," Jane said, laughing, "Hannah was never scared of anything on TV."

"Neither am I," Lewis declared. Flecks of mud were stuck to his forehead.

"Of course you're not," Conor teased him. "That's why you watched it last week with a cushion over your face."

"Didn't—"

"Yes, you did! Anyway, are we going to sort out this costume?"

Jane glanced at the assorted Dalek components that were

strewn around the floor: sheet of cardboard, cans of gold paint, a battered wicker laundry basket. Ancient armchairs and a sofa crowded the room. On the walls were drawings of stars and planets; Saturn's ring had been sprinkled with glitter. A sheet of black paper had been splattered with fluorescent paint and entitled The Univerz by Lewis. There was no sign of a mother, no hint that a woman lived here.

While Conor made tea, Lewis glared at the laundry basket. "It'll never be a Dalek," he muttered. "Dad said he'd help but he's always too busy working. It's not fair."

"It might help," Conor called from the kitchen, "if you didn't keep changing your mind. You wanted to be a Cyberman then a Martian then—"

"Yeah," Lewis retorted, "Gavin's going as a Cyberman and Robbie's a Martian. I want to be different."

Jane smiled, remembering Hannah being asked by a day care nurse at Nippers if she went to ballet classes. *No,* she'd retorted, *I'm different.*

"Mum used to make stuff for me," Lewis murmured.

"Did she?" Jane asked cautiously.

"Yeah." He pointed to the Univerz picture. "Now she's there."

"Oh," Jane said, "I'm sorry."

As Conor entered the room, she searched for some hint of how to respond. He placed mugs of tea on the table and rested his hands on his Lewis's shoulders. "What about these sticks?" he asked.

Lewis delved through the driftwood he'd dumped on the living room floor. The smoothest and straightest would be the sticky-out bits—the bits from which fatal rays would blast, should Lewis feel inclined to exterminate. "Can she help?" he asked.

"Jane," Conor said gently. "Her name's Jane."

She smiled and said, "Between the three of us I'm sure we'll come up with a completely terrifying Dalek."

"And you can stay for supper," Conor added. "If you'd like to."

"I'd love to." His eyes met hers over the top of Lewis's head, and the glow that flooded through her was so unfamiliar, she'd forgotten it was something her body could do.

31

*B*efore he was fully awake, Max was aware of every muscle and bone in his body. He ached all over. Even his *eyelids* ached. He opened his eyes slowly, trying to ascertain whether he was in the chalet or his bedroom at home. It didn't smell like home. It smelled as if vegetables were being overboiled in some distant kitchen. He was aware of hushed female voices, someone's hacking cough, and a soft rattle that sounded like an approaching trolley. For a moment, he'd decided he was on an airplane and a stewardess was bringing coffees and teas.

No, not on a plane. In a hospital ward. Of course; he'd been brought here at some point—it could have been an hour or a day or a week ago—aware of little more than a searing pain in his right leg. All he'd thought, while he was being examined, was that he wanted the fleshy-faced doctor to take his prodding fingers off him and let him sleep.

A nurse with her hair pulled back into a severe ponytail approached his bed. "So," she said, "awake at last. How are you feeling?"

"I don't know," he muttered.

She smiled pertly and checked the clipboard, which was attached to the foot of his bed. "Hungry?" she asked.

"Not really." Max had never been less hungry in his life.

"You're lucky your girlfriend was with you," the nurse added. "You'd lost consciousness after you hit the rock. You have a concussion. She's the one who called the rescue team."

Max had no recollection of any rescue team, and couldn't figure out who the nurse was referring to when she said "girlfriend." He was pretty sure Veronica hadn't been involved. For all he knew, he could have been brought here by dog-sleigh. "Where is my, um, girlfriend?" Max asked.

"She's been sitting with you, waiting for you to wake up. I think she's gone for a coffee."

Max nodded, then, feeling foolish, asked, "Where am I exactly?"

The nurse laughed. "Chamonix hospital. Don't you know what happened?"

A hazy image formed in his mind; of Hettie, with that spotty thing bunched around her neck, standing beside him at the start of the green run. He remembered the swill of nerves before he took off. After that, just pain and blackness.

The nurse poured him a cup of water from a plastic jug

on the table beside his bed. "You've ruptured your anterior cruciate ligament," she added.

At the word *rupture*, Max winced. "Is it serious?"

"It's very common. People like you, who go skiing without preparation or lessons—you take unnecessary risks. It might need to be operated on, but only if you'll need it—"

An anterior cruciate ligament sounded like something everyone needed. Max didn't relish the idea of being without one. "What do you mean?" he asked, panic rising in his throat.

"Some people find that they can recover and manage even if the ligament is damaged. But if you exercise a lot, especially running or cycling, then you'll probably need surgery…"

"I cycle," Max said faintly. "I have a cycling shop. It's what I do…it's my *life*." Put that way, it sounded pathetic. Thirty-eight years on this earth and what did he have to show for it? A bloody bike shop.

A cluster of children in bobble hats had burst into the ward and gathered around the bed of the coughing man. The man was hugging them and laughing. Max wondered if he'd ever laugh again. "Cycling might be difficult," the nurse continued. She checked her watch, adding, "I'll let you rest and come back with your painkillers in half an hour. Look, here's your girlfriend now."

The figure approached, smiled at the nurse and at Max, and perched on the edge of his bed. "So," Hettie said, "how are you feeling?"

"I've felt better," Max said.

"Poor you."

"Where's Veronica?" he asked.

"Um.... I'm not sure." Hettie shuffled awkwardly. "I couldn't reach her on her cell."

Her eyes held his for a moment. She was probably lying, but was also very pretty, he realized, with those soft blue eyes and dainty chin. Despite the nagging pain in his leg, her presence was making him feel marginally better. "Don't be too hard on her," she said gently.

Max shook his head despairingly. He must have been out of his mind to come on this holiday. What had happened to the old Max—the Max who'd made his own decisions and known his own mind? It had all started with the arrival of Veronica's hot meals. Jesus. He'd always thought of himself as a modern man—a sensitive father who cared about his daughter and ex-wife, who'd cared so much, in fact, that he'd taken the ludicrous step of buying a clapped-out house that was way beyond his means in a wretched attempt to lure them back. And what had happened? He'd been seduced by Veronica's tarragon chicken and pneumatic breasts. He was barely one step up the food chain from a slavering Neanderthal.

Max shifted his position in bed, groaning as the pain seared up his leg. "I don't understand," he groaned, "why it was so important for me to come."

Hettie studied her clipped, bare nails. "These past few years she's come with us. It's been fine—Veronica's an old schoolfriend and great company. To be honest, I get a bit sick of Jasper...."

"But he's your husband—" Max interjected.

She smiled tightly. "We've always welcomed her but I

know Veronica's always felt like a spare part—you know, a tagger-alonger…."

"So she wanted me to even out the numbers," Max said dryly.

Hettie shook her head. "She's crazy about you, don't you realize? You've been so good for her. You're the first decent man she's met since Anthony left and totally screwed her up…."

Despite the burning sensation at the back of his knee, Max was intrigued. "What did he do?"

"He was a shit, Max. He'd been seeing some other woman—some fancy banker woman—for years. Since Zoë was little, she thinks. You know what he said when he finally left her? That she'd never amount to anything without him. That's why she's so determined with this aphrodisiac stuff. She wants to show him she's…somebody."

Max reached for his cup and took a sip of water. "She doesn't give that impression. She's the most driven woman I've ever met."

"An act she's perfected over the years," Hettie said. "She's read all the articles in the women's magazines— followed them to the letter. She's reinvented herself, Max. It might sound weird to you, but I kind of can't help admiring her."

Admire her? Max supposed he could try. Yet admiring a person, and truly knowing them, were very different. He thought of Jane, who was probably striding along some windswept beach with her hair blowing all over her face. She'd be wearing her chunky black sweater and ancient jeans. Her hands would be grubby from working with lead and solder. He was aware of a different twinge of pain, this time from his heart. "Where is she anyway?" Max asked.

Hettie flushed. "She's a bit annoyed, Max. Said this wouldn't have happened if you'd listened…."

"Hettie, I had no idea how to ski! She zoomed off without me…."

"She thinks," Hettie added, "that you did it on purpose. To make a point."

Max covered his face with his hands. "Yes, that's right. I have a habit of storming off and deliberately rupturing my cruciate ligament."

Hettie frowned. "Is that serious?"

Before Max could respond, a hefty figure with sturdy thighs straining the seams of his trousers burst through the swing doors and strode jauntily toward them. "So," Jasper boomed, "some pickle you've got yourself into, eh, Maxy?"

32

"What does the inside of a stomach look like?" Lewis asked the following evening. He was breathing heavily over his kitchen table, squirting yellow paint from a fat plastic tube on to a sheet of black paper.

Jane laughed. It was her second visit to Connor's, and already she was comfortable there. "I imagine it'll be full of the shepherd's pie we've just had."

"No, I mean the stomach. The actual *stomach*."

"It's probably quite dark," Jane replied, "but maybe some light gets in there. Babies are supposed to be able to see a glow of daylight through their mums' tummies." She stopped. Was any mention of mothers out of bounds?

Conor had explained earlier that day, as they'd walked back to the studio after lunch, that cancer had stolen his wife. "It's at times like that," he had added, "when you're staring at a laundry basket with a can of gold spray in your hand that it hits you. You've no idea when it's going to happen. You can't prepare yourself." Jane had tried to find words to show that she understood, but the way he looked at her had suggested that she didn't need to say anything at all.

Lewis swirled gray paint over the yellow. "What are clouds?" he asked.

"They're tiny droplets of water," Jane said, "which look fluffy but are really—"

"Are you a mum?" he interrupted.

"Yes, I am."

"D'you have a baby?"

Conor glanced round from the sink where he was washing up. "Lewis, stop plaguing Jane with your questions."

"It's okay," she laughed, enjoying Lewis's perpetual chatter; he reminded her of Hannah, when being by Jane's side was all it had taken to make her happy. Since the lost shoe incident, the girls had filled their time by hanging around the village. "Hannah was my baby," she added, "but she's fifteen now—nearly a grown-up. You met her yesterday when you rescued the shoe, remember?"

Lewis nodded, splodging on a trail of shooting-star white. "When are you going home?" he demanded.

"Lewis! Don't be so—" Conor interjected.

"I mean your *real* home, in London."

"In four days' time," Jane said, trying to sound as if this were a positive thing; returning to her proper, grown-up life.

"Can we come and see you? I've never been to London…."

"Of course, I'd love to see you—"

"Great, 'cause we like you, don't we, Dad?" He turned to his father, who had busied himself by refreshing Lewis's water jar at the sink, even though the water hadn't needed changing.

Jane grinned. "I like you, too," she said, looking at the man, not the boy.

Over the next two days, Jane began to turn her favorite sketch into Max's panel. She worked with a new confidence, aware that Conor was rarely far away. In London she would deliberate for days over a single shade of glass, whereas here she went with her instincts.

When Conor had collected Lewis from school, he would find her drawing in Hope House grounds and invite her for supper. "Are you sure you don't mind me going down to Conor's later?" Jane asked Hannah on the fourth day.

Although Hanna shook her head, her eyes told Jane that she *did* mind. "It's okay," she said dully. "Mrs. McFarlane's rented us some DVDs from the village."

"Great. I'll definitely have dinner with everyone tomorrow night, okay?"

"Yeah, all right."

"Our last night," Jane added, though just uttering the words flooded her with sadness.

"So you're gracing us with your company at last," Nancy exclaimed the following evening."

"What do you mean?" Jane asked.

"All week you've eaten at Conor's instead of here with us." Nancy swirled meaty chunks around a frying pan with a wooden spoon.

"Not a problem, is it, Mom?"

Nancy glanced up from the pan. The meat appeared to be poaching in a mysterious fluid. "Of course it's not. You're an adult, Jane, you can do whatever you like…"

"Conor's just…been friendly," she said quickly.

Amusement glinted in Nancy's eyes. "Not had any of the others down for supper, has he? Not Dorina or Paula as far as I can make out…."

"Mum, he has a seven-year-old son. I've been helping him make a Dalek costume, you know, from Doctor Who?"

"Ah," she said, "I see."

"There's nothing *to* see," Jane retorted, remembering how right she'd felt in the tiny house, almost as if she belonged there. She shooed her ridiculous thoughts away.

"You know it's his father who's been tutoring the dry-stone walling course?" Nancy asked.

"Yes, Conor told me. How have you got on, anyway? Made friends with any stones?"

Nancy's mouth softened. "I've made friends," she said airily, dumping several tablespoons of gravy browning into the jug and sloshing it into the pan. "Set the table, would you? We'll need an extra place setting tonight."

"So," Jane said, "who's coming to dinner?"

"Archie. I've finally managed to persuade him. Ridiculous man thinks he can survive on whisky and cigarettes."

Archie piled in great forkfuls of Nancy's stew. "You could make so much more of this place," Nancy was reprimanding him, "if you'd get yourself organized. That studio, for a start—it needs a proper clear-out. How you produce anything at all is a complete mystery."

Hannah caught Jane's eye across the table and smirked. "Han," Jane said, "I saw you sketching this afternoon. It's great that you've started drawing again."

Hannah gave her a shrug, as if to say: *what else is there to do around here?*

"You could accommodate double the students you're taking now, Archie," Nancy cut in. "Running courses in the middle of winter is ridiculous. Get yourself organized and you could be packed out all summer long, then spend winters to concentrate on your work."

Jane glanced between Archie and her mother. Archie's mouth lolled open in faint surprise. "Well, Nancy," he managed to say, "I'd never thought of that."

"And what about your work?" she demanded. "I don't see any of it on display. Surely it's your greatest asset? It should be everywhere, inspiring your students. You're sitting on a gold mine here, if only you could see it."

"I'm not producing much these days," he muttered, laying down his fork.

"That's obvious…"

Archie's gaze skimmed the group. "Most of my work—including the pieces you saw at the Barbican, Jane—were destroyed in a fire."

"He'd been smoking in bed," Paula hissed into Jane's ear.

Archie picked up his glass, took a great gulp of wine. As he set the glass down, Jane noticed her mother nudging it away and filling his tumbler with water.

"I run an articles library," Nancy said, now addressing

the entire group. "It took me years to build up, then something happened. It was…destroyed."

"Why?" Dorina asked.

"That was burnt, too," Nancy said levelly. "He—*someone*—carried every file, every scrap of paper into the back garden and set fire to the lot. There was so much smoke, the neighbors came round and complained. It was blowing all over their washing, they said." Her eyes gleamed in the dim glow from the center light.

"Mum," Jane exclaimed, "that's awful. Who did that?"

"Who complained, you mean?"

"No, who burnt it."

Nancy threw her a look that said: *your father, who else?* "Just someone," she said.

A chunk of meat caught in Jane's throat. She hadn't known about the fire; she'd had no idea. Now she vaguely remembered overhearing a fight, late at night: *That library wastes a whole room!* Doors had been slammed, and someone had stormed into the archive room. Jane had heard things being thrown. She'd bunched the pillow around her ears and willed herself to sleep.

Dorina touched Nancy's hand. "That's terrible," she said.

"I never knew that, Gran," Hannah murmured.

Nancy emitted a short laugh. "Why would you? I didn't even tell your mother. She was only a child, and children shouldn't be dragged into their parents' difficulties. So, Archie," she continued, deftly switching subjects, "the reason I mention this is to show you what can be achieved if you put your mind to it. You can hit rock bottom and build yourself up. We're leaving tomorrow, but we'll keep in touch. A year from now I'll come to your studio and expect to see a wonderful display of your art."

Jane watched her mother's eyes burning in the shadowy room. As for Archie, who had now abandoned red wine for water—he was surveying Nancy as if she, too, were some breathtaking work of art.

33

"What d'you make of all that?" Zoë had pulled up the blankets to partially cover her face, muffling her voice.

Hannah shifted on to her side, waiting for her eyes to become accustomed to the dark. "I can't believe he did that to her. I was scared of Granddad—he always seemed cross—but never imagined he'd do anything so awful."

"My dad was like that," Zoë murmured.

"Like what?"

"A bully, a complete shit. Loads cleverer than Mum but, God, did he let her know it. The woman he went off with…I did tell you, didn't I, that he'd been having an affair for years—"

"Uh-huh," Hannah said, although Zoë had only hinted at her parents' troubles. It had taken this long—five months of friendship—for Zoë to tell her anything real.

"She was a lawyer or a barrister or a judge or something. Something to do with court anyway. That's why Mum ended up with nothing."

"It's hardly nothing," Hannah said, unable to stop herself. "Your house is lovely. Look at the horrible old wreck we live in."

"Yeah, but you should see Dad's place in what's-it-called valley. Swimming pool, games room, the lot."

"Don't go often, do you?"

"As little as I can." Zoë shrugged.

"Why?"

"I told you. My dad's a prat. When Mum got upset about him leaving, he said he'd found someone who had *direction*."

The rain that had been rattling against the cracked window was easing off now. "What about you, Zoë?" Hannah asked. "What d'you think you'll end up doing?"

"You mean, do I have *direction?*" She giggled. "Don't know. There's only one thing I'm good at, and I can't see myself making a career out of it. Hey, that reminds me, I've got something for you."

"What is it?" she asked eagerly.

"You'll see…."

"*Zoë,* you didn't nick anything from those shops in the village, did you?"

"No!" she protested. "I—I just *got* them. Turn on your lamp and I'll show you."

Hannah reached for the bedside lamp, shivering as her blanket fell away. Their last night on the island, and she still hadn't mastered the art of being warm. Zoë swung out of bed and delved into the shoulder bag that lay on the floor. She pulled something out, pouched it in her palm and padded over to Hannah's bed. "This is for you," she murmured, uncoiling her fingers.

On her palm rested a tiny oval-shaped box. It was yellow and decorated with delicate brushstrokes of pink and green. Hannah's heart lurched; she knew what was inside. "Worry dolls," she whispered, "just like the ones I had."

"Hannah," her mother had said, "I've got a present for you. Be careful with them, okay? They're not really for girls of your age because they're so small and a bit sharp and could be swallowed. I know you won't do that, because you're a sensible clever girl."

Hannah had assured her that she wouldn't try to eat them. She'd placed the five tiny objects on the palm of her hand, honored to be given something that wasn't for kids of her age. But then, her mother had never made her feel like a little girl. She'd made her feel big and powerful, as if anything was possible.

"They're called worry dolls," Jane had explained. "I bought them at a craft fair. The lady on the stall said, 'If you're worried about something, put one of the dolls under your pillow before you go to sleep. When you wake up, the doll will be gone.'"

"Where?" Hannah had asked. "Where does it go?"

Jane had laughed. "No one knows. Same place as teeth, maybe, when the tooth fairy comes. The important thing is it's gone, along with your worry."

Hannah had been five years old; it had been just before her parents had broken up—so long ago that she couldn't possibly remember the conversation. Yet her mother's words rang clear in her head. Hannah hadn't liked dolls apart from Biffa, but these weren't really dolls at all. They were splinters of wood bound with fragments of fabric and brightly-colored thread. When they'd moved to Albemarle Street, Hannah had left them under the floor at her dad's house. That way, she'd decided, part of her would still live there, too.

"Well," Zoë said. "D'you like them?"

Hannah lifted the dolls from the box and laid them on the palm of her hand. "I can't believe you bought these for me."

"I told you, I didn't buy them. They're not *like* the ones you had, Han. They're the *actual ones*."

Hannah stared at her. "They can't be."

"They are," Zoë said with a triumphant grin. "I went to your old house. Remember I asked you where you lived?"

Hannah nodded. It had seemed weird when Zoë had wanted to know not just the street name but house number, too. "So…how did you get them? You didn't break in, did you?"

"Don't be stupid. It was simple really. I knocked on the door and this woman came out. I said a friend used to live there and had left something really important…."

"What was my room like?" Hannah blurted out. "Was it just how I left it?" How dumb of her. She hadn't known Zoë when she'd lived there.

Zoë tossed back her hair. "Can't remember. It was pale pink, I think. Kind of messy. Anyway, I tried all the floorboards and the woman helped me and eventually we found them."

Hannah's vision had blurred. Everything looked misty and unreal; it reminded her of being drunk when she'd come out of the Opal. Her mind was racing now. She didn't want to sleep, but to be outside in the moonlight. "I can't believe you did this for me," she said.

"Hey," Zoë chided her, "don't start crying. I thought they'd make you happy."

"I *am* happy," she murmured, sliding out of bed. Suddenly she pulled on jeans and a sweater over her pajamas.

"What are you doing?" Zoë asked.

"I'm going out. I just feel like a walk, that's all."

"What, in the dark? It's pitch-black out there!"

"No, it's not," Hannah insisted. "The moon's really bright. I'm going to the bay to sit for a bit."

"You can't," Zoë protested. "Something might happen…."

"Like what? I'll be savaged by sheep?"

"I'm just worried…."

"Why?" Hannah asked, laughing now.

"Because," Zoë said, her eyes shining in the glow from the bedside lamp, "you're the best friend I ever had."

34

It was midnight and Jane was still packing. She'd worked late in the studio, polishing away fragments of solder, determined that the panel should be perfectly finished before they left the following morning. As if further delaying the moment of leaving, she'd tidied up the studio, neatly stacking glass sheets, placing books back on the shelf and sweeping the floor. She coveted Archie's studio with all of its light and space and view over Seal Bay and beyond. What *was* beyond? Jane had stared out into the dark, trying to decide what the next land mass would be—and figuring Canada—but being unable to focus beyond the pale smudge of Conor's house.

Her mother, who was muttering softly in her sleep, appeared to have made no preparations for tomorrow's departure. Of course, she hadn't even bothered to unpack when they'd arrived, and had merely plucked each day's outfit from the suitcase that lay open in the corner of the room. All week, she'd worn the same bottle-green sweater with an unraveling cuff.

Quietly, so as not to disturb her, Jane packed away her toiletries in the bathroom. Nancy, who didn't possess a toilet kit, stored her own belongings in a plastic freezer bag. Jane was overcome by a wave of sadness as she picked it up. Was her mother's life really so basic that her hairbrush, comb and nail scissors—her personal things—should be stored in a freezer bag with an opaque panel on which to write 'date' and 'contents,' as if they were leftover spaghetti bolognaise?

"Jane, is that you? What are you doing?"

"Just packing, Mum. I didn't mean to wake you…."

"Have you set the alarm?"

"Yes, don't worry." She heard her mother shuffling in bed then, eventually, the soft hum of her snores.

A postcard had been left on the side of the bath. It depicted one of Archie's works; slices of blue becoming gradually paler like sea merging into sky. Picking it up, Jane focused on the handwriting. It slanted violently forward, like trees bent in a gale, and at first she couldn't make out the words. Squinting, she finally deciphered the scrawl:

Dear Nancy,
I am aware that time is running out, and sincerely hope that you will take me up on my offer. I have enjoyed our time together immensely and hope that you will consider my proposal very carefully.
Sincerely and gratefully yours,
Archie.

Archie? What kind of proposal was he talking about? Jane gripped the postcard, feeling chilled and repulsed. Had something happened between them? Surely not. Jane pictured his weasely eyes and the beard in which a collection of food particles were perpetually nestling. Archie, and her mother? A drunk, washed-up artist…and her *mother*?

Nancy hadn't shown one jot of interest in another man since Jane's father had died. Yet perhaps—Jane shuddered at the very thought—he'd tried to kiss or manhandle her. It was too vile to contemplate. She knew, with absolute certainty, that her mother wouldn't have had any of it. Archie was a sad, delusional old man.

Jane stepped quietly back into the bedroom. She wondered if Conor might come up to the house early in the morning before they set off for the ferry. He'd made no mention of seeing her one final time before she left. She felt hurt, and stupid for expecting anything; if he did show up, it would be to say goodbye to the group, with whom he'd worked closely all week, and not Jane with her stupid crush and longing. Was she any smarter than Archie with his ridiculous infatuation with her mother? Conor would have some young nubile girlfriend to warm him during these hostile winter's nights. Even if there was no one on the island, in a few weeks' time a fresh bunch of students would tumble off the ferry, and he'd pick himself a new friend.

Jane zipped her suitcase shut. They would leave as early as possible, to avoid any potentially embarrassing goodbyes. She made a mental note to get up extra early to chivvy the girls along so there'd be no hanging about. They would set off before breakfast. It wouldn't matter if they had time to kill at the pier. All Jane had left to pack was the panel that lay on the studio workbench, ready to be packaged in bubble-wrap and sturdy cardboard. She could collect it in the morning, or be extra-organized and fetch it now. Checking that her mother was in a deep sleep, Jane pulled on her coat, stepped into the corridor and closed the door quietly behind her.

The striplight flickered to life, filling Archie's studio with bleak white light. Jane held up her panel. It wasn't remotely what she'd planned to do, not what Max had asked for at all. There were none of the reds or oranges he'd wanted. Instead she'd picked delicate blues, lilacs and turquoises—island colors. She examined it, aware of time ticking by, and that she should be getting some sleep in preparation for the long drive tomorrow.

"It's beautiful," came the voice.

Jane spun round to face the door. "I didn't hear you come in," she said, startled.

"Sorry," Conor said, "didn't mean to shock you. I saw the light on and came up to check. You know what Archie's like. Has a tendency to leave the soldering iron on, or he'll come in late at night and then leave a cigarette burning in the ashtray...."

Jane laughed and placed the panel flat on the bench. "Well," she said as Conor pulled himself up to sit on the bench, "I'd better get this packaged up."

"Where are you going to put it?" he asked, watching intently as she pulled a length of bubblewrap from the roll.

"It's not for me," she explained. "It's for my…it's for a friend."

Conor raised an eyebrow. "That's quite a present."

"Yes, I suppose it is." She knew then that she wouldn't charge Max for the window. She wasn't sure if he'd like it and, she realized now, she didn't really care either way.

"Well," Conor said, "he's a lucky man."

She looked up at him, at the eyes that gleamed like sea-washed pebbles on the shore. An awkward silence filled the studio. She wished Lewis was here, firing questions about comets and clouds. "I didn't say it was a he," she said quietly.

"So, is it?" Conor's eyes teased hers.

Jane sighed. "Max is…Hannah's dad. My ex-husband. Not even ex, really—we've never got around to getting divorced."

"So, he's…?"

She smiled. "I suppose you'd call him my best friend."

Conor's eyes met hers. "Like I said, he's a lucky man."

Jane's heart skipped as he raised a hand and pushed back a wayward strand of her hair. She could hear the buzz of the light. It felt too warm for February; the air was heady and thick. No sounds came from outside, as if the sky and the sea were waiting for something to happen.

"Where's Lewis?" she whispered.

Conor's fingers remained on her cheek, where he'd brushed the hair away. He was sitting on the bench, with Jane standing before him. "He's having a sleepover with a friend in the village," he said.

"Oh," she said, and a smile tweaked her lips. She could do it. The scene she'd played over and over since the first time he'd invited her into his home—she could make it real. In a few hours she'd be leaving; this moment would be gone, washed away like a footprint on the sand.

Conor had taken hold of her hand. She looked down at the fingers—his weather-beaten yet elegant, hers slender and pale. She was sick of worrying about how others viewed her: her mother, with her "you should make something of yourself" lectures, and Hannah, whom she'd placed at the very center of her universe for the past fifteen years. She was sick, she realized as recklessness surged through her, of doing the right thing.

It was Jane who slid her arms around his shoulders and kissed him. Jane who ran her hands through his hair, and Jane who kept kissing and kissing him, oblivious to the studio's harsh light. She could hardly believe they were her words— "Shall we go back to your house?"

He pulled away and smiled. "Let's go."

She felt so warm, so ridiculously happy, that she barely registered the blue-white flash of lightning, which was followed, seconds later, by a thunderous crack.

And the storm came.

35

*H*annah inhaled deeply, feeling cool air filling her lungs. She'd never imagined that she'd grow to like it here, to relish the sense of calm that had crept over her without noticing. Down at the bay, something shifted on a rock. A seal, perhaps, watching her.

The rain seemed to come from nowhere, a rumble of thunder spurring her return to Hope House. She walked briskly, noticing that a light had been switched on in Archie's studio. She froze. There were two people in there; people who obviously weren't there to work.

They were wrapped up in a tight embrace, clearly not caring who might be wandering around in the dark and see them. Hannah felt repulsed, spying on them like this, yet couldn't tear away her gaze. That kissing—it was virtually sex. She'd never seen anything like it—at least not for real. In movies, maybe. The schmaltzy films that Amy and Rachel were so fond of. No one, not even Ollie, had kissed her like that.

These people were *old,* too; they had to be. The only young people around Hope House were herself and Zoë. The couple parted, and Hannah tried to make out their faces. It was Conor, that man who'd been so friendly and attentive to her mother, and—

The woman laughed and took his hand as they made their way to the door. Hannah turned and ran. Of all the people to make a complete spectacle of herself—the woman who'd lectured her about getting drunk, and not completing her geography homework and, more recently, the shoplifting, which Hannah knew she'd never let her forget. *It's the last time,* Hannah thought, pelting through the sudden downpour toward the house, *you have a say on how I should live my life.*

She was drenched by the time she got back to the room. The rain hadn't built gradually but flooded down on her as thunder crashed across the island. Zoë stirred in bed as Hannah let herself into the room, but didn't wake up. She pulled off her wet clothes and, not bothering with pajamas, flung herself into bed and bunched the blankets around her.

Her own mother, behaving as if she were fifteen years old. Was she drunk or had she gone completely bloody crazy? Didn't she care that anyone could see with the lights blazing like that?

She fixed her gaze on Zoë's sleeping face. Wake up, she thought, desperate to talk to another human being. Zoë looked so peaceful, her face far prettier without its customary makeup. The sky flashed silvery white. In a few hours, Hannah thought, we'll be leaving, and her mother will have made a complete fool of herself for nothing. They were probably doing it right now. She was a *mum*, for crying out loud, and what were mums meant to do? Bake cakes, like her friend Sally—why couldn't she be more like Sally?—and make sure there was plenty of food in the fridge. Jane did none of those things. She had a crappy job, spent the best part of her free time messing about in a clapped-out shed, and snuck out in the middle of the night and had sex with a man she barely knew in a hut with all the lights on.

Hannah tossed and turned in bed, feeling as if she could almost vomit. She glared up at the bubbly pattern formed by dampness on the ceiling. Her chest felt tight, and her breathing was shallow and fast. Calm down, she told herself, steady now. She scrabbled on the bedside table for her bag and rummaged for her inhaler. No inhaler. She lay on her back, trying to rein in her breathing—bring it down to a steady pattern. It was coming, she could feel it, like that time in biology when she'd felt the tightening and fear. *Calm, calm, calm.* Her pillow was damp from her wet hair. She flipped it over but it still felt clammy.

She swiveled out of bed and opened her suitcase, which still contained the clothes she hadn't got around to unpacking. Naked and shivering, she grabbed them by the handful and flung them onto the floor. "Han," Zoë murmured, "what's up?"

"It's okay. Just need my inhaler."

Zoë sprung up instantly. "Are you all right? You sound

weird. You're really wheezing, Han. Has something happened?"

Hannah shook her head. *Don't speak,* she told herself. *Save your breath. Worst thing you can do is panic.* She remembered after the last attack, the doctor reminding her to avoid stressful situations or anything that might make her anxious. Zoë clicked on the main light and peered at Hannah's face. "I thought it was the storm," she muttered. "I thought the storm had woken me. Did you hear the thunder? You weren't outside in that, were you?"

"Yes," came Hannah's small voice.

"Han, this is scary—shall we get someone?"

"Think so."

"You'd better get dressed. Let me help." Zoë grabbed the sweater and jeans that were lying on the floor close to Hannah's bed. "These are soaking. I'll find you something else." She flung open a drawer in the wooden chest and pulled out clothes haphazardly. Hannah allowed Zoë to feed her limbs into trousers and sleeves. She felt like a small, helpless kid.

"Is it getting any better?" Zoë asked.

Hannah shook her head.

"Come on, let's get your mum." Holding her hand now, Zoë led Hannah along the corridor and hammered on Jane and Nancy's door. She pushed it open, and Nancy sat up abruptly. "What are you two—"

"Where's Jane?" Zoë blurted, staring at the empty bed.

Nancy followed her gaze. "I've no idea. I thought…what time is it?"

I know, Hannah thought. *I have a very good idea where*

Mum is and what she's doing right now… "Nancy," Zoë blurted, "Han's asthma thing's come on. We can't find her inhaler in our room…"

"Oh, love," Nancy said, tumbling out of bed and wrapping an arm around Hannah.

"Gran—" The worry dolls fell from her hand to the floor. She hadn't realized she'd been holding them.

"Shh, don't try to speak. You two stay here. I'll go down to reception, see if I can find a number for a doctor." Bundling herself into a threadbare dressing gown, she hurried out of the room.

The waiting seemed to take forever. Hannah perched on a chair at the window and tried to watch the lightening sky. The storm was over, and the sky had filled with great swathes of pink. Hannah could hear her own tight, strangled wheeze. Zoë touched her arm. "You'll be okay," she soothed. "Your gran's going to sort everything out."

Make them hurry, Hannah thought, not focusing on the sky now, but rigid with fear. *Make them hurry—*

"Han," Zoë cried, "your face, your lips…"

Hannah stared at her. They're blue, she thought, her head swilling with the horrible sound she was making—

My lips are going blue.

36

*C*onor's hand felt warm in Jane's as they walked beyond Seal Bay, turning inland where the ground swelled toward the Fang. She hadn't felt awkward as his lips and hands had traveled over her body, but crazily happy and hungry for him. His body had been so different to Max's; more sturdily built with broad shoulders and long, strong legs. She hadn't cared that it was gone 2:00 a.m. and dawn was creeping into his bedroom.

"Let's go out," Conor had said, "there's something I'd like you to see before you leave."

"What is it?" she'd asked.

Instead of answering, he'd kissed her again.

The church on the hill looked as if it had dropped from the sky. There were no other buildings around it; just swooping hills bisected by crumbling walls and dotted with sheep.

Built from rust-colored stone, the church looked solid and proud, despite its windows being in a poor state of repair. Some segments were either cracked or missing. Others needed careful cleaning to bring the colors back to life. Conor and Jane circled it, trying the locked door.

"So," he said, "what do you think?"

"It's beautiful," Jane said.

"It could be, if the windows were restored."

"Wouldn't Archie do it?"

Conor shook his head. "He doesn't do restoration work. Reckons it's not—" he chuckled "—art."

"I do," Jane said. "Just before I came here, I finished a rose window for a church…."

"Would *you* do it?"

"How? I'd have to take the panels out and transport them to London and—"

"You could do it here. It would take you, what, a couple of months?"

She laughed, then realized he was quite serious. "I've got my job, Conor. Hannah has school…we have a life."

"It needn't be forever. Just until you'd finished." His eyes seemed to search hers.

"And there's Mum," she added quickly, "I've got to take Mum back to London, and I've another commission to start as soon as we're home…."

So many reasons. As he placed his hands on her cheeks and kissed her again, Jane felt all her reasons for leaving being blown out to sea.

Hope House was waking up by the time Jane returned. She could see movement in some of the upstairs rooms;

people preparing to leave. A crow was perched defiantly on the cracked washbasin. Self-consciously, Jane tried to flatten her hair and smoothed down her clothes, trying to make herself look respectable. As if she'd just been for a walk, that was all. A walk until 6:45 a.m. with a man who'd kissed every inch of her body. Her lips were tingling. She hoped they wouldn't give her away.

She didn't feel remotely tired as she strode into the foyer. She was buoyant and giddy inside. Mrs. McFarlane looked up sharply from the desk. "*Here* you are," she barked. "We've been looking everywhere for you. You can't believe how worried we've been, what's been happening—"

"I only went for—" Jane began.

"Not you. We weren't worried about *you*. You've no idea, have you, what's happened to your daughter?"

Jane's heart shot to her mouth. "What? Where is she?"

"She's had an asthma attack," Mrs. McFarlane said briskly. "Doctor's still here, brought a nebulizer. She's fine now—at least better than she was. They're in your—" Jane was no longer listening but tearing along the corridor and bursting into her room.

Hannah was sitting up in bed, resting against propped-up pillows. Her face was waxy and pale and partially covered by a clear plastic mask attached by a tube to an oxygen tank. "I'm so sorry," Jane murmured, hugging her. "So sorry, darling. I had no idea." Hannah's body stiffened. Jane pulled away slowly, chilled by her daughter's glare.

An elderly man with a fuzz of soft white hair was sitting on the chair beside the bed. "You're the mother?" he asked levelly.

"Yes, yes, I am." She didn't know whether to stand or sit, what to do with herself. Hannah was making it clear that she didn't want to be held. Nancy and Zoë, who were perched on the other bed, were pointedly avoiding Jane's gaze.

"Hannah's breathing has settled," the doctor said, "but I'll stay for a little longer. You'll need this." He opened the bag at his feet, pulled out a pad of prescriptions and scribbled on the top sheet. He ripped it off and handed it to Jane; he was prescribing the same steroids—the ones that made her nauseous—that she'd had after the attack at school.

"We're supposed to be leaving this morning," she said. "Will Hannah be okay to travel?"

"Absolutely not. She needs another day's rest." He frowned at her, but his eyes had softened. "She'll be fine, Mrs. Deakin. The worst is over now."

The worst happened, she thought, *when I wasn't here.* Jane studied his kind, soft face for a hint of blame or recrimination.

"Out in the rain, getting herself soaked," Nancy muttered. "Did something upset you, Hannah, to trigger this off?"

"Unlikely," the doctor interjected, lifting Hannah's mask from her face. "Unlikely that it was caused by stress. This sort of thing is usually overexertion, perhaps hiking too much."

Jane felt her daughter's dark eyes boring into her. She didn't need to say a word, as her gaze said it all: *I needed you, and you weren't here.*

37

"*C*hicken or fish?" the air stewardess trilled as she shunted the trolley along the aisle. *Chicken or fish? Chicken or fish?* It was doing Max's head in. From his aisle seat— easier to get in and out of with his leg in a splint—he smiled wearily. "I'll have the chicken, please."

Veronica slid her eyes in the direction of the stewardess. "Just water, please." The stewardess passed her a bottle and cup. "Thanks," Veronica murmured, then returned to the pressing business of staring pointedly out of the window.

Max glanced at her. There'd been no row, no outburst of any kind, so he couldn't understand why she was being so frosty. It wasn't his fault he'd been concussed and ruptured a ligament. He hadn't damaged himself on purpose solely to wreck Veronica's holiday. He leaned forward, wincing as a twinge shot up his leg, and extracted the in-flight magazine from the seat pocket.

"We're an *ideas* factory," Jasper was booming to his neighbor in the seat behind. "That's the best way of putting it. Concept, branding, thinking outside the box. That's what we're all about."

He was talking in management-speak like those jerks Veronica had invited to Max's party. Max didn't even *know* any management-speak. It wasn't required in a cycle shop. He wanted to communicate with someone who spoke normally, but it looked unlikely that Veronica would be forthcoming. Her jaw was set firm, causing a tendon in her neck to protrude like a tree trunk poking out of the ground, relaxing only when she sipped her water.

He lifted the foil from his in-flight meal and hacked into the chicken. How did Veronica survive on so little food? he wondered. The snacks she carried around in little sachets in her bag looked like they should be sown in the garden, not consumed by ravenous human beings. He had a craving for curry—the mouth-searing, blow-out array of dishes he used to wolf down with Jane. *There* was a woman who knew how to eat. He couldn't imagine her acquainting herself with millet or goat's arse yoghurt. Max stole a glance at Veronica's notebook, which lay open on her flip-down table. *FoxLove on the go,* she'd written, accompanied by a scattering of sausage-shaped objects that looked like dismembered penises.

"I'm going to the loo," Max muttered.

Veronica flashed her eyes at him. "Fine."

Max sighed. "Veronica, what on earth's the matter? Why are you being so cold with me?"

"I'm not," she muttered.

"I didn't do it on purpose, you know." He pulled himself up from the seat and stepped gingerly into the aisle.

"That's him," Jasper bellowed. "That's the fellow I was telling you about. Ruptured himself, back of the leg, going to need some kind of reconstructive surgery. Rather him than me, I say! Feeling any better now, Maxy? Hope it's not affected your *groin*, heh heh…"

Max fixed him with an icy stare. Jasper was wedged between Hettie, who was immersed in a book, and the poor sod he'd been boring stupid about his ideas factory. "Actually," Max said, "it's agony."

Jasper's smile froze. "Ah."

"Did they give you painkillers to bring home?" Hettie asked, glancing up from her book.

"Yes, I'm just going to the loo to chug the whole bottle. About thirty should do the trick."

"Max!" Hettie looked aghast, then caught his eye and giggled.

Max realized that he, too, was smiling. Funny, he mused as he made his way along the aisle, he couldn't remember the last time he'd done that.

The taxi crawled through East London streets. It smelled faintly of cigarette smoke and Veronica's hostile vibes. Her skis lay diagonally in their zip-up case across the floor of the cab, forcing Max to fold up his legs at an uncomfortable angle. He was determined not to complain or ask her to move them. He would suffer in silence.

"What really gets me," Veronica muttered, "is this has

never happened with cycling. All the time you spend training and racing and there's never been a single injury."

Max frowned at her. Of course he'd had his share of tumbles and collisions. He'd skinned arms and thighs, had to pick gravel out of his knees. Perhaps that didn't count as serious enough. If he'd broken a leg or dislocated a shoulder, would that have made her happier? Maybe he should arrange it. "I don't know what you're talking about," he snapped.

"I mean," she said, "that you made it plain from the start that you didn't want to come. That you were humoring me." Her voice wobbled.

"Of course I—" He stopped short. She was right; he'd only agreed due to his overwhelming lust for the most gorgeous body he'd ever laid eyes on. What a shallow specimen he was.

"I thought it was going to be really special," she continued. "Our first holiday together. And you, being so fit and active, I thought you'd love—" She clamped her mouth shut.

"Veronica, please. Let's forget it." He patted her knee, a gesture that felt inadequate and vaguely patronizing.

She waggled the knee, shaking him off. "What do you think of me Max, really?" Her eyes were fixed on him. The cab driver was humming along to a song on the radio. Max blinked at the curly graying hairs that sprouted from the back of his pink neck.

"I—I think—"

"D'you think I'm stupid? That I don't have *direction?*"

"Of course not!" Max spluttered. "Look at your business,

what you've managed to do all by yourself. You've got your investor, you're full of ideas, you're nearly ready to go into production…."

"*You* wouldn't invest," she muttered.

"How could I? I don't have that kind of money flying about. And there's the shop…"

"Oh, yes," she said witheringly, "the shop."

Max glared at her. Was she implying he was a workaholic, or what? Just taken a whole week off, hadn't he? "Which number, mate?" the driver called back.

"Sixty-seven," Veronica said curtly.

Not her house, but his. Max studied her face. "Are you coming in?" he asked hesitantly.

She blinked at him. "I'll help you in with your stuff. I'm not that selfish, Max."

Max hadn't lived in his house for long enough to experience the faintest smidge of pleasure in returning. In fact, as he stepped into the narrow hall, he had an unsettling notion that he was trespassing.

A scattering of letters and leaflets—mostly junk mail and brown envelopes—lay on the floor. Max kicked them aside with his good foot. Veronica groaned behind him as she carried in his bag, even though it contained little more than a few clothes—no base layers, no salopettes, no buff. She dumped it on to the floor without comment.

Max ambled into the living room to check his answering machine messages—more to distance himself from Veronica's hostility than any thought that someone interesting might have called. He pressed the button. "Max? It's me. Listen, there's nothing to worry about. Everything's fine now. Hannah had a bit of an asthma attack but the doctor came and put her on a nebulizer and steroids and she's fine. We're having to stay on the island an extra day, just to make sure she's okay to travel, but we'll be leaving first thing tomorrow as long as the ferry's running. Weather's been pretty awful. Anyway, love, please don't worry about Han, she's fine—everyone's fine. It's been…good here. Hope you had a great holiday. See you soon."

Her voice: so familiar yet faraway sounding, even though she was only in Scotland. It could have been another continent. Max was gripped by an urge to replay the message, to reassure himself that everything really was okay, but was aware of Veronica observing him from the doorway. He turned and gave her a weak smile. "Han had an asthma attack," he murmured.

"Yes, I heard. I expect you'll be glad to have her back home."

He nodded, feeling awkward in this house that still felt unfamiliar and not quite his. Despite the skiing tan that stopped at the neck, Veronica looked drawn and tired. Her left eye had acquired some kind of tic during the cab ride. He was overcome by a sudden desire to put his arms around her, to comfort her, to say sorry—although he wasn't sure what for.

The tic had become more pronounced. She brought her hands to her face, sweeping them over her eyes and cheeks. To his horror, tears began to spill and form wiggly lines down her cheeks. She made no attempt to bat them away. "Veronica, what—" Max began. He wanted to hold her but she'd shrunk back, away from him.

"You might as well say it," she whispered.

"What?"

"That you don't love me. It's Jane, Max. You still love Jane." She was crying properly now: not silent tears but the great, gulping sobs of a hurt little girl.

Max opened his mouth to protest, but words failed him.

38

"Aren't you getting ready, Mum?" Jane asked.

"Things aren't quite as simple as that," Nancy said. She was scrubbing her walking boots with a wire brush, sending out a shower of mud particles.

"What do you mean? The doctor says Hannah's fine to travel. It looks like the eleven o'clock ferry's running on time. We should get something to eat before—"

"Jane, I'm not coming. I'm staying here." Nancy looked up from the boots.

A shudder ran through Jane's body. *I hope you will consider my proposal,* Archie had written. "Mum," she said faintly, "what's going on?"

"I have the wall to finish. Brian needs help to prepare for the next course, there's a lot of repair work to be done on the estate after the storm, and Archie—"

"Is something going on with you and him?" Her voice wavered.

Nancy jutted out her chin. "The man's a shambles, Jane, but thankfully he's seen sense. I'll be taking over the organizational side of his business."

"You'll be *working* here?"

Nancy frowned. "Why shouldn't I?"

"There's…there's your house, your life, your library, all your stuff…."

"They're only *things,* Jane." Her expression softened. "People move, don't they? They take stock of their lives and move on. They're not frightened to make changes."

Jane's head flooded with an image of Nancy's home: dark, grimy corners, the cooker with its temperature markings worn off. A house that had withered without anyone noticing. No wonder she didn't want to go home. "You can visit me," she added. "You and Hannah—you can come anytime. It's not that far. It's not—"

"I know, Mum. It's not Madagascar. So, this was Archie's idea, was it?"

"Initially, yes. First sensible thing he's come out with all week." She cleared her throat. "Conor's been looking for you, by the way. I told him you'd been keeping an eye on Hannah. Didn't think you'd want to be disturbed."

Jane nodded. Mrs. McFarlane, too, had told her that Conor had dropped by. She hadn't been able to face him. What had seemed wonderfully reckless now felt foolish, something she planned to erase from her mind. Hannah was communicating in cool, curt sentences, and who could blame her when her own mother had disappeared for an entire night? A fine example she'd set her. "Mum," Jane said, touching Nancy's arm, "are you absolutely sure about this?"

Nancy nodded firmly. "It's obvious that I'm needed here."

"What about your house?" Jane asked. *We need you, too.*

"Could you keep an eye on it, if it's not too much trouble? Drop by every so often? I might sell it or rent it out. Maybe you and Hannah could live there…."

It would make sense, Jane thought. No more rent and double the space. She tried to imagine returning to the house in which she'd lived as a child. "Thanks," she said, "but I'd like to stay where we are. It's close to school and work…."

"Well, it's yours if you want it."

Jane glanced at her watch. She should make sure the girls were ready to leave, check that Zoë's ceramic irons were cool enough to be packed. "Mum," she added, "it is just a business thing, isn't it—you and Archie?"

Nancy laughed raucously. "Of course it is. Gosh, what were you thinking? Filthy old sod had other ideas of course, but I've laid down strict rules, just like you do with a small child. I'll be having none of his nonsense. He's promised to give up drinking—at least, drinking before seven o'clock. If we're going to develop a proper program of events, he'll have to sort himself out."

"And where are you going to live?" Jane asked, awash with relief.

"Right here, of course."

Jane looked out at the hills that swooped down to the bay. The sun had come out, giving everything a feeling of newness. She thought of Conor, and how she'd barely left her room in case she should run in to him or Lewis. It would be a relief to get back to London and be normal again. "So," Nancy said, cutting into her thoughts, "aren't you going to say goodbye to Conor?" Her eyes flashed mischievously.

"There's no time," she replied.

She felt her mother peering at her as if trying to focus on something behind her eyes, something unreachable. "Okay," Nancy said, "but before you go, I've got something to show you. I hope you have time for that."

It was a ramshackle sculpture: stones of every color from darkest gunmetal through rust and yellowy golds. Spaces between the larger stones had been filled with delicate slivers of rock. "You made this?" Jane asked, astounded.

Nancy nodded, her eyes gleaming as if to say, *of course, what kind of townie idiot do you take me for?*

"Where did they come from?" Jane asked, touching a rust-colored stone that matched the dilapidated church.

"It's a quirk of the area," Nancy explained. "There are far too many types to be indigenous. Brian thinks that some of them might have been the ballast of ships that were wrecked and washed up on the beach."

Jane ran a hand along a top stone's rough edge, deciding that she wouldn't ask about her feelings toward Brian. "Well," she said, "it looks like it belongs here."

When she turned back to her mother she saw that her eyes were gleaming. "Like me," was all Nancy said.

They left in the bright morning sunshine. A cling-film-wrapped packet of sandwiches, which Nancy had insisted they take, sat on the passenger seat. Jane glanced into the rearview mirror and gave her mother a final wave.

Hannah and Zoë were curled up sleepily in the back of the car. "Feeling okay, Han?" Jane asked.

"Uh-huh."

"What d'you think about Gran?"

A pause, then Hannah said, "Good for her. Not like she has anything to stay in London for."

At least she's speaking to me, Jane thought. That's a start. "What if I'd done that?" she asked.

"Done what?"

"Decided to stay. To start a new life and all that." Jane laughed to convey the ridiculousness of the idea.

"That'd be different," Hannah said.

"Why?"

"'Cause you've got your job and me. You've got *responsibilities*." There was a bitter tinge to her voice.

"I know," Jane said briskly, "but say I didn't, and you didn't have school…. Anyway, there's a school on the island, and we could live—" She cut herself short. She had reached the end of the driveway. Instead of taking the right-hand turn, which would lead to the pier, she stopped the car and turned off the engine.

"What are you doing?" Zoë asked.

Jane scrabbled for an acceptable answer. She was gripped by envy, not because she wanted to *be* her mother, and definitely not be Archie's whatever-it-was, but because she knew she would never be half as courageous. Nancy's spirit was nothing to do with having no responsibilities. "Have we broken down?" Hannah demanded.

"No, love." Jane started up the car, turning left instead of right.

"Aren't you going the wrong—"

"It's okay, Han. We won't be a minute."

"We'll miss the ferry!" Zoë protested.

"We might," Jane said airily.

"But Mum—"

"I told you, there's plenty of time."

"It leaves in twenty minutes," Zoë muttered. "Mum'll go mental if I'm not back tomorrow. I can't *believe* this." She raked her hair distractedly.

Jane smiled to herself. She had pulled up a short distance from Conor's house. It didn't look as if anyone was home; no smoke drifted from the chimney, and Conor's car wasn't in sight. "Won't be a minute," she said, stepping out of the car and shutting the driver's door as quietly as she could. Sidestepping puddles, she opened the trunk and lifted out her stained glass panel. Even through layers of bubble-wrap and cardboard, she could see its swirling blues and greens: the colors of temperamental seas and skies. It was as if the shapes and shades had imprinted themselves on her brain.

Jane carried the panel to the side of Conor's cottage where there was no window, and therefore no chance of being seen. She propped it against the whitewashed wall, hurried back to the car and started the engine. "What was that?" Hannah asked.

"Just…something I had to drop off," Jane replied.

"But what—" she protested.

"Just something that belongs here, that's all." Jane started the engine, turned the car on the graveled area and headed back toward the main road.

"Was that your panel?" Hannah asked quietly.

"Yes, it was."

"I thought it was meant to be for Dad?"

Jane felt light—so light that she rose above the gusts of disapproval that were filling the car. "It wasn't right," she said. "Not the colors he'd chosen for that back room. I'll make him something else."

"Can't believe you just gave it away," Hannah muttered. "What will *he* do with it?"

"Just drop it, Hannah," Jane said.

The island seemed so still as the road snaked upward toward the Fang. The sky was a watered-down blue now, smudged with chimney smoke and pale, wispy clouds. Jane could see the ferry approaching, cutting through a cobalt sea, as the road dipped down toward it. A small collection of cars were already lined up and waiting to board.

A streak of smoke drifted from the ferry's funnel. It seemed to approach so fast, like a child's remote-controlled toy. Jane glanced back at the Fang's ragged outline and the silver-white crescent of the bay. She saw a rabbit, or maybe a hare, dive for cover into an overgrown edge. She thought of Sally and how she'd try to photograph it, but of course it was too fast, just a blur of gray.

She glimpsed a faint orangey spot on the hill. The church, with those windows crying out for repair. And she thought of a man and a boy finding the parcel propped against their house and carefully unwrapping it. *Dad, Dad, what's this?* They would open it together, and Conor would say, *It's a gift*.

Jane swallowed hard as she indicated right, and turned down the single-track road that led to the pier.

39

*O*llie's block looked even sadder than Hannah had remembered. Since coming home, she'd been sharply conscious of the *city-ness* of everything: her vast, faceless school with its gloomy gray corridors, bordered on all sides by uneven concrete—yet more gray—and teachers who, for the most part, nearly looked as desperate as she for the bell to ring.

A group of boys were booting a football against the wall of the flats. An elderly woman—Hannah could make out a small, angry face and puff of white hair at a window—rapped on the glass. The boys laughed and carried on kicking. No one had behaved like that on the island. In the village she'd seen clusters of teenagers hanging out by a drinking fountain. They'd been smoking and stuff, but it hadn't been like this—aggressive. The woman shouted something, but her words were swallowed by the boy's jeers. "Want a photo?" one of them yelled.

Hannah snapped back to the present and realized the boy was addressing her. She pulled herself tall and, fixing her gaze on the entrance to the flats, marched toward it. "Live here, do you?" the boy called.

She turned to look at him. He had pasty skin and closely cropped straw-colored hair. The other two boys were sniggering.

"No," Hannah said as she reached the block's entrance, "I don't."

"Visiting someone?"

"Yes." The straw-haired boy had rested one foot on the ball. Despite his jeering eyes, he no longer looked remotely threatening. Balancing a foot on the ball was making his entire leg wobble. Hannah felt a smirk coming but trapped it.

"Who?" he asked, seeming genuinely interested now.

"You won't know him."

"Why wouldn't I?"

She sighed, realizing that she'd allowed herself to be drawn into conversation. "Ollie," she said. "Ollie Tibbs."

A cackling laugh rattled out of him. She stared at his yellowy teeth. "'Course I know him. Everyone does." The other boys were acknowledging the fact that everyone knew Ollie. Hannah felt her cheeks burning. It was if there was some huge joke going on, and everyone knew the punchline except her. "Our friend Ollie," the boy added. "Don't tell me you're his girlfriend, pretty thing like you."

Hannah shook her head firmly. God knows what she was

to him. In the four days since she'd been back, she'd heard not a peep from him. Now she was sick of waiting; it was all she ever seemed to do. "Nice girl like you," the boy added, "shouldn't be hanging around with the likes of him." He kicked the ball across the yard.

Hannah shrank back into the doorway. *The likes of him:* it was something Granny Nancy would say. She felt the coldness of the glass through her blazer and shirt. The boy was coming too close; she could smell cheap, chemical aftershave. She glanced down at her school uniform: white shirt, blue-and-gray diagonally striped tie, black skirt and blazer. She hadn't bothered changing, because she'd come to tell him that it—whatever "it" was—was over. She just wanted to see him one last time, be mature about it, as they'd still run into each other at theater workshop and she didn't want any awkwardness. She'd felt pleasingly grown-up as she'd formulated her plan.

The boy was just a couple of feet away now, blocking the afternoon sun. "You're too pretty for him," he murmured. He looked embarrassed, as if the words had fallen out before he could stop them. Behind him his mates were making gurgling and choking sounds, like central heating pipes going wrong.

A flicker of concern crossed the boy's face. "Hey," he said, "you really don't know?"

"Know *what?*"

The boy shrugged. "He's a dealer, love. Knocks out hash for the whole estate."

She nodded, taking in the words.

"Nothing else, though. No crack or anything. Been

doing it for years from his flat up there—" he indicated the top of the building "—but not anymore 'cause the dumb fucker got busted last week. Looks like he's up for community service."

"Oh," Hannah said softly.

The boy grinned. "Asking for it, flash bastard. Reckoned he was doing it to support himself and that loony mother what's been in and out of mental asylums…."

She looked into the boy's eyes, which were blank and pale. She turned to push the door open and ran up the stairs, not wanting to hear any more.

Through the door to Ollie's flat she could hear faint music and the hum of a Hoover. A woman was singing. She had a clear, sweet voice. Hannah hovered, daring herself to press the bell.

The woman sounded happy, not like someone who was carted off to hospitals. The Hoover stopped and the music was turned up a notch. It felt wrong, bursting in on her when Ollie had been busted and all kinds of stuff had been going on.

Hannah jumped as the door opened. "Oh, gosh, don't do that to me!" the woman exclaimed.

"Sorry," Hannah stuttered, "I was…I've come to see Ollie, I—"

"Come in," the woman interrupted, "I was popping out to the shops but it's not important. I'm Celia, Ollie's mum. Have a cup of tea with me, tell me how you've been feeling."

Hannah frowned as she followed her into the flat. How she'd been *feeling?* Perhaps Ollie had told his mother about her. As Celia bustled around in the kitchen, Hannah sat gingerly on the sofa where Ollie had held and kissed her. "Here you go, sweetheart," Celia said, handing her a mug of weak tea.

"Thanks." Hannah glanced from the clip-framed photos to the real Celia, who'd arranged herself cross-legged on the floor. The two women weren't terribly different. The skin around her eyes was more crinkled now, and her shoulder-length curly hair was flecked with gray, but she had a sweet, dainty face with vibrant green eyes, which had barely aged at all. "I'm not sure when he'll be back," Celia said. "You know how hard he is to pin down."

Hannah dropped her gaze. What would it matter if she came straight out with it? Maybe the boy outside had been making stuff up just to keep her talking. Perhaps he, not Celia, was the mad one. "I was talking to a boy outside," she began. "He said Ollie's been…in some trouble." She met Celia's gaze.

"Yes, darling, but it's all being sorted out. It'll blow over." Her smile wavered. "He's a good boy," she added. "Works ever so hard. Pays the rent on this place, has done since we moved in. But then, you'll know all about that…."

Hannah nodded, as if she knew the first thing about Ollie and his financial arrangements. "I just hope he's okay." She really meant it. As she arranged the facts in her mind, she decided that it didn't make him a bad person.

"People get up to far worse around here."

"I know they do," Hannah murmured. The tea was too hot to drink, but she sipped it anyway, scalding her lip. The room seemed less disturbing now. In fact, it felt almost cosy.

Would she and her own mum ever be friends and equals, Hannah wondered, as Celia and Ollie clearly were? Imagine being cool about him being busted for dealing. Hannah remembered her mother's grief-stricken face at the police station.

"That's a pretty necklace," Celia added.

"Thanks. Ollie gave it to me for Christmas."

Celia chuckled and reached out to touch the silver chain. Hannah flinched as her cool fingertips brushed against her neck. "Naughty, isn't he, buying you something so expensive? Especially with the two of you saving up for a deposit on a flat…."

Hannah shrank away from Celia's touch. "It's okay," Celia added, "he told me about your plans. I'll be okay by myself. Doing much better these days, got a job and everything." She directed her gaze to Hannah's stomach. "I'm pleased for you," she added warmly, "though I do feel a bit young to be granny."

Hannah placed her mug on the floor, allowing her hair to fall forward. She couldn't let this woman see her face. She didn't know what to think or how to make sense of what Celia was saying. Was it a joke, she thought desperately, or had Ollie been making up all kinds of wild stories? She felt dizzy and stifled with the red walls around her. "You'll be okay," Celia continued. "I was young, too, when I had Ollie. Barely seventeen, just started college. Turned out he was the best thing that ever happened to me."

Hannah's eyes filled with tears as she stood up. "I've got to go," she managed. "There's stuff I have to do."

"Darling," Celia cried, leaping up from the floor, "you're all upset! Have I said something?"

"No, I—"

"You'll be fine, you know that? You've found a wonderful young man. You're adorable, you really are, just like Ollie said. And look at you—five months and not even showing! I was massive when I was carrying him, had to wear these gigantic dungarees from the army-and-navy shop... Thought of any names, sweetheart?"

Hannah blundered toward the door, not knowing or caring who Celia thought she was. "Hazel," Celia called after her, "don't feel you have to rush off, I can call Ollie on his mobile if you—"

She didn't hear any more as she clattered down the steps, wanting to be as far away as possible from Celia and her red living room with all those staring clip-framed pictures. "Hey!" the straw-haired boy yelled as she hurried away from the block, "looking for your boyfriend? Come back, come and talk to us...."

Hannah kept running until she reached the canal. She tripped down the steps, stopping to catch her breath beneath the curve of the bridge. She thought about Celia's words: *People get up to far worse around here.* She wondered who Hazel might be, and how she felt to be pregnant at, what, fifteen or sixteen years old? A girl in the year above Hannah had had a baby last year. "He's gorgeous," everyone had cooed, clustering round the old-fashioned pram with massive chrome wheels at the school gate. Ginny, the new mum, had tried to look pleased. Hannah had caught a look in her eyes, the look of someone who was trying to be brave when she desperately wanted to be young and free like everyone else. As they'd exchanged a glance, Hannah had realized she'd never met anyone who looked desperate to be *in* school.

A narrowboat chugging past along the canal. An elderly couple waved at her. *Look at them,* Hannah thought, waving back, *they don't have any worries. Life's so much simpler when you're old.* When they'd gone, she touched her pink crystal necklace, feeling the chain's silky coldness against her skin. Without undoing the clasp, she pulled it from her neck and flung it into the canal, where it barely made a splash, as if it had been nothing at all.

40

*M*ax couldn't pinpoint what irked him about trades-men. The electrician who'd come to fit extra sockets had been overly chatty and displayed too great an interest in Max's splint. "Buggered my hamstring," he announced gleefully, "last time I played five-a-side. That was the end for me. Got to face it, haven't you, mate?"

"Um, yes," Max had responded, not quite knowing what it was that he had to face.

"There comes a point," the electrician had rattled on, "when you've got to hang up your boots and admit you're finished." Max had blinked at him. He was thirty-eight years old. He'd barely got his head around the fact that he might be toppling toward the cavernous void they called a midlife crisis. Now, this stranger was blithely pointing out that he was *finished*.

The painter and the decorator, who'd come to finish the bedrooms now that Max was incapable of climbing a ladder, had given his emulsioning efforts a disapproving stare, as if an unruly child had sploshed paint randomly about the place. These people made you feel so incompetent, as if some doctorate in the Advanced Application of One-Coat Gloss should be gained before you attempted to paint a door frame.

Thankfully, there was no else in the house right now. Max sat on a straight-backed chair in the kitchen, dutifully performing his leg raises—twenty per leg, rest and repeat—figuring that the real problem was that he wasn't accustomed to having to ask for help. All these years he'd lived in a state of reasonable contentment—if depressed, he was only *mildly* depressed—cooking perfectly serviceable meals, trying to be a decent enough father while running the shop and fitting in a weekly cycle down to Kent. Even sex—he was pretty self-sufficient in that department, too. It was, he decided, hugely overrated. Most people said that after the first time, but his had been with Jane, and that had been anything but. When it was all over—approximately one-point-four seconds after it had begun—he'd wrapped his arms tightly around her. They'd fallen asleep that way, and woken up in the same position to a changed life. That had been the best part, waking up and finding her still there. He'd never come close to feeling that way again.

Max tried to summon up the energy for another leg-raise. This was so un-him, exercising for exercise's sake. He'd never done push-ups, owned a set of bar bells or belonged to a gym. Cycling wasn't about exercise, but about having the courage and mental capacity to push himself to the limit. It was about letting go.

He glared around his kitchen, which he'd had refitted in a whirl of pheromone-induced enthusiasm. Actually, it didn't even feel like *his* kitchen. It was Veronica's. She'd even picked the goddamn granite countertop. "So much more hygienic than wood, sweetheart, and don't you think laminate looks cheap?" she'd said. Now, whenever their paths crossed, she greeted him with a pert 'hello,' as she might with any of Zoë's friends' fathers. Not that Zoë seemed to have any friends, apart from Hannah. Since they'd come back from Scotland they'd hung out together as usual, although he'd detected a shift in their friendship. Hannah had stopped wearing all that atrocious makeup for a start.

The rap on his front door made Max jump. He hauled himself up from the chair and hobbled toward it. He realized it was Jane before he'd let her in, despite the fact that the lower half of her face was obscured by the bubble-wrapped panel. She lowered it, grinned at him, and the twinge in Max's leg melted away.

"Poor you," she said in the kitchen, resting the panel against the wall.

"It's not so bad," Max said airily. "Splint's coming off next week. There'll be physio for a few weeks after that...well, I should be shipshape again."

"So you'll still be able to cycle?"

"Hope so." They stood awkwardly for a moment. He saw her glance down at the panel. "So," he added, "can I see it?"

Jane nodded. He watched as she peeled off its bubble-wrap and carried it through to the back room. *How right she seems here,* he thought, *as if she belongs.* He knew, before she held the panel at the window, that he'd like it. Even if he didn't—even if she'd veered wildly away from the colors and shapes they'd discussed—he didn't care at all. He'd still live with it and love it.

"So," she said, "what do you think?"

His gaze traveled from her face to the swirling reds and golds. He walked toward it, feeling the colored light warming his face. "It's…it's perfect," he said.

Jane smiled, and he saw relief spread over her face. She placed it against the wall. "I'm so glad. You see, it's not the one I made for you. I made another one but it didn't seem right…." She looked flustered now; her cheeks were pink, and her eyes were avoiding his. Max was overcome by an urge to hold her.

"It doesn't matter," he said.

"Max," she continued, "something happened in Scotland, I met some—"

He did it then, not caring what she'd think; he took her in his arms and buried his face in her hair. "I told you," he whispered, "it doesn't matter."

She pulled away, still pink in the face. "I'll install it for you later this week."

"Whenever you have time," he said.

"Are you sure Veronica will be okay about it?"

He frowned at her. "What's it got to do with Veronica?"

"It's just…I know she's helped you do the place up. The kitchen and everything. And the window— Well, she might feel weird that your ex-wife—"

He laughed mirthlessly. "I never think of you like that. As my ex-wife—"

"Don't you?" she asked softly, meeting his gaze. "How do you think of me, Max?"

He cleared his throat. "As you. As Jane, that's all. Anyway, me and Veronica aren't really…a *thing* any more."

"A thing?" Jane asked, laughing.

Max lowered himself onto one of the two wicker chairs, the sole furniture in the room. Jane sat in the other, curling up her legs. "Things didn't go too well in France," he added.

She glanced down at the splint. "I can see that."

"I mean with me and her. She didn't take it very well— my accident and everything."

"How does one take an accident? It was hardly your fault," Jane protested.

"She seemed to think I'd been reckless—not listened to her. It's okay," he added quickly, "we're still friends…well, not friends exactly, but it's all right. It's not awkward." He realized his voice had acquired a slightly strangulated, un-deniably *awkward* quality.

"I'm sorry," Jane said, as if she really meant it. Max looked at her, yearning to tell her the real reason it was all over—how Veronica had seen his face when he'd played Jane's message. How she'd read thoughts in an instant. How she wasn't so dippy after all.

"You should get out," Jane said gently. "Go for a meal or see a film or something. You look like you've been stuck in here for days."

"Well," Max said sheepishly, "I have." Was she suggesting that they went out, just the two of them? In the evening, like a real couple? He pictured them in a restaurant—some friendly, unpretentious place—with Jane not shunting butterless asparagus around her plate, but wolfing her food, hungry for the hottest curry on the menu.

"Why don't you give Han a call?" Jane asked.

He frowned, failing to grasp what she meant.

"The two of you haven't spent time together for ages. I can't remember the last—"

"The aquarium," Max interrupted, trying to mask the crushing disappointment in his voice. "That's the last time I took her out. I don't think she wants to hang out with me anymore."

"You could ask her," Jane insisted. "Why not ring her— she'll be back from theater workshop by now—and see what she's doing later? Come on, Max—she could do with a treat."

Max studied her face. "Why, what's wrong?"

She paused, biting her lip absent-mindedly. "Something's happened since we came back from Scotland. I think there was some boy, and it's all finished now—maybe he met someone else while we were away. She's trying to be brave about it."

"Has she said something?" Max asked.

Jane smiled. "I'm her *mum,* Max. I just have a feeling."

Max felt a wave of shame. He was incapable of "having a feeling" where his daughter was concerned. Jane was right; for months, he'd spent their dad-and-daughter time either with Veronica, or Hannah had been holed up in Zoë's bedroom when she was supposed to have come to see him. He'd lost her and he hadn't even noticed.

"If you think she'd like to come out," he said, "I'll give her a call."

"Of course she'd like to," Jane said, squeezing his hand.

What struck him was how sweet and natural Hannah looked. Her purplish hair color was long gone, and now she seemed to have ditched the garish blue eyeshadow and overly glossed lips of her Zoë era. Her eyelashes looked normal, having lost their clogged-matchstick appearance. She had appeared at the door as his cab had pulled up outside Jane's place and skipped toward it, looking almost— no, *truly*—pleased to see him.

And she seemed to approve of his choice of restaurant, Max decided, glancing around the Opal's bustling interior, although it came to something when his own daughter seemed more at ease in such places than he did. He'd chosen it because it was new, not grossly expensive and he couldn't think of anywhere else. Their table had been squished into a too-small corner. Max felt ungainly, as if he should keep his elbows tucked in and somehow shrink into himself. He glanced around at numerous unlined faces. Max had started to feel horribly geriatric.

His crutches didn't help. Although he could manage to hobble around the house without them, he still needed them whenever he left the house. Hannah took a sip of her freshly squeezed juice. "Dad," she said hesitantly, "Zoë told me something about Veronica."

"What?" Max asked.

"She thinks she's seeing someone else. Her business

partner or something. Some guy with fuzzy hair and glasses who's invested in the aphrodisiac stuff. Pug-ugly, Zoë said."

Max pictured someone who vaguely fit that description from his party. Or rather, Veronica's party. "It's okay," he said, trying to keep a lightness to his voice. "We weren't very…well-matched."

"I didn't think so." Hannah grinned. Her face had changed over the past year or so; gone more angular, losing its childlike softness. He knew he should ask her about school, about exams and all those dad-type questions, but he suspected she wouldn't want to fill the evening with study-related small talk.

"You can still come and see Zoë anytime you like," he added quickly.

"I will. It's just with the show being really close, and all the rehearsals and costume fittings, I haven't really had time."

That was girls for you, Max thought. Fickle and unfathomable. "Anyway," he said, "how was Scotland?"

"Okay, apart from the end bit. I drew a lot—sketches of the hills and seals and stuff."

"That's great, Han. You'll have to show me sometime."

"They're nothing special." Max could detect a hint of tension in her smile. Perhaps he was capable of reading his own daughter after all.

"And Mum enjoyed her course?" he asked.

Pink patches sprang up on Hannah's cheeks. "I think so."

"Hannah," he started, "is there something—"

"She's thinking of leaving her job," she interjected. "Has she told you? She wants to do stained glass full-time."

"Really?" Max was incredulous. Was this something to do with Nancy's fit of madness? When Jane had told him about his mother-in-law's shock announcement—he did still view Nancy as his mother-in-law—he'd assumed it was some kind of sick joke. Abandoning her home, her entire London life—how could anyone behave so recklessly?

"She's been at Nippers for ten years," Hannah added. "She wants to try something new."

Max was silent for a moment. "What about you?" he asked. "Your mum said she thought something had happened. With some boy."

"Been discussing me, have you?" she asked. There was a tinge to her voice, as if something sour had landed on her tongue.

"No, it's just that—"

"Yes, Dad, I was seeing someone," she said curtly. "Turned out he was two-timing me."

He smiled inwardly at her use of such a teenage phrase. "Sounds as if you're best out of it."

"I know." She studied her menu nonchalantly. "Especially as the other girl's pregnant."

Max felt as if he'd been whacked in the stomach with his own crutch. "Pregnant?" he repeated.

"Yeah."

He didn't know how to respond. Had Hannah, too, been having sex with this two-timing jerk? He hadn't the first idea how to broach the subject.

"It's okay, Dad," she said, touching his hand across the table, "I'm not that dumb."

Max smiled weakly. "I'm glad to hear it."

"To be honest," she continued, "I feel sorry for her. Some poor girl landing herself with such a shit. And his mum—I went round to see him, and she thought I was the pregnant one. I felt sorry for her, too. She seemed kind of…fragile."

Max nodded, trying to appear interested, though mustering any sympathy for his daughter's ex-boyfriend's mother was beyond him. What was it about the female psyche that made them so fascinated about people they barely knew? It was too hot in here, Max decided, flapping the neck of his T-shirt. The food smells, plus the smoke that was drifting from a table with five cackling women crammed around it—it was all conspiring to make him feel quite unwell. He wondered where the waitress had stashed his crutches. "Dad," Hannah said, "are you listening?"

"Sorry, Han, I'm just feeling a bit—"

"What's weird," she continued, "is Celia seemed really nice. The kind of person, if I hadn't been so upset, I'd have stayed and talked to for longer…."

"Celia?" Max could feel a trickle of sweat on his temple.

"Yeah, Ollie's Mum. Celia Tibbs."

The waitress approached their table. As if his arm were mechanically operated, Max flapped her away. "What's wrong?" Hannah asked.

"Nothing. Nothing at all." He snatched a menu from the table, realizing his hands were drenched with sweat, and pretended to focus on it. *Celia Tibbs.* It was hardly a common name; she had to be the same person. Celia, who had worked in his shop for one hot summer, who'd hung around him after work and been there when they'd all gone out to celebrate a great review in *Your Bike* magazine. She had a child of her own—he'd have been seven or eight then. "Bet you're a wonderful dad," she'd told him.

They hadn't acknowledged him being a dad or a husband that night they'd staggered drunkenly into her bedsit off the Holloway Road. There'd been a child's bedroom, he remembered that much, but no son sleeping in it. "He's at his gran's," she'd told him, adding with a laugh, "Good timing, eh?" One little mistake, that's all she'd been. He could picture the well-worn teddy bear sitting on the bed, watching them reproachfully.

"I'll have a poached egg salad," Hannah said. "How about you?"

He tried to focus on the words. "The mushroom thing," he muttered, picking the first thing that leapt out at him.

"Ugh. Can't stand them." He felt her frowning at him over her menu. "Are you okay, Dad? You've gone really pale. Is it your leg or something?"

"I'm fine," he said, catching a waitress's eye and indicating that they were ready to order, even though there wasn't one hungry cell in his entire body.

41

Dear William,

I know things have been difficult these past few months. Now that you have promised to stop seeing Winnie, and have vowed not to contact her again, I hope that we can put this episode behind us and build a life together again.

*J*ane blinked at the neat, compressed handwriting. Winnie: the name was so old-fashioned as to be almost comical. Winnie and William—they could have been an old-fashioned comedy act. William seemed ill-fitting, too. Her mother had always called her husband Bill. Jane had almost forgotten that her father had been a William.

This isn't because we have Jane. If you and I were to part I am sure that, at eleven years old, she would cope with that. No, I want to make a go of things because I love you very deeply. You destroyed my library and have made a concerted attempt to destroy our marriage but I refuse to let it turn to ash as my clippings did.

I forgive you, William, and I am prepared to shut the past few months in a drawer, firmly lock it and throw away the key. What do you think, can we talk about this?

Love always,

Your wife Nancy

Jane folded up the sheet of blue airmail paper and slipped it back into the file where she'd found it. She hadn't intended to snoop through the drawers, hadn't even realized her mother kept personal things there. She had planned to spend an hour or so checking through her mother's mail, clearing out the fridge and doing a quick, superficial cleanup.

She forgave him, Jane thought, after everything he'd done. Her eyes had misted, and she wiped them against her sweater sleeve.

Her phone bleeped, and she fished it out of her pocket to read the text.

Window looks amazing know you won't let me pay u but I must thank u somehow love m x

One little mistake was all it had been. Like her mother, Jane could have forgiven, but now it was ten years too late.

"You've done *what?*"

Jane gripped the phone as she cleared away the pencils and half-finished drawings that Hannah had left scattered on the living room table. "I've resigned, Mum. Well, not completely. I'll do one shift a week until Sally finds someone else."

"You're misunderstanding," her mother barked. "Why not make a clean break from the place? What's all this one-shift-a-week nonsense?"

"Sally's my friend. I can't just leave her in the lurch." *And Hannah and I have to live,* she added silently.

"You're playing safe. If you're going to make a go of—"

"Mum, I am! Three shops are stocking my work. I've advertised, dropped leaflets and cards off at every local business I can think of, carted panels all over East London…"

"And in between that," Nancy added with a chuckle, "you've been salt-dough modeling or whatever it is you get up to with the kids."

"I *like* salt-dough modeling," Jane said huffily, wondering how this could possibly be the person who'd written such a forgiving letter.

"I suppose you have responsibilities," Nancy added dryly.

"Yes, I do." Jane sighed and gnawed the end of Hannah's charcoal pencil.

"Are you eating? Have I disturbed your meal?"

"No, Mum. Anyway, how are things? Have you settled in?"

A small laugh. "Busy as anything. A full summer program set up and running with bookings already coming in. I suppose you've seen our new website?"

"Yes," Jane lied.

"So, are you going to?"

"To…what?"

"Book a place for the summer school. We can offer a discount."

"I can't keep coming to Scotland! I've got stuff to do here, Mum, like—"

"What's so important that you can't give yourself a week off, now you're only working one day a week?"

Jane burst out laughing. "I've got…stuff."

Nancy snorted, then her voice softened as she said, "We'd like to see you."

"We?"

Nancy paused. "Conor asks about you. Thank goodness for him, is all I can say, working with this drunken imbecile…"

Something twisted in Jane. She wanted to say, *What do you mean, he asks about me? He could have got in touch if he'd wanted to.* "I popped into your house today," she said quickly. "It was strange, being in the archive room without you."

She heard her mother take a breath. "You could do me a favor and clear it out."

"What would I do with it all?" Jane asked.

"I don't really care. It's only *stuff*, Jane. I've had enough of hanging on to things that no longer fit into my life."

The house seemed too quiet after the call. Hannah was at Zoë's birthday do, and Sally was coming round later to share a bottle of wine. Stuff, Jane thought, casting an eye around the living room. So much stuff she'd accumulated since moving here ten years ago. The house had been pleasingly empty the first time they'd walked in. Plain pale walls, plain faded carpets, the only artifice being those window boxes filled with blowsy plants. She'd tried to remember to water when she noticed them reprimanding her with their sagging heads.

So he'd been asking about her, had he? Jane wondered if the laundry-basket Dalek was still in one piece. Lewis, unlike Hannah, struck her as a careful child who'd look after his possessions. She doubted if Conor had to rake under leaves for lost Dr. Who figurines.

Jane found a notebook between numerous drawing pads under her desk. The pages were the flimsy airmail kind like her mother had used for her Dear William letter. She found a pen on the table and wrote:

Dear Conor,
I'm writing to apologize for leaving without saying goodbye and for avoiding you after the night we spent together. As you know, Hannah had an asthma attack and I felt terrible for not being there when it happened. I know that my being with you didn't make it happen, but as a parent—as I'm sure you know—

you can always find a million and one reasons to blame yourself for anything.

Mum says she sees a lot of you. She seems to have settled in well and is keeping Archie in line. I think about you often, Conor, and especially that night we spent together. It might sound crazy, but since Max and I split I haven't met anyone who I've felt anything for, and there you were. I've felt quite restless since we came home—which has turned into a kind of productive whirl, and I'm inundated with work over the next few months. In fact, there's enough to keep me going until the end of the year. I have almost given up the day job as it's always been a reason not to throw myself into my business wholeheartedly—a kind of security blanket.

Why am I telling you this? I feel as if I know you, even though we spent such a short time together. Just that one night, and look what happened. I hope you and Lewis are happy and that the Dalek put in a fearsome performance at the costume contest. I also hope you like the panel I left for you, and that you have managed to find a home for it.

With love,

Jane

She looked down at the page. What was she thinking, spilling out her feelings to him? She'd been home for four weeks. He could have got in touch—found her number or e-mail on Archie's computer, or asked her mother for it.

As for the panel—couldn't he have thanked her, even if he hadn't liked or wanted it?

It was obvious, she realized with crushing certainty, that Conor had no plans to contact her again. A one-night stand—that's all she'd been to him. When the next batch of students arrived he'd pick one out to befriend, asking her round for supper and taking her up to the foothills of the mountain to see the broken-down church.

Tear pricked Jane's eyes as she reread her letter. They weren't the words of a responsible adult but a hormonal fifteen year-old who couldn't even keep geraniums alive. She ripped out the page, scrunched it up in her fist and fired it across the room, scoring a direct hit in the waste bin.

Then, telling herself that she had nothing to fear—that she was just late, and probably panicking over nothing—she headed upstairs to the bathroom to do the pregnancy test.

42

*H*annah wasn't sure how Zoë had managed to rake together a collection of friends for her birthday dinner. They were occupying the largest table in the Italian restaurant, tossing and flapping their hair like changing-room curtains. Veronica sat at the farthest end of the table like a queen surveying her subjects. Everyone, Hannah realized as she twirled linguine around her fork, was blond, apart from her. She felt like a different species. "So," whispered the girl beside her, "I presume you're the latest?"

Hannah frowned. "Latest what?"

"NBF."

"Don't know what you mean," she said with a shrug.

"New best friend." The girl grinned, showing gleaming pink gums.

Hannah tried to catch Zoë's eye, but she was too busy

laughing theatrically with a girl who kept throwing her head back, as if she were having trouble controlling her neck muscles.

"It's the way she operates," the girl added. "Gets super-close to someone, hangs out with them all the time, then drifts away and moves on to someone else."

"No, she doesn't," Hannah said hotly. Even listening to this girl's remarks was making her feel disloyal. No wonder Zoë preferred being with her if all her schoolmates were as bitchy as this.

"A toast, everyone!" Veronica was saying, standing up now and gripping the stem of her glass.

"We've all been there," the girl railed. "We've all been the NBF."

"To my beautiful Zoë," Veronica announced, "happy birthday, darling."

Everyone cried "Happy birthday" and, in perfect synchronization, a waiter glided toward them with an enormous platter laden with fairy cakes. Each fairy cake had been intricately iced with spirals of piped icing. "It's okay, Hannah," Veronica brayed over the table, "they're all natural colors. I was very specific about that. They won't set off your asthma or anything."

Hannah smiled tightly. "Thanks."

"D'you have asthma?" chirped the girl beside her.

"Um, yeah."

"That's a shame. Listen, some of us are going clubbing after this. Want to come?"

"No, thanks," Hannah said stiffly, "I'm going back to Zoë's. I'm staying there tonight." She tried again to catch

her eye—send her a let's-get-the-hell-out-of-here code—
but Zoë was swooshing away in the direction of the loo,
closely followed by her mother, who was clattering across
the polished floor in her Emma Hope wedding shoes.

Hannah had hoped they might lie around gossiping in
Zoë's bedroom, but Zoë seemed distracted, and more in-
terested in admiring herself wearing her new earrings.
"They're lovely," Hannah said. "Who gave you them again?"

"Amelia."

"Who's Amelia?" Hannah asked, aware of the strained
tinge to her voice.

"She's just started at our school. She's dead clever and
has this really cool family. You won't believe it but her
mum's a fashion designer. Amelia gets to pick anything she
wants from the collections. She's going to be a model."

"Oh," Hannah responded, picturing the girl who'd kept
throwing her head back and filling the restaurant with extravagant laughter.

"You'd like her," she added. "She's a laugh. Completely
mental."

Hannah watched Zoë twirling the earrings between her
fingers and checking her reflection from all angles. She
hadn't told her about visiting Ollie's flat, or Ollie's mother
blurting that stuff about the pregnant girl. "It's just fizzled
out," was all she'd said, "and I'm glad. He was just messing
me around."

"I'm proud of you," Zoë had said, and Hannah had felt
vaguely ashamed for being so grateful for her friend's
approval.

She picked up a copy of *Glamour* magazine but couldn't summon up the enthusiasm to read it. Hannah was aware of a hollowness inside her—a feeling of something missing. She could hear Dylan playing a guitar in his room. Zoë's cell phone rang, and Hannah saw her face light up as she took the call. "Hi Amelia. Yeah, I'd love to—what time? Okay if I bring Han?" Hannah kept her eyes firmly fixed on the magazine. Are Your Friends Toxic? the headline read. Find out if your buddies truly deserve you. "Honestly," Zoë continued, "I'm really up for it. There's nothing much happening here." She finished the call, her eyes gleaming excitedly. "We're going to town," she announced. "New club in Covent Garden. Amelia's mum knows the manager and he's put our names at the door."

"Our names?" Hannah repeated.

"Yeah. Zoë plus one. You do want to come, don't you?"

"I don't really feel like it. Anyway, I don't have any money." She didn't add that she'd had to scrounge money for the birthday meal from her mum—only to discover that Veronica was picking up the tab—as she'd spent her last fifteen quid on a lacy Top Shop vest for a present. A top that Zoë had merely glanced at quickly before dropping it back into the ripped remains of its wrapping and moved swiftly on to more extravagant gifts, like Amelia's earrings. Hannah wasn't in the mood for clubbing, or being anyone's plus one.

"Come on," Zoë pleaded. "It's my birthday. I'll get some money from Mum. You've got to—"

"I really don't want to. I'll see you over the weekend, okay? I'm going to phone Mum, tell her I'm getting the bus home."

Zoë's face drooped with disappointment. "Okay. Sorry, Han, but I'll have to hurry if I'm meeting Amelia at ten. See yourself out, will you, while I have a shower?"

Dylan was leaning in his bedroom doorway as Hannah left Zoë's room. "Want to see something?" he asked.

"I'm just going home."

"Come on," he urged her, "it won't take a minute."

She looked at him. Something about his expression suggested that the 'something' was really important. Hannah paused on the landing, hearing the shower being turned on and Zoë singing to herself. "What is it?" she asked.

"Come in. It's okay, I won't bite." The smile lit up his sweet, pale face.

"Okay. Just for a minute." Hannah stepped into his room. It looked like it belonged to another house. There were no calico walls, no golden letters spelling his name, no cluster of body oils on a dressing table; just colossal piles of magazines, books and rumpled papers.

"Hang on a minute," Dylan said. He opened his wardrobe and crouched on the floor, rummaging through papers and notebooks at the bottom. He dragged out a pile of folders and spread them on the floor. Hannah sat on the bed, taking in the details of his face: the dark brown eyes that shone vividly from luminous skin, the unkempt dark hair that looked as if he'd hacked at himself with blunt scissors. There was a faint smell—a boy's bedroomy smell— but it was warm and biscuity rather than outwardly unpleasant. "Here it is," he said, thrusting Hannah a folder. "Zoë said you're a really good artist. Tell me what you think."

He flashed a crooked grin. "You can say if you think they're crap. I can take it."

She took the folder from him and slid out the drawings. They were comic strips, featuring a girl with creamy skin and purplish hair. She was dressed entirely in black, with fierce determination shining out of her dark eyes, and looked eerily familiar. "Did you really do these?" she asked quietly.

Dylan colored slightly. "Yeah. I've been working on them for ages. I was thinking of sending them to a publisher or something, some company that does graphic novels, but maybe you think that's stupid."

"I don't think that's stupid at all," she murmured, examining the loose pages in turn. The girl, she discovered, had a friend. A blond, ditzy friend who wanted everyone's attention and sulked when she didn't get it. "Not based on your sister, is she?" she said, laughing.

"I, um, don't really base the characters on real people. They're just made up."

"So…what's the dark-haired one's name?"

"Haven't decided yet."

She nodded, and their eyes met. Usually Hannah hated clutter—her mother's clutter at least—but Dylan's felt quirky and interesting. She felt quite at home in the chaotic room. "So, what happens to her in the end? The dark-haired one, I mean?"

"I haven't decided yet. Maybe you could help me figure it out. If you've got time," he quickly added, "next time you're here to see Zoë."

Hannah heard Zoë coming out of the bathroom, humming to herself in her room now, getting ready for her night out. She thought of the assortment of blond girls around the restaurant table—the pretentious restaurant Veronica had chosen—and felt relieved to be here. "Don't you want to go?" Dylan asked, as if reading her thoughts.

"I don't like clubbing. It's never been my thing."

"Yeah." He took the drawings from her and spread them out on the floor. Then, as he raked through his CDs and selected one to play, Zoë swept past his open door—either not knowing or caring that Hannah was still there. "Anyway," Dylan added, "I'm glad you're not going."

"Why?" she asked.

"Because you can hang out here. If you want."

She liked the way he colored easily, the way she felt utterly unintimidated by him. It was good, she realized, to be with someone with whom she felt equal. "Okay," she said, checking her watch. "I'll see if Dad'll pay my taxi fare home." The front door banged shut, and Hannah heard Zoë clip-clopping down the stone steps.

"See you later, Princess," Dylan muttered under his breath.

"She's not so bad," Hannah said defensively.

"You don't live with her."

"She can be really sweet," Hannah added. "You know what she did when we were in Scotland? She gave me these." She rummaged in her bag and pulled out the yellow box. Since Zoë had given her the worry dolls, she'd taken to carrying them with her at all times. They'd worked, too. The weight of the Ollie stuff had fallen away.

Dylan took the box from her and lifted its lid. "Where did you get these?"

"I told you. Zoë got them for me. It's amazing, what she did—they used to be mine. I'd hid them under the floor at Dad's old house, but he moved out before I could get them." She glanced at Dylan, who was watching her intently. "Zoë went to the house and explained what had happened. That's how I got my worry dolls back."

Dylan bit his lip. "What is it?" Hannah asked.

"Nothing." He replaced the lid and handed the box back to her.

"Dylan, tell me...."

His eyes looked huge and deep. "I don't...she made it up, Han. The story about going to your dad's house..."

"How d'you know?" She was angry now—what was she doing, listening to Zoë's little brother? He was fourteen, for God's sake. A baby.

"Have a look at the dolls," he said quietly. She tipped them onto her palm and regarded him coolly. "Look at the blue one," he added. "See the thread stuff's unraveling?"

Hannah looked down and nodded. "If you unwind the thread," Dylan continued, "you'll see some writing on the wooden part inside it."

Slowly, Hannah unwound the thread. If this was a game, she was prepared to play along, if only to prove that Dylan was as weird as Zoë had said. She wanted to leave now, hurry round to her dad's and call a cab. A sliver of wood lay on her palm now. A sliver on which someone had written, in the same ultrafine black pen as Dylan had used for his comic strip. "It says Dylan," Hannah said, frowning.

He smiled warmly and touched her hand. "She nicked them from my room, Han. I had worry dolls, too. Those are mine."

B

*P*erhaps she'd done it wrong. Jane stared at the pregnancy test. Perhaps her pee had seeped into the wrong part of the stick, or she'd done it too soon for the test to be accurate. Or—Jane favored this version—she was in the midst of some hellish, hyper-real nightmare and would soon jolt back to safe, nonpregnant reality in her bed.

Of course the test could be faulty. Jane studied the box: "Proven to be 99% accurate", it said. Knowing with absolute certainty that she couldn't have another child, she clung to the hope that she represented that rogue 1%. She'd never wanted another baby after having Hannah. Hannah had been enough, all she'd ever wanted; with her baby, and Max, life had felt complete. Although Hannah had been unplanned—"Have you given a thought to your future?" her mother had barked—she'd never felt so certain, *so right.*

And here she was, fifteen years later, with dread coursing through her veins.

"Jane? It's me!" Sally's voice ricocheted around the house as she let herself into the hall.

"Won't be a minute," Jane called down.

There was some clattering downstairs, and a rustling of carrier bags. "I'll stick this wine in your freezer, okay? Can't understand why the store doesn't have one of those chiller machines, or at least put cheap white wine in the fridge and not just the expensive stuff…."

Jane was still gripping the stick. She didn't care about wine or chilling machines. Christ, by rights she shouldn't even be drinking. She examined her reflection in the bathroom mirror. She looked gaunt and strained, but not pregnant. She certainly didn't look like a woman who'd gone back to the house of a man she barely knew and had head-exploding sex on a tumble of soft blankets and sweet-smelling sheets while his seven-year-old son was being Chief Dalek at a sleepover party. If only she'd waited until morning to go to pack up her panel in Archie's studio. If only she hadn't been so mad that night she'd overheard Hannah and Zoë discussing her crumbling ovaries and booked a place on that wretched course.

"Jane," Sally called over the low music she'd put on, "are you okay up there?"

"I'm fine." Jane glanced at the bathroom bin into which she and Hannah dropped used disposable razors. No, couldn't risk her finding it. Grabbing a length of toilet paper, she wrapped it tightly around the stick. Now it looked like a miniature Egyptian mummy. Stuffing it into the back pocket of her jeans, she fixed on a too-bright smile, which she feared verged on the manic, and headed downstairs.

Sally was in the kitchen. She had obviously decided that chilling the wine in the freezer would be too long and drawn-out a process and was instead plopping ice cubes into two glasses. "I'm impressed you've got ice," she said without looking up.

Jane watched the wine swirling into the glass as Sally poured it. She wished she could feel pleased about having ice. "It's left over from Hannah's party," she said flatly.

Sally glanced at her. "God, Jane, you look washed out. Been working late?"

"Yes, a bit."

"I thought ditching your job was supposed to give you more time…you look beat…"

"Sally, I—"

"Bet you never used that massage voucher I gave you," Sally rattled on. "Come on, let's go through, get cosy. Where's Hannah tonight?"

"It's Zoë's birthday do. Veronica's organized some meal out…." Jane was aware of her voice, but it sounded as if it were drifting from someone else's mouth. A bunch of teenagers were throwing some kind of inflatable Frisbee across the park. Jane could feel Sally studying her, knowing there was something else. She couldn't tell her. Telling her would make it real, and a real pregnancy required decisions and explanations, even though what she'd done wasn't wrong— just sex, for God's sake…. Jane was aware of the hardness of the pregnancy test in her jeans pocket.

"Have you eaten?" Sally asked.

"No. I'm not really hungry. D'you want cheese on toast or something?"

"Please."

Relieved to escape from Sally's penetrating gaze, Jane headed for the kitchen, where she took the stick from her pocket and glared at it. Then she jammed it deep into the kitchen bin as if, concealed beneath a layer of bread wrappers, eggshells and carrot peelings, it would cease to exist.

41

*H*annah had imagined that a handful of people might wander into the launch of FoxLove Foods—the kind of mumbling weirdoes who hung about in libraries, twiddling on the computers because they had nothing better to do on a Thursday afternoon. In fact the conference room was full to capacity. Row upon row of women, and the occasional man in a T-shirt or ancient-looking sweater, were watching intently as Veronica demonstrated how Nibble 'n' Lick bars were made—as if each one you saw in the shops would have been lovingly prepared in her own kitchen.

"Each snack bar," Veronica announced from the stage, "represents a powerhouse of sexual energy to unleash your inner erotic resources." An image of her hand, swooping dramatically over glass plates of ingredients, was beamed onto the screen behind her. Hannah had agreed to spend two hours distributing samples, along with Zoë and Dylan—who, clearly, had had no choice in the matter—for the princely sum of five quid an hour. She glanced around the conference suite, a nondescript third-floor room in a faceless office building.

"No dairy in these, is there?" A skinny woman with a pale, pinched face peered at the gravelly lumps on Hannah's tray.

"No, they're all dairy-free," Hannah said, hoping that her smile masked the fact that she hadn't the first idea of what had gone into these things. It could be toenail clippings for all she knew or cared.

The woman picked up a gnarled-looking lump and sniffed it. "Yurumba bark?" she enquired.

"That's right," Hannah said.

"Great. You see, I have a mucus problem. Sinuses…" The woman tapped the side of her nose and bit into the lump. "Mmm," she said, giving Hannah a patronizing pat on the arm before bobbing back down onto her chair.

But now Zoë seemed to be enjoying herself as she toured the edge of the room with her trayful of libido-boosting mega-bites. Was this what the world was coming to, Hannah wondered, that to get in the mood for sex you had to stuff your face with horrible lumps that looked like old fish tank gravel bound together by PVA glue?

"Hey," Dylan murmured, sidling up to her with his own heavily laden tray, "want to escape for a bit?"

"How?" Hannah asked.

The audience had burst into spontaneous applause. Veronica held aloft a glass dish of sludgy stuff, and a cluster of people had surged toward the demonstration table. "This is the bit where she starts on about igniting libido, blood flow to the genitals and all that…." Dylan shuddered dramatically.

"How d'you know?" Hannah asked, laughing.

"I've heard her practicing in her study. Don't think I can stomach it again. Come on, let's sneak out for a bit. Mum won't miss us."

Hannah smiled. She liked his sweet, pale face, those dark eyes that radiated naughtiness and cheek. "Okay. Where shall we go?"

"I know a place," he said.

The graveyard wasn't spooky but filled with beautiful carvings of Madonnas and angels, their edges weathered to softness. Hannah sat on a damp wooden bench, enjoying the feeling of spring sunshine on her face. "So," Dylan said, sitting at a respectable distance beside her, "did you talk to Zoë about making up all that crap about the worry dolls?"

"Not yet." Hannah wanted to pick her moment. She hadn't seen Zoë all week, which was unusual. And today, with the opening night of *Little Shop of Horrors* a mere five hours away, she didn't feel up to a confrontation.

"Aren't you going to?" Dylan asked.

"Yes, of course I am."

He peered through his bangs at her. "Not scared of her, are you?"

"No, why d'you say that?"

"Because…you shouldn't be. She really looks up to you with your art and your acting and all that."

"My acting?" Hannah laughed hollowly.

Dylan looked hurt. "Yeah."

"Anyway," Hannah added, "she's hanging out with Amelia now…."

"No, she's not. They fell out. That's what happens with Zoë's new best friends. It gets really intense and competitive and—"

"It's not like that with me," Hannah interjected.

"No," he said, feigning interest on a blackbird that had landed on a gravestone. "You're different."

"What kind of different?"

He turned to look at her. Hannah was seized by an urge to grab some scissors and cut his hair so she could see his eyes properly. "You're just…you," he said.

Hannah smiled. She didn't fancy Dylan exactly—he was in the year below her at school, and thinking *anything* about him would be out of the question—yet hanging out here with him was hugely preferable to being trapped in that conference room and have people go on about their sinuses and mucus. "Dylan," she said suddenly, "d'you want to come tonight? To see the show, I mean?"

"What, and watch you being a Venus Flytrap?"

"Uh-huh."

His face brightened. "Is Zoë coming?"

"Yes, and my parents."

"Sure you want me to come?"

"I'd really like it if you were there. I'd feel better."

"Why?" he asked. "Not nervous, are you?"

Hannah sighed. "There's this boy, Ollie, who I was sort of seeing. He's in the show, playing the dentist."

"So…you dumped him, or what?"

"No, I went round to see him, soon after we'd come back from Scotland, and his mum mistook me for someone else—his *proper* girlfriend, who turns out to be pregnant…."

Dylan's eyes widened. "Holy shit."

"So," she continued, "I feel like a complete idiot."

"You're not an idiot." He touched her hand.

She smiled, enjoying the warmth of his ink-stained fingers. "Come on," she said, "We'd better get back. Don't tell anyone about the pregnant girlfriend thing, okay?"

"I don't tell anyone anything," Dylan assured her as they wandered along the grass path that cut its way between the gravestones—a path that Hannah would have followed happily for the rest of the day.

45

The waiting room had a sharp, chemical smell of new carpet. Jane gave her name at the receptionist's window and skimmed the room, estimating that she'd have to wait half an hour at least. Taking the only available chair, she grabbed a magazine from the table in front of her and opened it randomly, trying to focus on pictures of North African dishes—couscous, tagines—in order to blot out the real reason why she'd come.

"Well, if it's not Jane Deakin!"

Jane looked up to meet the gaze of the woman beside her. "How are you, Barbara?" she asked, mustering a smile. Barbara had been her mother's friend since childhood.

"Fine, Jane, apart from my cataracts. More to the point, how's that mother of yours, abandoning us all to live in a shack up in Scotland? Has the woman completely lost it or is there some man involved, hmm?"

"No, not that I know of," Jane told her. "You know Mum. There's no changing her mind once she's got an idea in her head…."

Barbara shook her head good-naturedly. "Complete nutcase, always had been. Not like you, eh, Jane?" Barbara's pointy elbow dug into Jane's side.

"Um, no." Jane felt her cheeks reddening.

"The sensible one, that's you. Most grown-up person in that crazy house, when you were a little girl. Always had your head screwed on." She laughed from the pit of her belly, flashing a glimmer of gold tooth.

Jane felt as if her tongue and mouth and even her throat had withered and were incapable of functioning normally. She smiled inanely.

"Are you okay?" Barbara asked in a quieter voice. "I don't want to pry, and do tell me it's none of your business but—"

"I'm fine," Jane barked, startling the auburn-haired girl opposite.

"Barbara Toner?" the doctor called around the door.

Barbara sprang up from her chair. "Yes, that's me. Lovely seeing you, Jane. Do take care of yourself—you're looking a little bit peaky if you don't mind me saying so."

"Yes, I will." Jane watched her leave. The auburn-haired girl caught her eye and smiled. She had a delicate face with a neat little chin and was wearing foundation that looked too orangey for her skin. She was pretty, Jane thought—around seventeen at a guess—with eyes of a pale, diluted green and the kind of sculpted lips you saw on Victorian dolls. In fact she looked like a doll, sitting there with pale hands clasped loosely on her lap.

A tall, good-looking boy ambled out of the loo. Finding nowhere to sit, he crouched down in front of the girl and rested a hand on her lap. "Feeling all right?" he asked gently.

"Yeah, okay," the girl replied. "Bit hot in here though."

He stood up, shook the stiffness from his legs and strolled across the waiting room to the water dispenser. "Get one for me, would you?" the girl called after him.

There was something about the young couple that transfixed Jane. The only un-doll-like thing about the girl, she realized now, was the faint swelling at her belly. The boy returned with a paper cone of water and bent to kiss her forehead. She looked up at and smiled her thanks.

It shocked Jane, the way her eyes misted instantly; she hadn't been prepared for it at all. She wanted the magazine—pictures of tagines to hide behind—but had put it back on the table from where it had been snatched by an obese man in a tight white T-shirt.

"Hazel Driver?" proclaimed a nurse.

"Ollie, that's us." The girl stood up, dropped the cone into the bin and linked her boyfriend's arm. They looked like a proper couple, Jane thought, trying to tear away her gaze. Like she and Max all those years ago. A couple who were happy and excited to be having a baby. They disappeared through the door to the surgeries, and Jane stared after them, even though there was nothing left to see. Here she was, probably two decades older than that girl—with her head screwed on, Barbara had said. She had a daughter who, in two or three years' time, would be leaving home. She had more work pouring in than she could handle, and the memory of a night in a cottage with the storm wreaking havoc all around.

"Jane Deakin?" the woman doctor said.

She stood up. "Yes, that's me."

The doctor smiled distractedly, and Jane followed her through the door and along the corridor to the farthest room. "So how can I help?" the doctor asked as Jane took a seat.

"I—I think I'm pregnant. In fact I know I am."

The doctor had a soft, kind face and wiry hair with grayness showing at the roots. "Have you done a test?" she asked.

"Yes." Jane glanced around the cool white room. She'd come to a room like this for her pregnancy test sixteen years ago. She hadn't known about home tests then, and wouldn't have trusted them anyway. It had taken three days for the results to come through but Jane had known already, just as she knew now.

"Is this your first pregnancy?" the doctor asked.

Such a typical London doctor's office, Jane thought, where you never saw the same doctor twice, despite her regular trips here regarding Hannah's asthma. "No, I have a fifteen-year-old daughter."

The doctor laughed softly. "That's quite a gap." *Quite a gap*—not only in years but in what she'd intended to do. To make arrangements to end it and get on with her life.

"It's not a planned pregnancy," Jane murmured. "The father and I, we're not together."

The doctor smiled sympathetically. "How are you feeling about it?"

Jane opened her mouth to speak, and her head filled with that auburn-haired girl and the handsome boy who'd rested a hand on her lap. "Fine," she said firmly. "Everything's fine."

"Well, that's good," the doctor said, sounding business-like now. "So, Jane, if you can tell me the date when your last period started, we can work out a due date and book you in for your antenatal care."

Jane felt something lifting—like a cloud, what were clouds made of again?—and said, "Thanks, that would be great."

46

"I'm sorry," Ollie said.

Hannah swung round from the table in the back room where Beth had been painting her face with lurid pink swirls to look like the center—the tongue—of the plant. "Are you?" she said flatly.

He perched on the edge of the table beside her. Hannah recoiled in her seat. Ollie was in costume, wearing the dentist's white tunic, which made his face look brown and healthy. "There's stuff I have to tell you," he added.

"It's okay," she said tersely, "your mum told me everything. What I can't understand—" the controlled fury in her voice took her by surprise "—is why you've said nothing since I came back from Scotland."

Ollie flushed and dropped his gaze. "I didn't know how."

Hannah glared at him. How different he seemed from

the confident Ollie in the Opal who knew about wine. "So why bother now?" she snapped.

"Because I might not see you again. I won't be coming back to theater workshop after the show. I've got...other stuff going on."

"Yes, I know."

"It's not like that," he protested.

"So, what is it like?" Hannah turned away, trying to blot him out of her consciousness and thinking instead of her mum, dad and Zoë waiting in the hall. And Dylan, who thought she was different, and that was okay.

"I'd finished with her," Ollie said. "It was all over when I started seeing you. Neither of us knew she was...you know."

"Yeah, I know." Across the room, Beth was tonging Emily's hair into Audrey-style waves.

"It just happened, Han. We were unlucky...." She checked her watch, unbuckled the strap and slipped it into her bag. Man-eating plants didn't wear watches. "So we're making a go of it," he added lamely.

"What about the other stuff?" she asked.

"What other—"

"The drugs stuff."

Ollie frowned. "You might think it's a big deal. It's not. Just a bit of hash I was knocking out, nothing else. I was..."

"Unlucky."

"Yeah. It's not something I do for fun, you know? Mum has depression. Really bad, manic depression, and a lot of the time she can't work and I have to support us, if you can imagine what that's like."

"And that's why you're a dealer—"

"What d'you suggest I do," he snapped, "get a paper round?"

"Ten minutes to curtains," Beth announced. A hush fell like a blanket on the room. Ollie slipped from the edge of the table and, without a backward glance, marched off to deliver what Hannah realized would be his second sterling performance of the day. Uncurling her hand, she looked down at the five tiny dolls that Dylan had insisted she kept, saying he'd stopped believing in them a long time ago.

"Ready, Han?" Beth asked.

"Yes." Hannah stood up, checked her reflection in the full-length wall mirror and tried to mentally prepare herself for being encased in knobbly papier-mâché. Even sharing the stage with Ollie, and having a best friend who told outrageous fibs—not to mention a mother who was acting like she was on drugs or something, and could barely look her in the eye—even with all *that*, everything was going to be just fine.

Funny how big things shrank into piddling little things when you were about to morph into a ravenous man-eating plant.

47

*J*ane seemed different, Max thought as they left the church. Distracted, as if present only in body, with something weighing heavily on her mind—something of gargantuan proportions that had overshadowed Hannah's performance in the show. His daughter had been brilliant, Max thought, considering her only lines had been, "Feed me!" and "Feed me, Seymour!" about thirty times over. She'd even managed to make a Venus flytrap funny—surely no mean feat—and had outshone by miles that dentist guy who'd wandered aimlessly around the stage and muttered into his chest.

"Okay if Han comes back to ours?" Dylan asked from the backseat of Jane's car. Jane was driving them home. Although Max's knee was healing well after surgery—he'd been told to "take it easy" for some unspecified period—he was still, irksomely, relying on her to ferry him around.

"Sure," he said, "that okay with you, Jane?"

"Uh-huh," she muttered.

He wanted to catch her eye, to signal: *isn't this good, that Hannah's started hanging out with Dylan instead of acting like some Zoë appendage?* Max had grown fond of this kid with his unkempt fringe and bizarre comic strips who, he suspected, had learnt to accept his lowly position in the family food chain.

"What's it to you what Hannah does?" Zoë crunched hard on a boiled sweet.

"I just—" Dylan began.

"I mean, asking Han back to ours? Like she's your…*friend* or something?" she snorted witheringly.

Hannah was sandwiched between Zoë and Dylan, sipping from a bottle of Lucozade. "I am his friend," she said levelly. "Maybe we could watch a film or something, the three of us…."

"The *three* of us?" Zoë repeated faintly.

The car's interior hummed with ill-tempered vibes. This wasn't what Max had bargained for at all. He'd left the church in a buoyant mood, despite the fact that Jane seemed to have floated off to some distant planet—and was now trapped with a carload of bickering teenagers.

Jane pulled up outside his house. "I'll cook you some supper if you like," Max said, hoping she hadn't detected the tinge of desperation in his voice.

"Sure," she said brightly, "that'd be lovely."

He needn't have worried. She wasn't even there.

Max brought mugs of tea into the back room, where low evening sunshine eked through Jane's stained glass window.

"So, are you happy with it?" she asked, curling up in one of the wicker chairs.

Max followed her gaze. "Of course I am...."

"But...?" she prompted him.

He glanced at her. She didn't just look different; she *was* different. He sensed a distance between them and yearned to pull her back in, but didn't know how. "I can't help wondering," he murmured, "what made you abandon the first panel and start again."

She picked up her mug and blew across it. "I didn't abandon it."

"So...what happened to it?"

"I gave it away." Her cheeks flushed, and tension flickered across her brow.

"Why?" he asked.

"I—I wanted to leave something. On the island..."

Max felt as if certain internal organs—his stomach, perhaps, certainly his heart—had sunk a little. "Jane," he asked softly, "did you give it to...that person you met?"

"Yes, I did."

"So...it wasn't just a fling?" *It's none of your business,* he scolded himself. *What are you thinking, asking her about this stuff?*

"It was a one-night stand actually." Jane forced a brittle smile. "I'm thirty-seven, Max. How does that sound, that I spent the night with someone I barely know?"

"There's no law against it," he muttered, his head swilling with lurid images of rough, tough Highlander types with indecipherable accents and grappling hands. He felt quite nauseous.

"It...just happened, Max."

"Right." *Or maybe one of those crackpot aristocratic landlords,* his brain ranted on. *Lairds, did they call them? The ones who'd inherited vast, crumbling estates and had nothing to do but slug whisky all day and—*

"Don't look at me that way," Jane said desperately.

"I wasn't," he protested, realizing that he'd been staring— no, *glaring*—right into her startled eyes.

He looked away, not knowing what to do or say next. The evening sun had been dulled by a cloud. She said something then—something that sounded like *repugnant.*

"What?" he snapped.

"Max, I said I'm pregnant."

He felt faint, as if he'd been whacked on the head with a stick. Years ago he'd hit black ice and come off his bike, cracking his head against a traffic bollard or so he'd been told later; he couldn't remember the bollard bit. Only the *thwack,* then the clouded dizziness as some young mum with a toddler in a backpack had struggled to help him up. "Are you sure?" he managed to say.

She nodded. "I've done a test."

So Jane was having a baby. She'd conceived a child with some drunken maniac in a derelict castle.

"Congratulations," he said flatly.

"Please, Max, don't be like that."

He stared at her, transfixed by the tear that wobbled like mercury in her left eye, then spilled over and formed a wiggly line down her cheek. Just like Veronica's tears after the holiday. Jesus, he really knew how to make women cry.

He reached for her hand and squeezed it. "I've really fucked up," she murmured.

"No, you haven't."

"You hate me…."

"Christ, Jane, how can I ever hate you? I love—" Suddenly he didn't care what she'd done on that island. She was a free woman—a gorgeous, sexy, single woman—and hadn't he spent recent months having mind-blowing sex with a woman with whom he had less than zero in common? Where did that place him, on the scale of fucking up?

He came out of his chair, perched on the arm of hers and pulled her toward him. She felt skinny and fragile, not like someone carrying a baby at all. He wanted to kiss and tell her that everything would be okay, and not caring that Hannah or Zoë or Dylan might stumble in and find them. "So what are you going to do?" he asked gently.

She wiped her face with her hands. "It's stupid, and it's not a good time—not that there's ever a good time to have a baby with someone you've no intention of seeing—"

"What's his name?"

"Conor."

"Does he know?" Max asked, turning the name over in his head. Conor didn't sound like an alcoholic maniac.

She shook her head fiercely. "He has a son, a boy of seven years old. I can't mess up their lives." A small voice in Max's head said, *It's okay, she wants the baby but she doesn't want him. This Conor person. That makes it almost—no, really— all right.* "What about Han?" he asked.

"I haven't told her yet."

He saw dread on her face then, mixed with defiance; she was going ahead with this, no matter what. "Jane, d'you know why I bought this house?" His voice faltered. Jane shook her head. "You didn't really believe I took it on as a challenge, did you?"

"No, but—"

"I bought it for you, Jane—you and Han." He stared at her. She looked aghast but Max didn't care; he didn't give a shit about anything.

"Why?" Jane whispered.

"I had an idea—you probably think I'm mad—that if there was some place that could be ours, for the three of us...not the old house where the bad stuff happened—"

"You thought I'd come back?"

He nodded, looking helplessly around the room. The house still felt hollow and empty no matter how hard he tried to fill it with chairs and standard lamps and oatmeal throws. "See that?" he asked, pointing to the stained glass window. "I thought, if I asked you to make it, then you might feel as if you belong here."

He looked down at his hand, which was holding Jane's. He did it then—kneeled in front of her and held her face in his hands, then kissed her lips, as if they were students again in a corridor, vaguely aware of someone whistling and laughing and neither of them caring. "Max." Jane disentangled herself and stood up.

"What—" he began.

"I can't...."

"You don't understand," he protested, scrambling up and following her through to the hall. "I want you to know it'll be okay. *We'll* be okay."

She blinked at him. "We?"

"Why shouldn't we have another baby?" The words had flown out of his mouth.

"But it's not your…"

"I don't care," he charged on. "It doesn't make any difference. It's yours and I love you and we can be a family—"

"Max," she said softly, her face pale in the shadowy hall, "I can't go back. I'm so sorry."

Max stopped. There was no point in saying anything else, because he knew he'd blown it now. He took in Jane's look of despair and—the worst part—pity. He'd poured them all out, the feelings he'd bottled for years, and she pitied him.

The front door opened slowly. Hannah stood on the front step, her face chalk white. "Mum," she said quietly, "I want you to take me home."

48

*H*annah was silent in the car. She had nothing to say—at least, nothing that could possibly convey the disgust that saturated every cell in her body. She had plonked herself in the back, as if her mother were merely a cab driver and Hannah the passenger, with no blood tie to link them. "I'm sorry," Jane said levelly, "that you had to find out like that. I was planning to tell you, when the time was right—"

"When would have been the right time?" Hannah glared at the back of her mother's head.

"When we were alone," Jane murmured. "Just the two of us. If you hadn't snuck up your dad's steps like that…"

"I didn't *sneak* anywhere," Hannah snapped. "I'd come to get some pens from my bag. Me and Dylan were working on…" She tailed off and stared gloomily through the grimy window. What did her mother care about the ideas she and Dylan were working on together? That he'd had an encouraging response from a proper publisher of graphic novels, and a request to see more of his work? None of that would mean a damn thing to someone who was more concerned with having sex—unprotected sex, and after all the cosy little talks her mother had given her—with men she hardly knew.

Of course, it had to be that Conor on the island. Conor who'd been so friendly and attentive with that hyperactive kid who'd rescued Zoë's shoe. Conor who'd hung around her mother like a bad smell, inviting her to his cottage for dinner. Dinner! Hannah almost laughed at the hideous absurdity of it all. Charming, artsy-fartsy Conor who'd gone and done it with her mother while Hannah was having a full-scale asthma attack. The thought of middle-aged people having sex made her feel like vomiting right here all over the backseat. It was so wrong, so unnecessary, so…what was the word? *Inappropriate.* That was a word that adults were especially fond of using. The concept of old-people sex was no better than seeing cows doing it in a field.

"Well," Jane said, her voice fraying a little now, "I wish it hadn't happened like that. You overhearing, I mean. And I'm sorry."

Hannah didn't bother responding to that. *Sorry, Han, there'll soon be baby things strewn all over the house, as if it weren't a shabby old pigsty already. Sorry—the entire house will stink of sick and nappies and be filled with relentless screaming. Sorry, did you say you were trying to revise for your exams? Babies can't help crying, you know. And it's only your GCSE coursework, after all.*

God, it would be no better than living at Nippers with the interminable noise and all those kids with snot dangling out of their noses and horrible stinks coming from their bums. "What about him?" she asked bluntly.

"Who?"

"Him. The father. Conor."

Jane paused.

"How...how'd you know it's Conor?"

"I'm not stupid," Hannah snapped. "It was obvious, unless of course there've been other men you haven't mentioned..."

"Of course there haven't!" Jane snapped.

Hannah glimpsed her mother's moist eyes in the rearview mirror. "What about Dad?" she challenged. "I heard him, Mum. He said he'd help you bring up the baby and we could be—" her voice wobbled, and she batted at tears with her fingers "—a proper family again."

"Han, sweetheart, I can't—"

"*Why not?*" Hannah yelled. "What's wrong with him?"

"Nothing!"

"Then why—"

"Please," her mother said, "let's stop this. We'll talk when we get home."

Hannah gnawed at a fingernail. "So," she muttered, "have you made up your mind?"

"About what?"

"Whether you're having the baby."

"Yes, of course I am."

"Aren't you even going discuss it with me?"

Jane signaled right onto Albemarle Road and pulled up abruptly in front of their house. "Hannah," she said, swinging round to face her, "it's not something we discuss, like why I need a computer or whether we should get a new TV."

"Why not?" Something ragged caught in Hannah's throat.

"Because…it's not a *thing*."

Hannah blinked at her, then flung the door open and marched toward the house. Already she felt stranded and stupid; she couldn't storm upstairs to her room until her mum had unlocked the door, and right now she was showing no sign of getting out of the damn car. Hannah glowered at a cluster of old men playing boules in the park.

By the time Jane had let them in, and Hannah had flung herself, drained and exhausted, onto her bed, she'd become aware of the sensation of acting a part. It felt creaky, not unlike Ollie's portrayal of the dentist. She rolled over and sat cross-legged on her bed, wondering what to do next. Glancing up at her shelf, the spine of a book caught her eye. *The Glass Heart.* Hannah would gather up all the kids' books that had cluttered her room for too long, and dump them in her mum's room for the baby. It was the least she could do.

No, she corrected herself, it was *all* she would do. Her mother had got herself into this, and all Hannah could do was insulate herself from the awfulness of it all. She kneeled up and pulled *The Glass Heart* from the shelf, flicking it open at a random page.

Broken things, she read, *can be fixed so they're as good or even better than before.*

She stared at the delicate illustrations of princesses in

pretty dresses. She had never been that sort of girl. Not pretty, despite the gargantuan efforts she'd made with Zoë's tweezers and eye shadows and ceramic hair irons. Yet she could fix things. She wouldn't let the minor matter of her mother's unbearably embarrassing pregnancy ruin her life. Her dad had bought her this book, all those years ago. He hadn't figured out that she didn't like princess stories, hadn't really known her at all. Yet he'd know what to do now. He'd look after her. He couldn't cook, but neither could her mother so she'd be no worse off. She would live with him in that massive house.

Yes, Hannah thought, sliding *The Glass Heart* back into its space on the shelf, that's precisely what she would do.

49

In the months while Jane grew rounder, Nancy had taken up knitting. Miniature sweaters had begun to arrive, with curious lumpy bits and smelling vaguely of sea. "There's a problem, isn't there?" Sally said, examining a stripey orange-and-purple hooded sweater with unnecessary toggles on the front.

Jane nodded. They were sitting on her back step in the cool evening sunshine. "I don't think the baby will need a hooded sweater, even in December. Mum must've forgotten it's warmer down here...."

"You know what I mean," Sally chided her.

"Of course I do." She set down her mug and watched a swollen bee drift around the garden. Although she suspected her mother had guessed, Jane was grateful that she hadn't quizzed her about the baby's father. *Just a fling,* she'd told her. *And, yes, I'm old enough to know better.*

"How can you visit your mum without seeing Conor?" Sally asked.

"She's planning to come down," Jane said firmly, "when the baby's born." *Of course I can't go there,* she thought. *On the island there's nowhere to hide.*

"How many weeks to go now?"

"About ten."

"And Hannah hasn't said if she's coming home?"

Jane shook her head. "I thought she'd come back after a couple of weeks, get sick of living in her dad's place...I thought she'd want to be here, with all her things around her...."

A crow landed on the studio roof and eyed them, brazenly. "You thought she'd want you," Sally said gently.

"Yes."

"It's that Zoë girl," Sally muttered. "I knew, right from the start, that she was a bad influence...."

"No, Sally, it's not Zoë. It's me."

Jane watched the crow deposit a spectacular splat on the glass wall of her studio, then fly away with a squawk. She was aware of frequent flutters inside, reminders of the baby who had pushed Hannah away. Yet she couldn't help smiling, when it happened. It was living and growing, despite everything. "Well," Sally said, "I think you should talk to her...."

"You think I haven't tried? I've taken her out, phoned her, even written to her at Max's." She rested her hands on her swollen belly and added, "Sally, I've got to accept that there's nothing else I can do."

Sally squeezed her hand. "Oh, hon, I wish I could help...."

"It's fine." Jane said. "Really." She didn't add, as Sally left, that she'd give anything to have Hannah—the old Hannah—back with her now. The Hannah who loved to be held, and would bury herself in Jane's lap during a scary episode of *Doctor Who*. She remembered now that, even when she'd started high school, Hannah would occasionally wake from a nightmare and hurtle into her room. Jane would half wake—the way she did now, with the baby's movements—vaguely aware of her daughter snuggling against her.

These nights, she wanted to drive to Max's, just to creep into Hannah's room and see the dark lashes against her pale skin as she slept. Of course, she couldn't do that. It was too late to make things right. And it was certainly too late to tell Conor—to turn his life with Lewis upside down.

This one she'd have to deal with alone.

Hannah had never noticed so many pregnant women before. Now it seemed as if they were everywhere: lumbering around parks and shops, touching their bellies, wearing vast, unflattering dresses or dungarees. They looked hot and often seemed breathless, as if the baby was pressing upward against their lungs. Her mother wasn't like that. She'd been even more energetic than usual, and had worn normal clothes until a few weeks ago. Now it was T-shirts, cardis and stretchy skirts. Although it irked Hannah to admit it, pregnancy actually suited her mom. She had more color in her cheeks, her hair looked thick and glossy and she hadn't gone fat all over like some of those women, who clogged up buses and tube carriages. Yet Hannah still pre-

ferred to meet her in the West End, minimizing any chance
of being spotted by anyone from school. That would be a
step too far.

There were babies, too, babies everywhere Hannah
looked. She'd been aware that small people existed—after
all, her mother used to look after them—but had never
noticed so many around her. Today, as she sat alone on a
park bench in the afternoon sunshine, a girl ground to a
halt in front of her. She had the sort of frizz-attack hair that
looked as if a powerful electrical current had zapped
through it. Attached to the girl was one of those old-fashioned prams with a scruffy hood and huge chrome wheels.
Inside the pram, judging by the frantic wailing, was a baby.

"It's okay, darling," the girl said, scooping the child from
its pram and cradling it in her arms. "Mind if I sit here?"
she asked, indicating the space beside Hannah.

"No, of course not," Hannah said, wanting to spring up
and escape the baby's screams but sensing that she should
stay put for at least a few polite moments.

"Are you hungry, sweetheart?" the girl asked her child.
Glancing at her, Hannah realized now that she wasn't much
older than herself. Sixteen, maybe seventeen. Surely she
hadn't planned this—to be traipsing through the park with
a battered old secondhand pram when she should be—well,
doing other stuff.

The girl had lifted her top a few inches and positioned
the baby on her breast. Although she couldn't really see
anything, Hannah averted her gaze. Would her mother
feed the baby like this, she wondered? Yes, probably. She
could imagine her being as earth-mothery as they come.

The baby had stopped crying and looked relaxed and floppy in his blue velvet romper suit. Hannah allowed herself a quick peek. His face was partially tucked under his mother's top, his pink fingers loosely coiled. Such tiny hands. Last time she'd been to see her mum, she'd glimpsed miniature mittens that granny Nancy had sent from Scotland. They looked like dolls' gloves. It was amazing, Hannah had thought, that this new person wouldn't be much bigger than Biffa, that tatty old doll of hers.

"Good boy, let's get the windy-pops up," the girl murmured, positioning the baby over her shoulder. He burped loudly and, despite herself, Hannah burst out laughing.

"Does he always do that?" she asked, incredulous.

The girl nodded and smiled. "Yeah. Wouldn't believe such a big noise could come out of such a small person, would you?"

"No. How old is he, anyway?"

"Three months."

"What's it like," Hannah asked, unable to stop herself, "looking after a baby all the time?"

"Well, my mum helps," the girl said, kissing the baby's head and placing him back in the pram. "She's brilliant with babies. And my boyfriend's really good, he looks after him while I'm at school…."

School? thought Hannah. How can you be so happy about all of this when you're still in school? Her own mother flicked into her mind: tall and elegant with her cute little bump, and cursing under her breath when she couldn't fit the flat-pack cot together. How could she be capable of making beautiful windows, yet be unable to construct a simple cot?

A lump formed in Hannah's throat, and she gulped it down. She'd never imagined she'd miss her mother so much. "God," the girl said, checking her watch, "I'd better go. I was meant to meet my boyfriend in the park café five minutes ago."

"Oh," Hannah said, feeling faintly disappointed. There was something about the girl that she liked—her cheery manner, her easy way with the child. It made babies seem less scary somehow. After all, the child had been bawling just moments earlier, and she'd satisfied him with a feed. Maybe Hannah's mum would let her feed the new baby with a bottle sometimes, or let her help in other ways. She thought of the stranger's child's tiny fingers, and wondered how her own brother or sister's would feel, coiled around hers. "He's a lovely baby," she added, but the girl was already striding away toward the café.

Hannah didn't know what made her get up and follow her. Curiosity, probably; she wondered what the boyfriend of this pretty, tired-looking girl might be like—if he'd look as young as she did. She reached the café and peered through the window. The girl was in the queue at the counter, with one hand on the pram's handle and the other resting on the arm of the boy beside her. Hannah froze for a moment, telling herself that it couldn't be him, that it just looked like him, and that her vision was misted by the steamy windows. Yet there was no mistaking this boy as he turned and smiled at the girl.

Ollie. A real father now. Before he could spot her staring in, Hannah hurried away.

50

"*Y*ou shouldn't be doing this, you know."

Jane spun round in her studio and peered at the door. She had taken to leaving it open when she worked late. With a few weeks to go now, she craved the cool evening air. "Han?" she murmured.

Hannah stepped into the studio and eyed her mother. "I'm sure you shouldn't. Work with lead, I mean. Couldn't it get into your blood through your hands and poison the baby?"

Jane blinked at her, amazed by her daughter's concern. "I wear gloves. Look." She showed her hands, which were tightly encased in beige-colored latex.

"Very attractive."

A smile tweaked Jane's lips. "What are you doing here, Han? It's gone midnight…"

"I thought about it—what you're doing. Looked it up

on Dylan's computer. All this scary stuff about old, lead-based paint when you're pregnant. I thought, what about Mum, getting that stuff all over her hands every day?"

"Thanks," Jane said, "but I'll be okay."

"Maybe you should get a mask," Hannah added, perching on the edge of Jane's workbench. "You shouldn't take any risks." She paused. "I could help you. You could still do the designing and glass-cutting, but I'd do the lead-cutting and soldering and all that…."

"How could you?" Jane asked.

"Easy. You showed me everything when I was a kid."

"I mean time, Han. There's your studying, your exams… you don't even live here, remember?"

"I…I could stay here sometimes. Just when you need the help."

Jane stepped forward and placed her hands on Hannah's shoulders, conscious of the bump between them. "If you're sure…"

"Shhh." Hannah flinched.

"What?" Jane asked, letting her hands drop.

"I heard a noise. There's something outside."

Turning slowly, Jane peered through the glass wall to the garden. Something moved among the plants. "A fox," she whispered. It emerged from the border and pottered across the overgrown lawn, sniffing the ground. Jane followed its movements across the garden to the back door of the house.

"Is it a boy or a girl?" Hannah murmured.

Jane laughed, and the noise was enough to send the fox darting across the garden—just a blur now—and disappearing between the slats of the fence. "It wasn't close enough to tell," she said.

"No, Mum. The baby." Hannah indicated the pinboard covered with fabric snippets and Quality Street wrappers and, almost lost among the muddle of color, the monochrome image of Jane's twelve-week scan.

Jane looked from the scan picture to her daughter. One child who hadn't yet come into the world. The other who might—just might—be on the verge of returning to her. "I don't know," she said. "They didn't tell me. Anyway, I don't want to know."

"Thought of any names?" Hannah asked.

"No," she said tentatively, "I thought you might be able to help me."

Hannah frowned, as if trying to conjure up some suggestions. "Where will it sleep?"

"With me for the first few months. I think, though, that we'll need a bigger place. The offer's still there on Mum's house—she wouldn't even charge us rent—but I don't think it would feel right, and it's too far from school...."

Hannah nodded, following Jane out of the studio and waiting as she locked the studio door. "I think," Hannah said, "that somewhere new might be better. A fresh start for us."

They headed back into the house, Jane linking her arm through Hannah's. "Yes, for the three of us," she said, a smile breaking her lips.

51

"What you need," Andy announced from his cross-legged position beside the upturned silver racing model, "is a nice normal bird. Someone to have a laugh with and go home to and get cosy." He flung a spanner onto the filthy concrete floor.

"Thanks," Max said, leaning against precarious floor-to-ceiling shelving. "Thanks for your sage advice."

Andy looked up at him. *It's all right for you,* Max thought, *with your sweet, pretty girlfriend and five-year-old son and terraced house in Stoke Newington. All manageable, normal things. All the right boxes ticked.* "Ever tried that Internet dating?" Andy asked.

"You're saying I'm desperate?" Max retorted.

Andy grinned at him. "Yeah, I'd say so."

To distance himself from Andy's appraisal of his love-life,

Max installed himself at the lopsided desk at the far end of the workshop where he could at least pretend to catch up with accounts. It was weird, he thought, opening a drawer that was stuffed with mangled paperwork and quickly shutting it again. Jane's pregnancy: there was no avoiding it, obviously. Her growing bump, discernibly bigger each time he saw her—he'd expected to find it unbearable, seeing her like that. Yet it hadn't been unsettling in the slightest. If anything, it had forced him to get a grip on himself. She had enough to contend with without having him wittering on, trying to entice her back as if they were a couple of teenagers with no ties or responsibilities. It was time, he'd realized, that he got himself a life.

Maybe Andy was right, he mused, flicking through invoices that were long overdue for filing. What he needed was a nice, normal bird. Although he hadn't the first clue how to respond, he was aware that customers flirted with him occasionally. They'd bring in battered old bikes for minor repairs and start asking about the top-of-the-range models that were lined up in the window. Bikes they had no intention of buying. "Should have got her number," Andy would tease him when one of these women had finally run out of questions and left the shop. "She was well after you, mate. Should have asked her out. Kept the customer satisfied."

"The thing with the Internet," Andy was informing him now, "is there's millions of women out there, all actively looking to meet someone. You can't lose."

"Has it ever occurred to you," Max said, aware of the superior tone that had crept into his voice, "that I'm actually happy being by myself?"

Andy's laugh rattled through the workshop. "Yeah. You're bloody ecstatic. Anyone can see that."

Max scowled as he pushed back his chair and strode through to the shop. "You think I'm too fussy, don't you? That I should lower my standards and go out with anyone who happens to cross my path, because I'm a desperate sad case who—"

He stopped dead. A lone customer was standing in the middle of the shop. She looked stranded, as if she'd intended to buy a loaf or sausages and had found herself wandering into a cycle shop by mistake.

"Hi," Max said, conscious of his reddening cheeks.

"Hi, Max." The customer was Hettie. She wasn't wearing a padded red all-in-one thingie, but a white cotton shirt and softly faded jeans. A nice, normal bird, as Andy would put it.

"I was just—" he began.

"I have to say," she interrupted, "*sad* and *desperate* aren't the words I'd use to describe you." Her smile verged on the shy.

Max laughed, conscious of Andy clanking around in the workshop. Martin, the new sales assistant, was polishing the inside of the front window. He'd dumped the cloth at his feet and was peering quizzically at Hettie, then Max. Max cleared his throat. "So, Hettie, how can I help you?"

"I was just passing. Wondered how you were, after the accident and everything."

"Fine," Max said brightly. "Cycling again, against doctor's orders. How about you—are you or Jasper looking for a bike, or d'you need a repair—"

"No," she said. "My office is at the other side of Vicky Park. I've been meaning to drop in…." Her voice hushed to a murmur. "Jasper and I…we split up, soon after the holiday."

"I'm sorry," Max mumbled.

"I'm not. It had been a long time coming. Funny, sometimes it takes a holiday—being somewhere new, away from the usual distractions—to see things clearly."

Max nodded, wishing that Martin would get on with cleaning the window, or at least eavesdrop less blatantly. He could hear Andy humming in the workshop. "I was wondering," Hettie added, "if you're not too busy, maybe you'd like to come and have a bagel or something in the park…."

"I don't usually stop for lunch," Max said, unsure of what to do with his hands or his face.

"Okay. Maybe some other time." She smiled, and cute little dimples formed on her cheeks.

"Sure." He watched her leaving the shop and striding jauntily past the plate-glass window.

Martin picked up his cloth. "Nice girl," he said.

"Yeah," Max murmured.

A moment later, Andy emerged from the workshop clutching a tire. "I think," he said, raking his hair with his oil-smeared free hand, "we can manage without you for an hour or so."

"But I—"

"Off you go. Lovely day and all that. Vicky Park, she said. She's probably down by the Swan Pond. I'd get down there if I were you." He grinned, winked, then turned on his heel and disappeared back into the workshop.

Max was about to protest when an image popped into his mind. Jane's mother, Nancy, in Camden Market. He and Jane had only split up a few months before. He'd spotted Nancy and had tried—and failed—to duck in to a shop whose doorway was festooned with Peruvian knitted hats.

"Max?" Nancy had called sharply. "How are things?"

"Fine," was the only reply he could muster.

She'd frowned at him, those beetly eyebrows scooting down toward the bridge of her nose, and said, "For goodness' sake, you look terrible. You need to start taking care of yourself."

Max had been shocked. He'd expected a diatribe about letting down Jane, letting down Hannah—a furious detailing of his numerous shortcomings. "You look half-starved," Nancy had added. "Come back with me. I've got half a steak pie in the fridge. It's only a few days old—I'm sure it's perfectly fine."

He'd smiled, awash with relief, and said, "Thanks, but I'm meeting a friend for lunch." *A male friend,* he'd wanted to yell after her, but Nancy had already disappeared into the crowd.

And now, remembering her words, he heard himself telling Andy and Martin that he wouldn't be long—half an hour at the most—and would have his cell if anyone needed him. He stepped out of the shop, into the dusty afternoon and walked, as fast as his knee would allow, in the direction of Victoria Park.

Maybe, he thought, aware that he was smiling inanely, *this is the kind of thing the sad and desperate get up to on a Thursday afternoon.*

52

*T*he sound juddered through the room. Jane shifted in bed—the only way she could be remotely comfortable was to lie on her side—and glanced at the digital clock on the bedside table. 5:47 a.m. Saturday. Too early to wake up; not even properly morning.

It came again, swelling and gripping her—not a noise after all but a pain, heavy and all-engulfing. Catching her breath, she pushed herself up in bed. Braxton hicks, she told herself. Hannah had, rather sweetly, told her what they were at breakfast a few days ago: practise contractions that could occur weeks before labor. She'd read about them in the library and assured Jane that they were nothing to panic about. After all, she had more than three weeks to go.

Jane tensed, focusing on the pale, gray dawn as she waited for another wave. 5.58 a.m. In an attempt to steady herself, she focused on ordinary, Saturday things: taking preliminary sketches to Father O'Reilly at St. Saviours Church. Hannah and Dylan had planned to take a train to Brighton for the day. He loved the seaside in winter, Hannah had told her. Of course, Zoë had snorted that hanging out on a beach at the tail end of November was stupid and pointless, but gaining Zoë's approval no longer seemed to feature on Hannah's radar.

Another wave came, even fiercer this time. Jane's breath caught like a web in her throat. She swiveled out of bed and stood up unsteadily, placing one hand flat against the bedroom wall. She focused on sounds: the hum of distant cars, a bunch of people laughing, maybe coming home from a club. It was too early to wake Hannah. No point in disturbing her for a false alarm.

Jane made her way on to the landing and downstairs to the living room where she sat in semidarkness. Hannah had insisted she stopped working in the studio— "What if there's lead dust in the air, Mum?"—so she'd brought much of her equipment into the house. It was oddly comforting, being bossed around by her daughter, being cared for. A piece of hardboard, on which she'd been cutting glass segments, dominated the living room floor.

A bath. That's what she'd have: a soothing, chocolate-scented bath. It might ease the contractions or make them fade away entirely. She headed back upstairs and started to fill the tub. She checked the chocolate truffle deluxe foam, but the bottle was empty.

And another wave came. *Breathe. Breathe.* Jane crouched on the bathroom floor, her arms out in front of her, gripping the bath's cold edge. *Breathe. Breathe.* Another wave, more urgent this time, leaving only a short space for her to compose herself in preparation for the next. Then there was no preparation, no thinking time; just her own voice crying, "Han? Hannah!"

And suddenly her daughter was there beside her, her hair sticking up at odd angles and her eyes filled with fear. "Mum," she cried, "what's happening?"

"I don't know. I'm getting these pains but it can't be labor because it's too early to—"

"What if it is?" Hannah put an arm around her back. "What if the baby's coming?"

"You'd better phone someone…."

"Who?"

"Anyone. Max. Call your dad. Han, please."

Hannah hurried downstairs, returning moments later. "No answer. He probably didn't hear his machine. I tried Zoë's number, too, in case he's round there, in case they're back together—"

"The hospital," Jane cut in. "We'd better phone the hospital."

She pulled herself upright, the thin cotton of her nightie clinging to her back. Gripping each other's hands, they made their way downstairs. There, Jane scrambled through her ancient phonebook for the hospital's number and tapped it out on the phone. "I—I think I'm in labor," she blurted out.

"Are you having contractions?" came the prim, female voice on the line. She sounded so ordinary, like a hairdresser might speak—*so what can we do for you today?*

"Yes," Jane said. "They're—how far apart are they, Han?"

Hannah's bewildered expression said: *how should I know?*

"I'm not sure," Jane said.

"Have your waters broken?"

"No, I—"

"And your due date is…" The woman sounded bored now, as if Jane's situation lacked the urgency required to keep her attention.

"Not for another three weeks," Jane said. "But—" Another wave. Jane slammed down the phone and sank onto the sofa.

What happened next came so thick and fast she was aware only of each contraction juddering through her. Random thoughts like hot towels—should Hannah get some hot towels?—shot through her head. Hannah was on the phone again, but her voice was muddled amid Jane's cries. "It's okay," Hannah soothed her, "it's okay. I've called the ambulance, they should be here any minute…."

The door flew open, and it wasn't a paramedic but a blond woman who'd clearly shot out of bed. Despite an overwhelming urge to push, Jane registered pink spotty pajamas with a sweater thrown over the top.

"Veronica?" she gasped. "What—"

Veronica clattered toward her and crouched to grip her hand. "I came as soon as I heard the message, Jane. Is it coming? Have you called—"

"Yes," Hannah snapped, "of course I've called an ambulance."

"God, Jane," Veronica cried. "The baby really is coming. I can see the head…."

There was a huge shifting downward, and a pain so acute that it almost felt like nothing at all—like standing under a shower so scalding it actually felt cold. Jane knew what was happening, knew that no one could stop it, even had there been medical people here instead of just a sixteen-year-old girl and a woman who concocted aphrodisiac snacks. She was no longer scared because she could feel the baby being born, hear its cry.

It sounded so new and tiny. Jane sank to the floor as Veronica placed the baby, still attached by its cord, in her arms. She could smell the child—a soft, sweet smell, as if it had been born ready-powdered. Jane felt high—the woozy high that followed white wine on a hot summer's day—and lost track of all time.

More people had arrived now, wearing white jackets with fluorescent strips on their arms. A silver case was opened, the cord cut. Jane looked down at the sleepy face with dark, penetrating eyes and a shock of sticky black hair. "Congratulations, Jane," came a voice, someone's voice she didn't know.

"It's a boy, Mum," Hannah murmured. "I've got a brother, Mum. It's not just me anymore."

"Are they okay?" Veronica was asking.

Jane gazed at the big eyes that had fixed firmly on hers, vaguely registering someone say, "Everything's fine, but we'll take Jane and the baby to hospital. Jane, would you like your daughter and friend to come with you?"

She looked up. "Yes," she said, smiling, then returning to those eyes, "of course I'd like them to come."

53

*T*his wasn't a Max thing to do at all: take an impromptu Saturday off work and be driven to Cornwall by a woman who he'd known—at least, known properly—for just a month. It wasn't Max behavior to book into a small hotel, agree to stay a second night, then find himself staring into an estate agent's window in a sleepy fishing village.

To rent: charming two-bedroomed cottage with small garden overlooking Darling Bay. All amenities including newly refurbished kitchen and loft currently being used as a studio.

They'd come to the village where Hettie had grown up. He hadn't known Hettie was from Cornwall when they'd been in Chamonix; he'd written her off as a fluffy PR or media type, in a Veronica mold, the type of which there were millions in London. In fact, on holiday he hadn't given her much thought at all. That lunch in Victoria Park had changed all that. He'd noticed nothing *but* Hettie. The time had whooshed by, and by the time he'd checked his watch it was 5:00 p.m. and he'd missed a whole afternoon's work.

They hadn't discussed when they'd meet up again or whether she'd come back to his place for supper. It had just happened. They'd picked up chicken, salady bits and white wine on the way home. They'd cooked together, chatting and sipping wine, and she'd stayed the night. They'd had breakfast together—she hadn't scoffed at the Coffee Time biscuits in his cupboard—and the first thing he'd done after work that day was call her and ask her to come over. It had been as easy as riding a bike.

"D'you want to look at it?" he asked her now.

She tore her gaze away from the picture of the cottage and looked at him. "I don't know, Max. I'd made up my mind to move back here after Jasper and I split up—he was the one who'd wanted to live in London. But now…" She shrugged.

"Looking won't hurt," he told her.

"Are you sure about giving up the shop?"

Max nodded. He wouldn't be giving it up as such; just handing over the reins to Andy, who was as obsessed with cycling as ever. It was different for Max. Since the accident, he'd known he wouldn't ride competitively again, but it no longer seemed to matter. He'd spent sixteen years building up the business and could have expanded, opened a second branch, yet he had never had the push to make it happen. Maybe that should have told him something—that someone else, someone with more drive and ambition than he could ever muster, should steer Spokes to greater things... world domination, maybe.

Hettie smiled reassuringly and squeezed his hand, then pushed open the estate agent's door. Max followed her in, Jane's offer ringing clear in his head: *You could take over Mum's clippings library. It just ticks along these days—it wouldn't take all of your time. She'd be happy—she has no intention of coming back and wanted it tossed—but it seems such a shame, after all those years' work. What d'you say, Max?*

The thought of living here, far away from his miserable street with its overflowing skips, made him feel lifted and free. Hannah could spend the summers here. Jane could come down with the baby. And Dylan—weren't he and Hannah always jaunting off to the coast? The cottage was tiny but he'd squeeze each of them in somehow.

The young estate agent was on the phone but motioned for Max and Hettie to sit down at his desk. Hettie caught his eyes and grinned, and Max tried to quell the excitement that whirled in his stomach. Was he really such a screw-up when, somehow, through all the mess with Jane and Veronica he'd somehow wound up here?

The estate agent finished his call. "Sorry about that. Now, how can I help you?"

Max was aware of the smile flickering across his lips, and Hettie's fingers brushing against his as he said, "We're looking for somewhere to rent."

54

"*How* ow did you know Conor would be okay about the baby?" Dylan asked.

He and Hannah were lying in the park, even though the grass was damp and the promised Spring heatwave hadn't materialized. Luke, Jane's baby, was four months old now, and the most charming, smiliest child that Hannah had ever met. Not that she'd met many babies. Now, though, she knew that they were capable of doing all kinds of things apart from crying and pooping: like smiling. Every time she looked at him, this walloping, toothless grin surged across his face. She wondered if babies possessed a limitless supply of those kind of smiles, because so far he was showing no sign of running out. "I know," Hannah said, "because he told me."

"You've spoken to him?" Dylan exclaimed.

"Not exactly. I wrote to him without telling her. It

seemed wrong, him not knowing about his own kid." She paused, thinking of Ollie in the park with his girlfriend and their baby.

"And he wrote back?" Dylan asked.

She nodded. "Said he's never been able to forget her and can't wait to see her and the baby."

"God," Dylan murmured. "You're lucky your mum doesn't read your letters. Mine rips them open the minute they drop through the door. Like that one from the publisher. The one with the check in it."

"Maybe," Hannah laughed, "she was worried you'd blow it all on drugs or something. Anyway, I had to make sure I grabbed the post before Mum saw it. She's usually still in bed with the baby first thing, so it wasn't that difficult."

Dylan paused. "You know what, Han? You're pretty smart, buying her train ticket and everything...."

"Well," Hannah said firmly, "I guess I'm lucky that she's been so wrapped up in looking after Luke, otherwise she'd have wondered why I'd been saving my allowance all these weeks, and why I suddenly don't have any money." She grinned at Dylan and flicked a ladybug from his sweater sleeve. It landed on the grass, and she flattened her finger for it to walk onto.

"You're mad," he said affectionately. "How did you know she'd actually agree to go?"

"I'm her daughter, aren't I? Sometimes you just know these things...."

"No, really," he protested.

Hannah sighed. "She'd been writing to Conor for months— ever since we came back from the island. Of course, she never sent the letters. That would have been far too bloody sensible. All she did was scrunch them up and throw them in the bin, which she never empties—you know how messy she is."

Conor plucked a piece of grass and chewed it. "Does your dad know she's gone?"

"Yeah. He gave me the last twenty quid."

Dylan shook his head. "Your parents are weird. And him, when's your dad moving again?"

"Next weekend. We promised to help him pack, re-member?"

"Yeah, okay."

Hannah rolled from her front to her side and pulled the small yellow box from her pocket. "I never told Zoë, you know," she murmured.

"What?"

"That I knew she'd made up that stuff about going to my old house. That she'd nicked the worry dolls from you."

Dylan leaned forward and pushed Hannah's growing-out bangs from her eyes. "That's what I like about you. You could've made her feel embarrassed and stupid, and you didn't."

Hannah shrugged. "She's chuffed, isn't she, getting work experience on *Cosmo*?"

"Un-bloody-bearable," Dylan replied, laughing. "You'd think they'd made her the editor."

Pulling herself up, Hannah said, "Come on, let's get a bagel or something. I'm starving." She knew, as she took his hand, that Dylan's success with his comic strip had infuriated Zoë. Still, at least it had spurred her onto badger editors with e-mails, resulting in the *Cosmo* job.

"Don't forget your dolls," Dylan said, indicating the yellow box on the ground.

Hannah followed his gaze. "Remember when Zoë nicked that doll's head and left it on a picnic table for someone to find?"

He nodded, and the smile sneaked across his face.

"I know they're yours really, but if you don't mind…I'm not really a doll person anymore, Dylan."

"Me, neither," he said.

"And I don't have any worries right now."

He touched her face, and she felt herself glowing all over, just as she had last Sunday when he'd kissed her on the Brighton Pier. Suddenly, she wasn't hungry at all. "I'm glad about that," he said.

"Come on, let's go back to mine. Mum left the place in a right state—clothes all over the place. You should've seen what she was packing. Just T-shirts and stuff, no warm things at all. Having a baby must do something to your brain."

He sniggered and said, "So you put her right…."

"Someone had to! I made her pack wellies and proper walking boots."

They started to walk across the park, leaving the yellow box on the grass. "Good job she's got you to look after her," Dylan added.

"Well," Hannah said, stopping to kiss his warm, sweet lips, "someone's got to be the grown-up around here."

55

She didn't leave in the night, but on the first train from King's Cross to Glasgow, then took another train north, which snaked perilously close to the sea as it approached the ferry port. Hannah had booked her a room in a pub where a disco thumped on until 2:00 a.m. Luke slept in Jane's bed. He'd been in his own cot at home for weeks now, but Jane was grateful for the excuse to sleep beside him again. It was those eyes of his. She'd wake at odd hours and see him sleeping, then his eyes would pop open and reassure here that everything was going to be all right. She needed to believe that it *would* be all right. It had been awkward when Conor had called her. So much had happened, she hadn't known where to begin. As she'd pictured him with wind in his hair, he'd seemed further away than ever.

"So you'll definitely come?" he'd asked her.

"Yes," she'd said, knowing she had to, if only this once.

Next morning, with Luke in a sling and their clothes in her backpack, Jane followed the winding lane to the ferry port. She shouldn't have come away, with her in-town restoration job almost complete, but what could she do when Hannah had planned everything so meticulously? "You don't have to go," Hannah had retorted snarkily. "You can rip up the ticket and waste all my money and never know what might have happened."

Jane had been lost for words. She'd already hurt Hannah's feelings by explaining that Biffa—that filthy old doll that had acquired a rather unpleasant odor over the years—wasn't really suitable for a baby.

And now, here she was, with nothing to lose. The ferry crossing was smooth, the sea flat as glass, and Jane felt lulled by the grumble from the engines. She wondered if Conor had managed to persuade anyone to restore the windows of that church. Someone who'd go to painstaking lengths to source the right colors and textures and degrees of opalescence. That's what was needed with restoration work. A perfect match.

There were only two other passengers on the ferry—a man and a woman who were dozing on each other's shoulders, her brown hair merging with his blond like some curious dual-colored animal. Jane fed Luke his bottle and stood up, watching the island looming large before her as he snoozed into her neck. Would Hannah be okay on the train to Cornwall, she wondered? "Of course I will," she'd retorted. "I'm sixteen, Mum. Not a baby. Anyway, Dylan and Amy will be with me." Jane was glad she'd picked up her friendship with Amy. It was as if she'd been patiently waiting for Hannah to come back to her, after all this time.

The ferry was docking. Steadying herself with the handrail, she climbed the metal stairs to the deck. She could smell smoke from the cluster of ramshackle cottages by the pier. It wasn't an acrid burning smell, like burnt toast or a ruined birthday cake, but woody and sweet.

The ferrymen were setting up the gangplank. Jane stepped onto the wood, then the pitted concrete of the pier. Luke stirred against her chest. She started walking alongside the road that led to Hope House, figuring that it would take her forty minutes or so; she had no intention of hurrying, even if she'd been able to with Luke and the backpack. Clouds gathered and swirled as if blown by a wind machine. A seagull squawked, and a gentle wind caused the branches of trees to sway and dance.

Jane's breathing came shallow and quick. She tried to calm herself by replaying Max's words to her: *You know you have to do this, don't you? You have to see him*. Then he'd made a quip about her not being allowed to waste the ticket that Hannah had bought her. Max seemed so different since he'd been with Hettie. It was as if he had finally forgiven himself and been able to let go of the past.

Jane turned the corner. She expected to see Conor then, but there was only a gull swooping slowly, as if suspended by invisible thread. Conor had known she planned to catch the eleven o'clock ferry, and she'd imagined he'd meet her at the pier. His cottage would come into view in a few moments. Despite having spent only five days here, she remembered every bend in the road, every kink in the jagged outline of the Fang. The island was etched in her brain. She wished Hannah were here, walking beside her and talking about the stuff they'd been discussing at home. Like whether Hannah might go to art school, and how she'd begun to work on comic strips with Dylan.

She saw Conor then, a tall figure in the distance, not hurrying, but almost dawdling. She tried to smile, but it felt as if it didn't fit her face. From her backpack, Luke's fingers teased her hair. Jane waved to Conor but he seemed distracted, and kept looking over his shoulder. Her heart quickened as she remembered how awkward they'd been on the phone. It was as if so much had happened and neither of them had known where to begin.

Something else appeared around the corner. A smaller being—not a person exactly, but an alien whose body armor consisted of a laundry basket covered with cardboard and sprayed gold, with a sink plunger sticking out of its front. Jane felt relief wash over her, and a smile flooded her face. She could see now that Conor was grinning, too. He quickened his pace—the laundry basket stumbled to keep up—until he was practically jogging toward her, the Dalek lagging behind now. Then he was right there, kissing Jane and Luke saying, "I've been waiting for you."

Jane took his hand, which felt so warm and right in hers, and said, "I've been waiting for you, too."

Keep your friends close…
and the blondes closer.

Jodi Gehrman

When her boyfriend, Coop, invites her on a romantic road trip
from L.A. to Mendocino where his college chums are getting
married, Gwen regards it as good news. After all, she typically
enforces a three-month expiration date in her relationships;
the open road and some QT just may be the antidote to break
her of the cut-and-run cycle this time around.

Enter the bad news: not only will Coop's best friend, stunning yoga
celebrity Dannika Winters, be joining them as the blond Satan behind
the wheel, but Gwen's about to feel like the third one, so to speak.
Hello, jealousy. So in an effort to avoid committing blondeicide, she
decides to record her every thought…from the backseat.

Notes from the Backseat

**Available wherever
trade paperbacks
are sold!**

A Rachel Benjamin Mystery
Jennifer Sturman

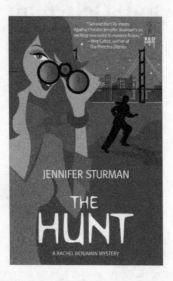

Rachel Benjamin's weekend of meeting her future in-laws
turns out to be quite challenging when she discovers her
friend Hilary is missing. As someone orchestrates an elaborate
scavenger hunt across San Francisco, dangling Hilary as the
prize, Rachel must track down her friend while proving to her
future in-laws and her fiancé how normal she really is!

The Hunt

"Sex and the City meets Agatha Christie!"
—Meg Cabot, author of *The Princess Diaries*